Outcasts in Time

Books in the *After Cilmeri* Series

Daughter of Time (prequel)
Footsteps in Time (Book One)
Winds of Time
Prince of Time (Book Two)
Crossroads in Time (Book Three)
Children of Time (Book Four)
Exiles in Time
Castaways in Time
Ashes of Time
Warden of Time
Guardians of Time
Masters of Time
Outpost in Time
Shades of Time
Champions of Time
Refuge in Time
Unbroken in Time
Outcasts in Time

This Small Corner of Time:
The After Cilmeri Series Companion

A Novel from the *After Cilmeri* Series

OUTCASTS IN TIME

by

SARAH WOODBURY

Outcasts in Time
Copyright © 2021 by Sarah Woodbury

This is a work of fiction.
All rights reserved. No part of this publication may be reproduced, stored in a retrieval system, or transmitted in any form or by any means without the prior written permission of the author, nor be otherwise circulated in any form of binding or cover other than that in which it is published.

www.sarahwoodbury.com

To Dan
*for walking this path with me
for thirty years*

Dearest Reader:

Thank you for waiting so patiently for this book.

The *After Cilmeri* series is a labor of love, and sometimes, as in labor, the birth process doesn't go as smoothly as one would like. I needed a year between books to make this story the best it could be. I know the wait has been painful. For me too!

I also realize that, as with most of my books where time travel (world shifting) is involved, it is written in two threads woven together: Avalon and Earth Two. I am aware that you may be tempted to skip chapters in one world or the other because you are anxious to know what happens in one world or the other.

I'm here to tell you that's okay.

A book, once written, is in a sense no longer the property of its author.

You, as much as I, have made this series come to life, and what happens between the pages of these books can shape your life as well as mine.

But once you've read the book all the way through the first time, in whatever order you see fit (I'm looking at everyone who skips to the end after the first chapter because they can't stand not knowing!), I would hope you would enjoy it again from the beginning.

Happy reading!

--Sarah

Cast of Characters

On the Plane

David—pretty sure you know who this is! King of England; time traveler.

George—revealed to be a CIA agent tasked with abducting David's son, Arthur; former employee of Chad Treadman; came on the plane (in *Shades of Time*) with Anna; worked with Andre, the pilot, and Sophie, who time traveled back to Avalon in *Refuge in Time*.

On the River Seine

Lili—David's wife; Ieuan's sister. Mother of Arthur and Alexander.

Bronwen—first appeared in *Prince of Time*, archaeology graduate student; married to Ieuan.

Ieuan—started out as the captain of David's guard; he and Bronwen are parents to Catrin and Bran.

Jacob—the liaison from Paris's Jewish community to the English court.

Rachel—arrived initially with Anna and Meg on the Cardiff Bus in *Ashes of Time;* physician; was imprisoned in Paris with Samuel and Aaron.

Darren—also arrived on the Cardiff bus; married to Rachel; former MI-5 agent.

Mark Jones—came to Earth Two on the Cardiff bus, stayed behind in *Guardians of Time*, and returned with Anna in Chad Treadman's plane; technical officer at MI-5.

Livia—Former MI-5 officer, married to Michael, David's bodyguard. We first meet her in *Shades of Time* when she is an assistant to Mark Jones; arrived in Earth Two in *Refuge in Time*.

Aaron—Jewish physician whom David's mother met when she returned to Earth Two (detailed in *Footsteps in Time* and *Winds of Time*). He has been an adviser to the Welsh court ever since.

James Stewart—Scottish nobleman and mentor to Christopher and his friends; has had significant roles in *Exiles in Time, Outpost in Time,* and *Champions of Time.*

Christopher and his friends (also currently on the Seine)
- **Christopher**—David's cousin; traveled to Earth Two in his car in *Masters of Time*; the Hero of Westminster; his family came to Earth Two with Anna in *Shades of Time*: Uncle Ted, Aunt Elisa, and Elen.
- **Isabelle**—Christopher's new special friend who happens also to be the daughter of Matthew Norris, the Master of the Paris Temple.
- **Huw**—Welsh companion we first meet in *Footsteps in Time* when David is abducted.
- **William de Bohun**—heir to the Earldom of Hereford; he has been part of David's court since *Crossroads in Time*; famous for *you've got to be kidding me!*
- **Robbie**—Grows up to be Robert the Bruce. We first meet him in *Exiles in Time* as one of the Bruce men all named Robert. At the time, he is dubbed *Baby Bruce* by Bronwen, along with *Daddy Bruce* and *Grampa Bruce.*

In Paris
- **King Philippe**—King of France; we first meet him in *Masters of Time* when he and David fall from the battlement at Chateau Niort. It is this meeting that also brings David into significant contact with the Templars.
- **Guillaume de Nogaret**—King Philippe's henchman and mastermind behind all sorts of schemes.
- **Matthew Norris**—Master of the Paris Temple.
- **Henri**—Templar first met in *Masters of Time*, who rode across France with David.
- **Thomas Hartley**—Templar first met in *Prince of Time* when David and Ieuan were imprisoned at Carlisle Castle. As nephew to the castellan, he freed them; David met him again in *Masters of Time.*

At the monastery guesthouse near Vincennes
- **Venny**—The captain of David's guard.
- **Mathew**—A member of David's guard.
- **Cador**—a Welsh archer.
- **Constance**—Lili's bodyguard; Cador's wife and an archer in her own right.
- **Matha**—son of Gilla, an Irish chieftain, first appearing in *Outpost in Time*.
- **Samuel**—son of Aaron the Physician, first appearing in *Footsteps in Time*.
- **Rhys**—a Welsh member of David's guard; Venny, Mathew, Cador, and Rhys were all imprisoned in Beeston Castle during the conflict with Roger Mortimer and John Balliol starting in *Shades of Time*.
- **Michael**—David's bodyguard from *Champions of Time*; married to Livia (a former MI-5 agent who is also floating down the Seine with David's wife, Lili); arrived in Earth Two in *Refuge in Time*.

Map of France

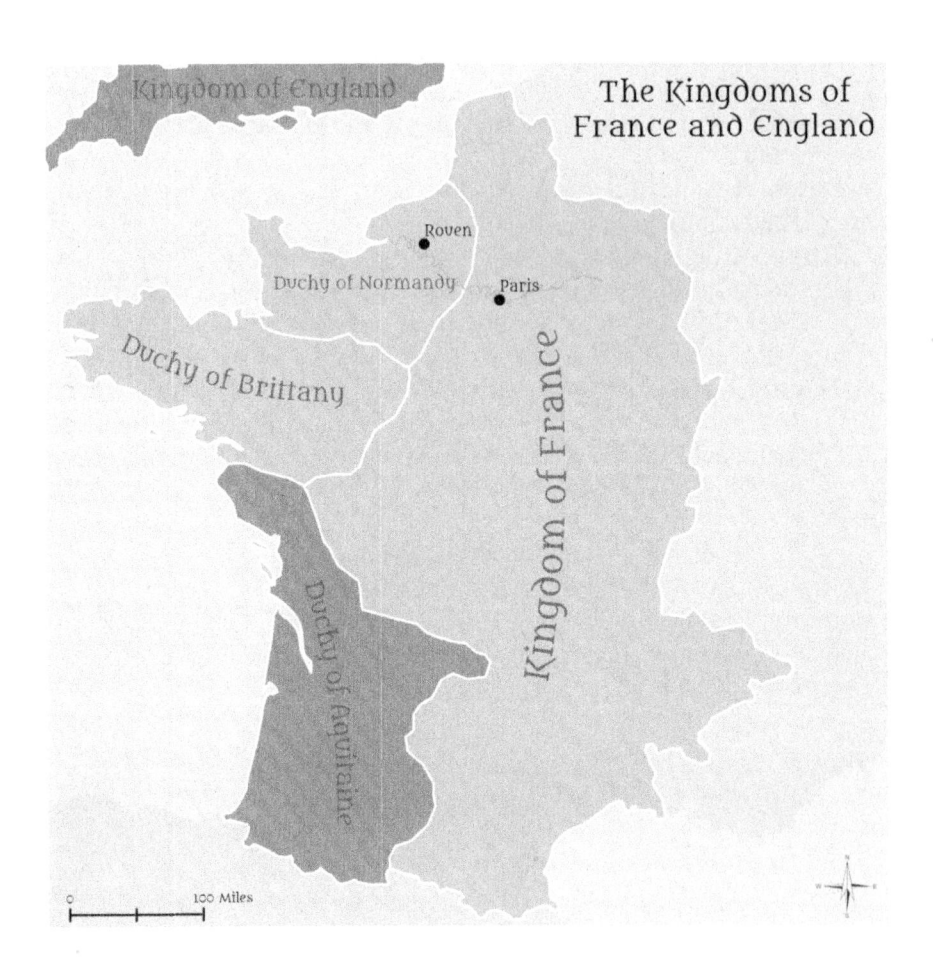

Map of Rouen

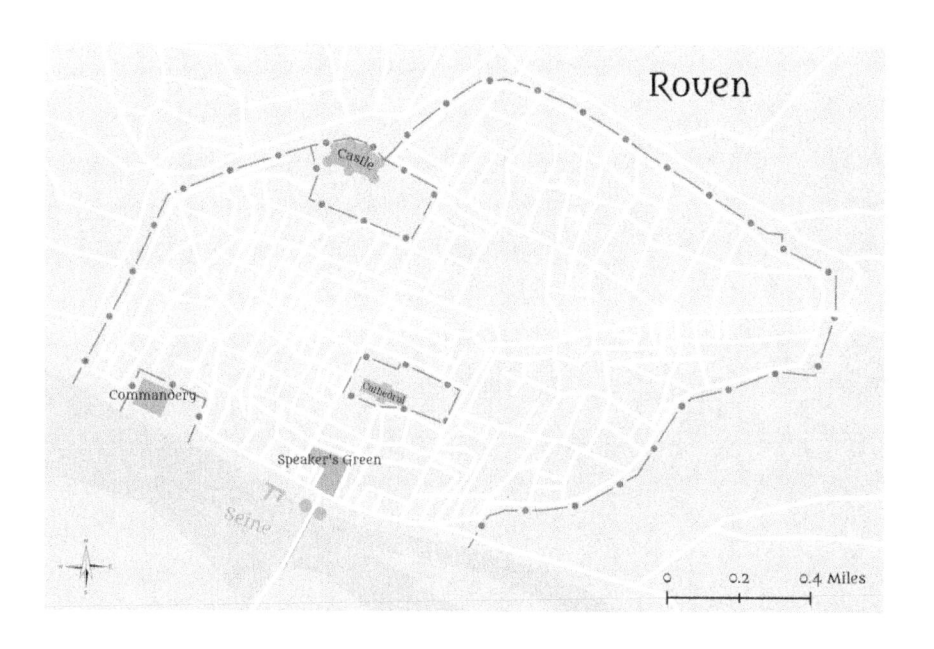

1

August 1295

Day Three (continuing from *Unbroken in Time*)

George

George checked Andre's pulse one more time. He'd tried to get the dosage exactly right, but he'd had to estimate Andre's weight. The older man had lost quite a bit of girth since he'd arrived in Earth Two and was now more George's size. Or so George guessed. At least Andre was sleeping well. Other than a headache when he woke, he should be fine.

If he wasn't, George would regret it. From the start, Andre had been an ally in Earth Two. Sophie had gone home because she couldn't hack the absence of hot showers, not to mention the lack of respect for women, in this forsaken place. Always playing his role, George had been dismissive of her complaints, but he shared them fully—less in terms of respect for women than for the amenity part. It was shallow, he knew, which was why he had never mentioned his irritation to anyone but Andre.

Unlike Sophie, George had discovered that he was not only very good at his job (she had been too), but that he really enjoyed it—up until very recently. He'd deceived an entire planetful of people without too much effort. He'd infiltrated the highest levels of power, both in England and in France. It was shameful how easy it had been to manipulate everyone. Nogaret was a piece-of-work, there was no doubt, but George's knowledge of seven hundred more years of spycraft had given him the upper hand at every turn. Still, at this point, the only reason he was finishing his mission was because he'd burned so many bridges in the pursuit of it that there was no turning back. He reminded himself yet again that everything he'd done would pay off in the end.

Which it had better do, considering what it was costing him.

The question before him now was who would be the first to come out to the plane, and how many of them he'd have to subdue to get to David. If enough of his men disappeared, eventually David would come. George didn't have an infinite supply of darts, but he had enough to render a dozen men unconscious, if David even had that many companions with him. While George had full permission to kill, *á la* James Bond, he never took pleasure in it. Unlike some of his colleagues, he saw it as a last resort.

Andre had parked the plane in a shed two fields away from the abbey guesthouse. The plane's nose faced the road, ready for immediate departure. George crouched at the entrance to the shed, which was open to the elements, his eyes on the guesthouse door. At long last the circumstances were exactly right. And then, as the guesthouse door opened, he allowed himself a low chuckle to see David himself exiting the building and making a beeline for the shed. He didn't slow down once he was away from the guesthouse either, but marched right up to the shed's entrance.

As he waited for David to come all the way inside, George retreated into the shadows behind a stack of crates, putting aside his dart gun and unholstering his pistol instead. The weapon would be more likely to impress upon David the importance of cooperating.

"Andre?" David called into the interior and took a few steps inside. "You in here?"

"I was wondering when someone would come." George stepped out, almost grinning in relief to see David alone and that capturing him, in the end, had been easy. "Honestly, I didn't think you'd be stupid enough to come out here by yourself." He finally allowed himself to laugh out loud—more in relief that this all was finally over rather than with mirth—and gestured with the gun in his hand.

For David to have come alone was exactly like him. Likely he hadn't wanted to bother his men, or he wanted a moment alone with Andre. David's problem was always that he was used to being the cleverest person in the room. Granted, he usually was, but even a clever man can occasionally be out-thought.

"Are you really CIA?" David didn't move other than to put up his hands. "Or am I dealing with some other organization?"

George had training, so he knew not to get close enough to David to give him a chance at taking away his gun. He'd seen that little move in action during a practice session with Callum. David was a physical specimen, more so even than George—and that was saying something. "I'm CIA."

George didn't see any harm in admitting it. They were returning to Avalon, so David would find out the truth soon enough anyway.

Back in the spring, David had sent George to Europe to negotiate with Marco Polo, a task which George had entirely ignored. David cared about trade routes, which, as a king, was smart of him, but George had bigger fish to fry. The specific details of his plan up until now had all failed—but it sure didn't look like failure now. While David's goal had been to outwit Philippe, at which he appeared to have been successful, given that he was out of captivity and at the abbey, George's intent all along had been to get David alone, right here, right now.

To everyone else, the plane had been left near the abbey in case David and his family needed a quick pathway out of the country. That's why they'd befriended the abbot of the Vincennes monastery, and ultimately why David had decided to come here after he'd escaped Philippe's clutches.

Somehow, George couldn't be surprised that David had eluded Nogaret. Now, there was someone who really was too big for his britches and thought he was smarter than everyone else. Yesterday, George had warned him that things weren't going to go the way he'd planned. Nogaret hadn't listened. He'd believed he had everything well in hand. George briefly wondered if David had killed Nogaret and then thought not. David had killed before, George knew. But, like George, he knew that killing had repercussions that rippled out from the initial event like a stone thrown into a still pond.

"Let's go." George motioned again with the gun, this time indicating David should move towards the plane.

David walked stiff-legged up the stairway to the door, which was open. Once inside, he glanced into the cockpit to his left and let out a sigh to see Andre's body slumped in the co-pilot's seat.

George tsked. "He isn't dead, just drugged. Drag him into the back."

David obeyed that order too, compressing himself a bit to maneuver Andre, who was shorter than he but stockier, out of his seat. Then he dragged him down the aisle. Andre was too heavy to lift onto the couch, so David left him face up on the floor. He looked peaceful, and he was breathing.

George tossed a set of handcuffs to David. "Cuff yourself to the handle."

David sighed again but did as George asked, sitting in a chair on the left side of the aisle and cuffing his left hand to the handle above his head. It put him behind the pilot's seat and kept his right hand free. George decided to let him have that little victory rather than order him to change seats. There was something he'd learned from David: *with leadership, less is more.*

Now that David was contained, which was the main thing, George moved to the pilot's seat and set about preparing the plane for departure. He needed to get on his way before David's men started wondering what had become of him.

"You were going to kidnap my son." David sounded genuinely angry.

George respected the emotion. Most of the time, David showed none, which was one of the more irritating things about him and made George want to needle him, just to see if he could get a response.

He'd never done it. He'd had a persona to protect. It was a relief to finally throw it off.

The cockpit had a little mirror that allowed George to see a portion of the cabin behind him, though only the right half of David's body, since the headrest of George's own seat blocked the rest of the view.

George looked into the mirror and said, affecting a British accent, "Sorry, old chap. Needs must and all that."

"Are you sure you can fly this plane? You served breakfast on the flight that took Anna home."

George scoffed, even as he was also pleased that his low profile had so effectively lulled even David into a false sense of security. "It was worth my while to pretend to be other than I was. The CIA can fabricate any story, you know."

"You mean you weren't really with the Chicago police before you joined Chad's organization?"

"Of course I was." George, in fact, had been one of many agents sent to infiltrate organizations interested in time travel. Chad

Treadman had simply been the one to win the lottery. Given that Chad had hired David's uncle Ted, the odds had been in George's favor, if in anyone's. "You forget that your parents showed up in that clinic in Aberystwyth seven years ago. We've had time to plan. My bosses wanted Arthur rather than you, but they'll settle for you, and I'm pretty sure they'll realize soon enough you're the better option. Even my outfit can get antsy about exploiting a kid."

As far as George was concerned, David had always been the better option, something he'd explained to his bosses from the start. They'd sent George in with the order to take Arthur anyway. He was going to tell them he tried, but they were just going to have to make do with what they got.

Having prepared the plane for departure while he'd been talking to David, George began taxiing out of the shed towards the high road to Paris, all the while keeping an eye on the door to the guesthouse. Whoever had come to the abbey with David, Michael for sure but probably Venny as well, would be getting worried. Even if the plane's engines were quiet, thanks to Chad's super-duper technology, the noise of their departure would carry through the medieval morning air.

It was a relief to be committed. David hadn't known that George was a pilot, and, admittedly, George hadn't flown for a while, but he could handle this. Crashing once they reached Avalon would defeat the entire purpose of the endeavor, since it would bring them right back to Earth Two.

Unless, this once, David's luck ran out, and it killed them. George supposed, if that were the case, he wouldn't be alive to know it. He felt remarkably at peace with the idea. While he very much wanted to live—and was looking forward to seeing everyone's faces when he brought David back to Avalon—he'd accepted long ago that he couldn't control everything. That was another thing David was right about.

The plane reached the road and turned onto it, heading east, against the wind, and began to pick up speed. It was still early in the morning, but a farmer was in his field, and his dog ran down a lane, leapt a low stone wall, and nipped at the tires. The plane lifted off the ground.

"I considered flying into the Alps," George said in a conversational tone, "but then I thought, *why bother?* This will be more fun." And he turned the plane until it was headed back towards the city. He glanced into the mirror to see David leaning into the aisle, so he could look through the front windshield.

"Don't—" David stopped, and since he didn't finish his sentence, George ignored him. They were on their way, and there was nothing David could do about it.

Within a minute they were soaring over the outskirts of the city. The engines roared.

"You can't be serious!"

George glanced into the mirror to see David trying to work his hand out of the cuff—or at least that's what it looked like he was doing. The only way he'd be managing that was by breaking his own thumb. Even David wasn't that committed ... or was he? George let out a laugh to think that David might still outwit him, and then he laughed again at how high and near hysterical his voice sounded as it came out. "You're afraid this won't work?"

"I'm always afraid it won't work." David appeared to have given up his efforts, since he leaned back in his seat and closed his eyes.

Plans and opportunities, George mumbled under his breath, ironically quoting David himself. Then he returned his attention to the view ahead of him, his total focus on the bell tower of the cathedral of Notre Dame. These were the old towers, rising towards the sky in all their medieval glory.

He didn't dare look away, even when every impulse in his body howled at him to flinch. A hundred yards ... fifty ... twenty ... they were so close he could see the carvings. George thought he might be screaming. It didn't matter. They were going to destroy Notre Dame in a fiery inferno seven hundred years too soon.

They plunged into a darkness so complete George couldn't breathe. He'd been through it before, but somehow he'd forgotten how terrifying it was to feel so much weight on his chest and at the same time to feel nothing.

One, two, three ...

2

August 2023

Day Three

David

Between one heartbeat and the next, the darkness dissipated, as it always did. Instead of the City of Paris or the fields of France, Chad Treadman's plane soared over a very different terrain, this one all browns and yellows, with a very large blue river making its way west towards snow-covered peaks shining white in the morning sun.

George sent up a cheer. "We did it! My God, we did it!"

David was thankful too, though he doubted George was really praising God, given his total lack of concern so far about anyone other than himself. That said, plenty of men throughout the ages had justified the means with an end result and called it holy. David also spared a wry thought for George's use of the word *we*.

As David stared down at the wide river below him, he allowed his heart to constrict for a single moment for Lili and his boys, floating down the Seine. One of the reasons he'd chosen this hour to leave

Earth Two was because they would be out of communication for at least the few days it would take them to reach Rouen, where they hoped to meet Amaury de Montfort and resupply, before making the last push down the river to the ships that were waiting to take them to England. With the shortwave radio packed away in a box in the hold of one of the boats, Mark Jones couldn't communicate directly with either London or Angoulême, so nobody would know David was gone until Michael and the rest of his personal guard left behind at the abbey reached them in Rouen. The last thing David wanted was for one of his family members to decide, as Cadell had done a year and a half ago, that he needed rescuing.

Before that could happen, if things went according to his plans, he'd be back with them. For now, the less anyone in Earth Two knew about what he was doing, the better. For months, he'd carefully asked questions of his recent companions from Avalon, grilling them about various aspects of their organizations and their lives in the third decade of the twenty-first century, plotting how to trap George into taking him to Avalon without letting him realize he'd been trapped.

Some percentage of Paris must know that something spectacular had just happened, even if they didn't know exactly what. It would have been hard to miss George driving the plane into—and then through—Notre Dame. King Philippe, if he hadn't believed the stories about David before, would have to now.

David pressed his nose to the round window next to his seat. He'd flown over this terrain a long time ago—a lifetime ago, really—

and knew where he was. By the jubilation coming from the pilot's seat, so did George. David had a rising excitement in his chest too, though not at all for the same reasons.

He had done it. And he was glad about it.

Could be he was also incredibly stupid. He would find out soon enough.

In a nutshell, David's plan was to allow the CIA to do with him as they pleased. They were going to force him to time travel, he was sure, but when they did, David was also sure that nothing about that traveling was going to go exactly as the CIA expected. Eventually, if they failed enough times, they would realize that working with David was better than working without him. He had developed this plan because he believed absolutely that coming here to allow them to do their worst to him was the only way to protect his family.

He still thought so, even if, in this moment, he was dreading what might come next.

As the plane flew south, George spoke into his headset, which had come to life now that they were in the twenty-first century. David couldn't hear most of what was said, but the conversation was lengthy and seemed to be about more than just the flight. George kept saying *Yes, sir* and *Thank you, sir*. There was even a *Sorry it took so long, sir*, which implied to David that he was talking to his superior officer—or at least *a* superior officer.

It was an interesting choice, really, for whatever power that controlled David's world-shifting, to drop him yet again into Eastern Oregon. Back in 2012, David's mother had been flying through this area when the pilot, Marty, had crashed the plane into the Wallowa mountain range. Cassie, now a staunch companion, had been hunting with her grandfather when she'd been caught in the plane's wake and transported to 1284 Scotland. David's mother had ended up at Hadrian's Wall.

It was to this region of Oregon also that David's mother and sister had traveled a second time, weirdly again at Marty's instigation, seven years later. The CIA had not been an ally that time either, and it was occurring to David only now that agents had followed so closely on his sister's and mother's heels because they had a base in the area.

George circled the plane to land at a substantial airport. It was larger than David would have expected to be associated with the adjacent small town, nestled in a river valley to the south and east below the plateau on which the airport was built. In point of fact, the plane could have landed on grass, since Chad Treadman, who'd designed it, had thought of everything.

Well, except for this, since he'd been the one who'd hired George in the first place. When next David saw him, they were going to have a conversation about his vetting procedures. The CIA was good, but Chad Treadman had always prided himself on being better.

Trucks and jeeps, colored the characteristic green of the U.S. Army, were parked near the airstrip and associated hangars. Other areas were covered with green and gray tarps or netting, which, given the brown and yellow wheat fields all around them, were the wrong color for the job. Maybe the camouflage worked better in the spring when the wheat was green.

George pointed the plane's nose towards the end of the runway and, in short order, brought it in for a graceful landing. He proceeded to taxi not towards the public airport buildings, but up to a giant hangar located at the opposite end, near which several men waited on the tarmac.

George then braked, flicked a bunch of switches, and took off his headset. Turning around, he grinned at David and said with an irksome degree of sauciness, "Welcome to Avalon, your highness."

3

August 1295

Day Three

Michael

Constance jogged past Michael, who was standing in the little lane which ran from the guesthouse to the road. "Come on!" She waved an arm. "What are you waiting for?"

"There's nothing to wait *for,* Constance." A wealth of curses welled up inside Michael as he watched the airplane take off. "You might as well not bother."

She ran a little farther anyway before cupping her hands around her mouth. "Andre!" But the plane didn't stop, as, of course, it wouldn't. Constance swung around. "Why is Andre taking off?"

"I don't think it's Andre. In fact, I'm pretty sure that was George in the pilot's seat."

"George?" She was thinking very slowly for Constance. "So ... where's the king?"

Michael couldn't blame her for refusing to believe what her eyes were telling her. Michael didn't want to believe his eyes either.

Cador and Samuel had each run towards the road too, but now Samuel diverted to the shed, loping along with haste at first and then slowing as he came to understand, as Michael already had, that he wouldn't find David there. Michael respected Samuel's need to check.

Constance was still working it out. "I know little about these things, but George once told me that he didn't know how to fly the plane."

"He lied." Michael was making her work for the truth, which wasn't fair, but inside he was fuming, and he was afraid he would take his anger out on her if he imparted more than the barest information at any one time.

"So—"

"George forced David into the plane," Michael said. "He has to have done."

Constance herself wasn't one to curse, and she didn't this time either.

Her husband had come to rest beside her, however, and more than made up for her lack. He finished with a final curse and then added, "We had one task, and we failed!"

Michael was reminded of a meme that had gone around the internet a few years before he'd come to Earth Two, the text of which read, *You had one job!* below which would be an image of a bathroom faucet installed upside down.

With David's disappearance, they were well beyond plumbing issues. The plane circled above them and turned towards Paris. Michael watched it until it was out of sight, at which point his brain finally started working again.

He turned to the others. "Why did David go to the shed in the first place?"

Constance's brow furrowed as she thought. "He said he was going to speak to Andre."

By now, Samuel had reached the shed, entered, and come out again. He made a motion with both arms like an American baseball umpire indicating the baserunner was safe at home plate, but since Samuel was medieval and would never have seen a baseball game, Michael took him to mean that nobody was there.

No Andre. No David. No George.

No surprise.

Michael gritted his teeth and deliberately wiped away his thoughts, refusing to allow them to churn inside his head like they wanted to. Instead, he turned on his heel and strode back into the guesthouse and then up the stairs to the room in which David had slept. Nobody had managed anything close to a full night's sleep, not with how late they'd arrived at the abbey. Michael's four hours were luxurious compared to what Venny, Matha, and Mathew had achieved. Those three had taken Nogaret to the dungeon in Paris and thus had arrived back at the abbey even later.

As Michael stood on the threshold of the chamber, Venny appeared, smoothing down wet hair he'd just dunked into the basin of water in his room. In all, eight of them remained at the guesthouse: Michael himself, Rhys, Samuel, Constance, Cador, Matha, Mathew, and Venny.

"What happened?" Venny had been the captain of David's guard for some time now, a position he hadn't attained by being slow to understand when something was wrong.

Michael told him.

Like Constance, Venny didn't curse. In fact, he didn't appear to react at all, though Michael knew him well enough to know his innards were churning like Michael's own.

Thinking to give Venny a minute to come to terms with his new reality, Michael entered the room and began to go through the few possessions David had left behind. They hadn't carried much in their saddlebags to begin with and had merely collapsed into their beds when they'd arrived at the guesthouse. David's bed was typically mussed, and Michael threw back the sheet and blanket, shaking them out just in case something had dropped from David's pockets while he slept. His cloak hung on a hook by the door, and the sword he'd been wearing when he arrived at the monastery was propped in one corner in its sheath.

The presence of both gave Michael pause, and he stood a moment, looking from one to the other.

Venny noted his attention. "What's wrong—I mean, beyond the obvious?"

"When David came downstairs for breakfast this morning, he was dressed in shirt, trousers, and tunic."

"So?"

Michael made a gesture to indicate his own attire. "I have not lived among you as long as he has. Perhaps because of that, I am very aware of what is required to look the part. What knight belts his tunic at the waist but doesn't wear his sword?"

"No knight." Venny's eyes narrowed as he looked at the sword and then back to Michael. "You're saying David took the sword off the belt? Why would he do that? He's the one who's always hammering on at us about being prepared."

"That's just it. He wouldn't."

"But he did."

Michael let that thought settle for a second before saying, in a somewhat gentle tone, "Which means he meant to."

"What would make him—" Venny cut himself off before he could finish the thought.

Michael didn't stay to discuss it, not that at this point they needed to, since the look on Venny's face was one of stunned comprehension. Instead, Michael headed back down the stairs to the dining room, where he found the rest of David's men (and Constance), clustered around the breakfast table. Mathew and Matha were awake now too. Nobody was eating.

Samuel, typically, was pacing, but he stopped as Michael entered the room and correctly read the message in his face. "He's gone. He's really gone."

Matha was irate. "We have to get him back!"

He still didn't see the full extent of what had happened.

Michael wasn't sure any of the others, even Venny, did yet either. "We can't," he said flatly.

"Of course we can." This was from Mathew, whose plain face wore a puzzled expression. "We just have to follow the direction the plane was taking and keep going until we find him. They were headed back towards Paris, though I don't see how George could have thought he could land the plane in the city."

Michael looked around the room. Over the last year and a half since he'd come to Earth Two, these people had become his friends and companions. To a man (and woman), they were loyal, honest, and upright. Some could be cynical at times. They'd fought in wars and killed men, so they had experience dealing with the worst the world could dish out.

And that meant he needed to take the time to explain as best he could what he thought had happened. To some degree he was guessing too, but he thought his guesses might be pretty good.

"I don't know how many of you know that David has been suspicious of George for months, if not from the moment he arrived from Avalon with Anna. He never talked outright about his concerns to me, beyond the bare minimum required to stop me from asking questions. But I could not be at his side as much as I have been since Livia and I arrived and not know that he was worried. George worried him."

The mention of Livia made Michael's heart clench for a moment, thinking of her sailing down the Seine without him. At the same time, he knew she was one hundred percent capable of taking care of herself. While he certainly would have preferred to have her beside him, he wasn't going to wish he was with her there instead, since he was clearly where he needed to be. And that meant she was too. Given that David was gone, Lili would need her more than he did.

"I knew that too," Constance said.

Everybody else in the room bobbed their heads in agreement, and Matha punctuated his nod with a snort of disgust. "Of course he didn't trust George. Anyone could tell that George wasn't committed to our missions the way we all were. I wondered more than once why the king didn't cut him loose, as I've heard Lord Callum say."

"George is from Avalon," Michael said flatly, "and that made him dangerous."

Constance was chewing on her lower lip. "You are certain George was flying that plane?"

"As certain as I can be." Michael wondered briefly what had happened to Andre and hoped he was still alive. He didn't mention his concern to the others. It would cause fruitless speculation that would do none of them any good at this late hour.

"What does George want with the king?" Cador was standing beside his wife and was fully dressed to the point of wearing his bow and quiver, which were slung together on his back. "If he meant to kill David, he could have done it in the abbey's shed."

And with that question, Michael realized the extent to which his friends still didn't understand what had happened—and what might be happening even now. Every one of them knew that Avalon was another world. Not all of them understood exactly what that meant or that David, Anna, and Meg had thought, when they first arrived, that they'd time traveled to their world's past. Truly, Michael himself didn't really understand how it all worked. But, while the idea of multiple universes wasn't something the medieval mind could truly grasp, his friends did understand that Avalonian society was more *advanced,* technologically speaking, than Earth Two, and that David's origin in Avalon gave him an awareness of events in Earth Two's future that he had spent much of the last thirteen years trying to avert.

Their knowledge didn't go beyond that, however. It couldn't. Michael was the only one among them who not only was Avalonian but had ever been to Avalon.

He closed his eyes, gathering his thoughts in an attempt to explain as fully and succinctly as possible the first time around. "I cannot know everything in George's mind—or in David's, for that matter—but I am as near to certain as I can be that George is not flying David to Paris or back to England. He intends to crash that plane, where or how I couldn't say, and force David to take him to Avalon."

This news was greeted by dead silence.

Then Rhys, who'd been typically silent up until now, cleared his throat and asked the only question that really mattered: "Why?"

4

August 2023

Day Three

David

George had spoken mockingly, as of course he would.

First of all, David wanted to say, *nobody in the Middle Ages says,* your highness, *as you well know, and second, you never called me* my lord, sire, *or even* sir *the whole time you were there if you could possibly help it.*

David didn't say what he was thinking because, from this moment forward, his intent was to be disgustingly cooperative until such a time as it stopped making sense to be so. For now, he simply looked at George.

George, however, wasn't looking into David's face but at his hands. "Where are the cuffs?"

David pointed to where he'd tossed them onto the seat across the aisle.

A little *v* formed between George's brows. "If you were free, why didn't you attack me? You could have brought the plane down."

"Then we would have travelled to Avalon anyway." David's reply had come smoothly, but inside he was kicking himself for misreading the situation right off the bat.

George snorted. "Well then what about afterwards? We could have travelled back to Earth Two immediately."

"I've been doing this for thirteen years. Do you think I learned nothing in that time?" David turned his previous mild look into a glare and made sure his voice dripped with venom. It wasn't all that hard to do, because he truly despised George. It just wasn't the way he ever spoke—or how he'd planned to be speaking to George in this moment.

George's brow smoothed, and David heard genuine astonishment in his voice. "You were afraid the time traveling wouldn't work."

David sniffed and looked away, out the window. Men were moving purposefully towards the plane. His time alone with George was coming to an end. At most, he had a few minutes left. He had to make them count.

"Of course I thought it would work. It always works. But while I could have overcome you from behind, I don't know how to fly a plane, so I'd be stuck in the air until I crashed. I can return home any time I want to, but I certainly don't want to do it with *you*."

"Practical as always." George said, as if being practical was a bad thing. "Heaven forbid you allow your emotions to dictate your actions. It's a wonder they don't call you *the robot king*."

George headed down the aisle to check on Andre, who still seemed to be breathing, giving David a moment more to think. David's answer had been accurate, but George's question had been a good one. It wasn't so much that David had underestimated George, but that he needed to make sure he didn't confuse what he thought people were thinking with what they were actually thinking. The more intelligent the person, the more difficult it was to predict what they were going to do or say. Just because he'd understood George well enough to get this far, didn't mean he really understood him, especially now that he'd taken David to *his* territory. David shouldn't get cocky.

For starters, he should have re-cuffed his hands once he saw where they'd ended up. George was right that he'd uncuffed himself in case he needed to overpower him, but only if the time traveling gods had made them appear some place like a forest or an ocean, where George would have had to manage a crash landing.

Once David realized his mistake, he had quickly changed tack. More than anything, he didn't want George (or anyone else) wondering if David had manipulated George instead of the other way around. George was about to tell his masters in great detail what had gone on in Earth Two and, very likely, boast about how he'd completed his mission. It would be best for David's plans if his opponents continued to think themselves clever and underestimate David himself. Nobody needed to know just yet that he had chosen to be right where he was.

Once again, at the moment of contact with the enemy, his *oh so clever* plan hadn't gone exactly as he'd planned, just as he'd warned his own companions and been warned himself by Callum.

The issue with the cuffs was too late to fix, but it wasn't too late to fix his second mistake, which was to think George would meet cooperation with anything but distrust.

"If they knew what robots were. Which they don't."

George barked a laugh. "I'm going to miss you."

David had said exactly the right thing.

He needed to keep on saying it, so he gritted his teeth and added, "Then get back in that cockpit and fly me out of here!"

The anger was just below the surface, so it took no more than a breath to call it up again.

George shook his head. "I cannot do that, sir." The *sir* was mocking, as it would be. "Aren't you the one who always says you arrive where you're meant to?" He raised his eyebrows at David. "If that's true, what does your guardian angel think of you now?"

David turned his head to look out the window again, afraid he would give himself away with his expression. Because, of course, his mind and his guardian angel's, as George had put it, appeared to be one and the same. David knew what his goals were, and it seemed his guardian angel agreed with them. He was *exactly* where he needed to be. That was the whole point.

With that thought, a wave of relief coursed through David, and he let out a long, silent breath that relaxed his shoulders and eased the muscles in his neck. As the minutes had ticked by, they'd been tightening themselves with tension like winding up a clock. Really, he'd been carrying that tension for a long while now, if only because he hadn't been able to tell anyone what he was planning, not even—or maybe, especially—Lili.

The evacuation of Paris's Jewish community had required the orchestration of many moving parts, which he and his companions had gone over together dozens of times, modifying and fine-tuning, before their arrival in Paris. In the end, they'd treated the overall mission very much like the heist it became. Unfortunately, the movie he was in now wasn't the same. Really, it was unlike any movie David had ever seen before. He knew how he wanted it to go, but even more than in Paris, he feared for the disruption of his plans now that he was here.

At a minimum, he wanted the CIA to stop interfering in Earth Two. Even better would be if they stopped *wanting* to interfere. As he'd told the world in that interview a year and a half ago, Earth Two was not Avalon's past. It had its own destiny, and while he was very much in the middle of it, affecting the course of its history, it was clear that *some* entity wanted him to continue to do exactly that. The CIA—and every other organization or government—needed to understand that David was the champion of that world, and they meddled with it at their peril.

All things being equal, he would also be happy to help out Avalon if he could. The seeds that even now were stored in the compartment under the couch seat, beside which Andre was lying, were a start in that direction. Bringing seeds, however, was not the same as allowing companies to exploit Earth Two's resources. Human greed had already destroyed huge portions of Avalon. Those who wanted to continue that exploitation would view taking over Earth Two as their God-given right.

That would be happening over David's dead body. Literally.

And really, the sad fact was that the CIA had been a problem for a long time. At first, they'd been merely troublesome, but not so much David refused to try to work with them. Back then, he'd (foolishly) seen them as basically impotent and not much more than a nuisance. Later, they'd become allies, conjoined with MI-5. That had been in the days Callum was still working for the British spy agency.

Unfortunately, those days were gone—and had been for a while.

For both organizations, new leadership brought new ideas, and very often those new ideas rehashed bad old ones. The impulse to take advantage, to exploit, ran deep and wide, and seemed to run deeper and wider in people who sought power and endeavored to wield it in secret. Maybe that was simply human.

What David had come to understand since his talk with Chad Treadman, during their walk along that dirt track in Wales, was that it was long past time he put an end to CIA interference in Earth Two. The day of that walk, he'd thought he was taking some positive steps towards that goal. It was why he'd allowed Chad to convince him to go public with his story. According to Chad (and confirmed later by Michael and Livia when they'd arrived in Earth Two), more than half the planet had tuned in to watch his interview. That was something Chad would know, since Treadman Global owned enough news and media outlets to ensure that the story reached every corner of the world.

The interview couldn't have been enough for George, of course, since he wasn't even in Avalon at the time. His mission was long term, and a feel-good interview he hadn't even seen wasn't going to change him or his goals. But David had retained a sliver of hope that it could change the CIA's. Maybe, in the time George had been gone, they'd realized the error of their ways and scrapped this mission entirely. Ideally, as soon as George opened the door to the plane, they would treat David as a valued guest. Maybe they would even consult with him about *his* vision for their alliance. He was pretty sure they didn't know that David wasn't actually a hundred percent against authorities like the CIA or MI-5 having a connection to Earth Two. As Chad Treadman had argued, what went on there could be advantageous to this universe and vice versa.

Even so, as David watched the half-dozen men, some in army fatigues and some in suits, gather on the tarmac, waiting for George to open the door, he wasn't holding his breath.

He glanced back to George, who had taken the time to change out of his medieval clothing and into the suit he'd been wearing when he'd brought Anna to Earth Two. It was a bit of vanity David hadn't expected, but it was also something he understood: medieval clothing would put George at a disadvantage with the people outside, and he knew it. He wanted to be believed and respected.

Don't we all.

In light of his change of clothes, it was hypocritical for George to have been so disparaging of David's own pragmatic approach to governing, one he'd worked very hard to cultivate. Why would anyone want a mercurial king? Did George think that David never wanted to be vindictive? That plenty of times he hadn't raged in private at those who'd betrayed him? Didn't he think David *wanted* to reward his friends beyond what was reasonable? Though, thinking about it more, George definitely would have wanted David to be less logical because it would have made him more controllable. Honestly, his snipe at David sounded more like sour grapes than a genuine criticism.

Still, it was odd to be despised for a quality David valued in himself.

With George's approach, David stood up, not willing to sit any longer and ready to face what was coming next. The question that lay before him was exactly *what* was coming. He was well aware that every time he'd returned to Avalon since he was fourteen years old, the Americans who encountered him had treated him like a kid instead of the nobleman he was in Earth Two. Initially, David had been *only* a prince, but he'd been the King of England for nearly seven years. Increasingly, it was hard to accept how little respect anyone in Avalon afforded a twenty-six year old man.

Thus George's suit, clearly.

Before walking out to the abbey's shed, David had laid out in his own mind how he needed to behave while in custody and exactly the way all this was going to go. But now George's reaction to his initial attitude had him questioning everything. The goal was both to play to his opponents' expectations of him and to defy them at the same time. The stakes couldn't be higher. The survival of Earth Two depended on him.

"Come here." Having finished tying his tie, George snapped his fingers at David. His expression had settled into his usual superior amusement.

David had known from the start that George, of all Chad Treadman's people, resented the relatively fixed hierarchy of Earth Two. But even with George's mission to capture David's son, David hadn't realized how much George resented him personally. And then, with a flash of insight, he realized that *George* looked upon David as an unqualified twenty-six year old kid who didn't deserve to be whatever he was (in this case, the King of England).

Honestly, it was a wonder George was willing to take orders from anyone, even Chad Treadman, who was youthful too. Maybe, because George worked for the CIA and was undercover, he considered everything he'd done up until now in the service of that mission. He could kowtow if he had to for a greater good. The irony was that David—and likely Chad Treadman—had never asked for obeisance. David would have been happy to be George's friend.

For all that David had spent far too much time thinking about George and his motives, he had learned more about him in the last fifteen minutes than in the whole time George had been in Avalon. For the first time since they'd met, George was showing David his true self. Finally, the veil had been pulled aside, and George wasn't going to give way to David—or anyone else—ever again.

So David obeyed—stiffly, as if it was the last thing he wanted to do—turning around and putting his hands behind his back as George indicated. A moment later, the cuffs were on again.

David had no chance of getting to the key in his pocket. Not that he was disposed to try. On one hand, he felt like he'd aged fifty years in the five minutes since they'd landed. On the other, he was genuinely curious to see how things were going to go from here on out.

One of the men outside cupped his hands around his mouth and shouted towards the plane. "Hanson! You in there?"

The voice was so American, David almost laughed. The United States wasn't home to him anymore, but there was definitely something about those flat 'a's that made him feel like he knew where he was. Then he had to remind himself, sternly, that he didn't. It was 2023 now, and the last time he'd spent any length of time in Avalon was 2010. That last time he'd come to Avalon he'd learned what a mockery those thirteen years of absence had made of what he thought he knew. In 2010, when he and his sister had come to Earth Two for the first time and saved his father's life, they'd still been using flip phones.

"Strap in. This ride might be bumpier than the last one." George shot David a look that was more ironic than amused and went to open the door, spinning the lock that kept it closed in flight.

Contrary to what David had expected from the dryness of the fields surrounding the airport, as well as the blueness of the sky, the air was pleasantly cool at this early hour of the morning. The weather was also a far cry from the rain they'd experienced the last few days in medieval Paris.

Standing in the doorway of the plane, he realized he didn't have to wonder anymore why the powers-that-be had brought him here. Though Army (or perhaps National Guard) personnel were everywhere, along with some lesser men in suits, the two men who'd come to greet them on the tarmac had neat haircuts, polished shoes, and dark suits with white shirts that were so similar they were practically a uniform. Their demeanor screamed *feds*—or rather, they fit David's television-watching stereotype of feds. If one hadn't been black and the other white, they could have been twins. They even moved similarly.

Internally, he dubbed them *Thing One* and *Thing Two* (from the Doctor Seuss children's book he'd read to Arthur only last week from one of the digital tablets) until such a time as he could learn their names.

George grabbed David's elbow and urged him down the stairs that led from the doorway. He didn't have the gun out anymore, but he didn't need it, and he knew it. David didn't exactly shake him off, but he made a motion with his shoulder to imply that he'd like to.

George only held his arm tighter (which had been David's intent), and they descended the stairs in tight formation. At no point did David want George to suspect that he hadn't captured David fair and square.

As David reached level ground, the two newcomers stepped back to give him room, both of them eyeing him from head to foot. His medieval clothing was making Thing One's lip curl. George had known what he was doing. His suit made him one of *them,* while David's odd (to their eyes) outfit made him the enemy.

David had, in fact, dressed very carefully that morning. In particular, he'd left off his cloak, armor, and sword and wore clothing in the fashion of what Anna called *kingly light.* His shirt was cream-colored and went well with his blue overtunic, brown pants, and brown boots, though after the night he'd had, everything was a little worse for wear. The boots in particular were seriously overdressing for Eastern Oregon at the end of August, and even at sixty degrees Fahrenheit, his feet were sweating.

In retrospect, the only reason his companions at the abbey hadn't noticed anything amiss was because he hadn't given them time to think. As a king and a knight, he routinely wore his sword to breakfast and insisted all his companions do the same. Not that he needed, in general, to insist on any such thing. Knights slept with their swords. Like any soldier who'd seen combat, they knew that remaining alert to danger saved lives, and, as the king's guard, their particular job was to keep David breathing and in one piece.

Thankfully, David's personal sword was back in London, since he hadn't wanted to risk bringing it to Paris only to have it confiscated by the King of France. The weapon he'd been wearing last night had been taken off the unconscious body of one of Nogaret's guards.

Michael should have discovered by now that David had left his sword and cloak in the room at the monastery and would be in the midst of a major freak out. It wasn't as if he could have missed seeing the plane take off. He, at least, would know instantly that David was on it and where George was taking him. It might take some time for the others to understand, but David trusted that Michael would take care of them and any questions they had. That Michael was among his guard was part of what had allowed David to walk away as easily as he had.

Given the terrain around Vincennes, David didn't think they would have been able to see the plane dive into Notre Dame and disappear. Still, at the very least, a quick trip into Paris should put to rest any concerns about where he was.

He was sorry he'd left them without fair warning about what he was doing. Ieuan would give him a good chewing out for it at the first opportunity.

David had every intention of giving Ieuan that chance.

But first, David had to neutralize the CIA.

No biggie.

5

August 1295

Day Three

Michael

Rhys's tone was the closest any of his companions had come to a wail, and Michael appreciated that none of them were actually gnashing their teeth or even cursing, beyond that initial impulse. Perhaps he should have been concerned that they were *too* calm.

"You know why, Rhys," Michael said gently. "You all know why."

Rhys wasn't convinced. "I thought George wanted to abduct Arthur."

By now, the story Christopher had relayed about overhearing George's plan for abducting David's son had been disseminated to all the companions. Even thinking about it made Michael's stomach churn.

"He did." Michael had everyone's full attention. "My friends, there are powers in Avalon that seek to control us here. David has fought them every time he has left us. As I'm sure you recall, Livia and I evaded men who tried to abduct Prince Cadell, and they were instrumental in forcing us to leave Avalon with him."

Everyone nodded. They knew that part at least. Nobody was likely to forget that Anna's son, Cadell, had taken it upon himself to rescue his uncle after an assassination attempt had sent William de Bohun and David to Avalon. They also knew that Cadell had been targeted by men who wanted to use him for their own nefarious purposes. The CIA's plan to abduct one of the children was illegal in any universe. Legality did not appear to be a top priority for these agencies, however, no matter what country they were from or operating in.

"What may not have been made clear before was that these men hoped to ride Cadell back and forth between Avalon and this world. That's why George wanted Arthur, and that's why he has taken David now."

"Ride—" Matha bit off another curse. "Like a horse?"

"Or more like a boat crossing a river. David's ability to travel between worlds allows everyone who accompanies him safe passage too."

"As in the River Styx," Samuel said.

Heads nodded all around. Most of them wouldn't have read any of the original myths, but the ancient Greeks had some of the best stories, when good stories were few and far between.

Michael continued, "In so doing, their intent would be to bring men and equipment here, enough to—" He paused as he thought about how to phrase what needed to be said next.

"Take over?" Venny supplied, in something of a dry tone.

"Exactly."

Venny scratched at a thin cut near his nose, one Michael hadn't noticed before and which he must have acquired in the night. If that was the worst of their wounds, they were doing really well. As it was, the scratch had scabbed over, but traces of blood remained on his cheek. "The king was truly worried about this?"

"I was with him when he learned of it, and he has mentioned it several times since."

"Why didn't he say anything to us?" Mathew was a bit worked up now. "We are his guard!"

"I cannot speak for him, but my guess is that the king was reluctant to discuss what he saw as an imminent threat because at the time it was something about which he could do nothing." That was a very roundabout way of saying that David didn't want to worry everyone. Michael needed them to keep trusting David, which he didn't have much doubt about, but he also needed them to keep trusting *him*. That meant he needed to lead them to conclusions they couldn't come to on their own, without telling them outright what they were.

Venny wet his lips. "I'm getting the sense that you believe the king thought he would find George in that shed. He meant for George to capture him and take him to Avalon."

"Yes."

Samuel's eyes were so narrowed they were almost slits. "He went to the shed not to see Andre but because he thought George might have found the plane. That's also why he left his sword behind. He thought George was there, knew what he wanted, and was going to let him capture him."

None of that was a question, but Michael nodded anyway. "Yes. He did this on purpose."

Now came the uproar, or as much uproar as seven experienced soldiers ever made.

Michael let them express themselves, and he was about to interrupt to get them to let him speak again, when Venny did it for him, slicing through the air with one hand in a cutting off motion that everyone in the room took for the command it was.

"This is actually good news."

"How can you say that?" Constance was the most upset of any of them. "He didn't tell Lili either! How is she going to feel when she finds out?"

"You can't worry about that right now, and to do so is borrowing trouble, since it will be some time before she does know. You may even be the one to tell her, and you will deal with it then." Cador put an arm around his wife's shoulders. "Besides, I wouldn't be surprised to learn that Lili already does know, whether because the *sight* has told her or simply because she's been married to the man for seven years."

Michael didn't want to be the one to tell Lili that David had gone missing again either, but someone had to do it. Ideally, David would return within a day or two, as had often been the case in the past. When Michael and Livia had come to Earth Two with Cadell, he'd been in Avalon for all of twelve hours total.

But they couldn't count on that happening again, and if David was gone for some time, they would have to reconsider their plans. Someone like Lili, Nicholas de Carew, Math, or Ieuan would have to become regent until Arthur came of age. As he was only six years old at present, there was a good chance David would return long before then.

But Michael also knew, more than any of his current companions, what was possible in Avalon. The CIA, if that's who was pulling George's strings, could lock David up and throw away the key. Michael believed that David had gone into that shed and allowed himself to be taken captive on purpose, but Michael was also worried that David had underestimated the CIA's resolve.

Michael himself was married to an MI-5 officer, and Livia's tales of intrigue and deception within the agency far exceeded what went on outside it.

David had heard those stories too, and not just from Livia. He was surrounded by former MI-5 officers.

And yet, he'd allowed George to capture him.

Venny drew in a long breath through his nose. "David meant to go, which means he had a plan."

"He always has a plan," Matha said.

"David did say something to me last night." Rhys hadn't spoken again since his wailing question, and now he was staring at the floor, frowning. "His words struck me as odd at the time, but I don't understand half of what goes on in his mind, so I didn't think anything of it."

"What did he say?" Mathew demanded.

"Os dw i eisiau denu gwenyn, rhaid i mi dod yn flodyn."

This meant nothing to any of them but Cador, since Rhys had spoken in Welsh.

Cador tsked through his teeth. "*If I want to attract bees, I must become a flower.*"

Rhys's head came up and met Cador's gaze. "I assumed he was talking about the way he'd drawn King Philippe's attention to himself to distract from what else was going on in Paris, but now I'm wondering if he didn't mean something else entirely. He could have been sending me a message I wasn't yet able to understand."

"He definitely said *want* not *wanted*?" Mathew asked.

"The past tense is a completely different construction." Cador made a dismissive motion with his hand. "Welsh isn't like English."

Michael went to the doorway and stood looking out at the fields, trying to get his brain to work. At any other time, Cador's explanation would have deserved mockery, something along the lines of *obvious much?* But not today. Michael had slept too little, and although he'd eaten breakfast, there'd been a distressing shortage of coffee, as the small stash they'd hoarded was currently sailing down the Seine with Livia.

David's disappearance had briefly put all thoughts of last night aside, but Michael could only hope that Philippe really had backed down and had both ceased to hunt David and abandoned his designs on Aquitaine. David had done him a great service in freeing his wife and children. Regardless, it wasn't something Michael could do anything about now, and he wasn't going to take bets on how long that goodwill would last. Gratitude and loyalty weren't in Philippe's nature.

By the time Michael returned to the room, several of his companions had settled somewhat dejectedly in seats around the table and begun to pick at the food that remained on it. Preparing to sit too, Michael pushed back a plate that was too close to the edge of the table before he realized it contained David's half-eaten sandwich. Michael had been seated when David had wolfed down in a few bites the bit of it he'd eaten. Michael wasn't even sure David had sat down to do it. They were all so casual around him now, at David's insistence, that they hardly did more than come off their seats two inches when he entered a room. If they did any more than that, he invariably waved a hand to tell them to sit again.

It was this same casual attitude that had allowed David to leave the guesthouse on his own. Even then, they hadn't been completely lax. Samuel had been standing guard outside, and, as David had left, Michael had risen and gone to the door to watch that he made it safely across the field to the shed. He'd been a bodyguard only since meeting David, but he should have known better. That said, it was hard to protect a man who didn't want to be protected.

David hadn't wanted to be protected.

The implications rattled around in Michael's mind as he tried to think like David himself. Every one of David's companions trusted David with his own life—in the same way David trusted them with his. Really, that wasn't even because David was the King of England. He had proven himself, time and again, to be entirely suited to wearing the crown. They followed him because to do otherwise would be counterproductive and idiotic.

And Matha was right that David always had a plan.

As those realizations came together, Michael's eyes focused for the first time on what David had left on the table.

"It's a note." He found himself laughing.

The others stopped their side conversations and stood up as Michael pointed to a handful of raisins strewn across the table in front of David's plate. Or rather, at first they looked as if they'd been strewn at random. The dish in which they'd been kept was in the center of the table and was half full. While Michael knew for a fact that David wasn't hugely fond of raisins, he'd been assuming they'd spilled when he'd grabbed a handful, because more remained on his plate.

"What are you talking about?" Venny stepped to Michael's side.

Mathew, who was larger than both Michael and Venny and twice as broad as well, poked his head above and between theirs so he could see better what David had carefully written as plain as day, now that Michael was looking.

"T. R. U. S. T. M. E."

Michael let out a sigh. "He knew us well enough to know that after he'd gone we'd be standing around the table like this."

"Why didn't he just tell us then?" Matha said.

Rhys shook his head. "He was afraid we'd stop him."

"That was smart of him because we would have," Samuel said.

"So he's really gone to Avalon? Just like before?" Matha had been in Ireland when Anna had arrived a year and a half ago, and he had witnessed the miracle of the plane's sudden appearance. David himself had disappeared shortly thereafter, in full view of many of his men, though none of those here had been present to see it. Venny, Rhys, and Cador had been imprisoned in Beeston Castle at the time. Michael, of course, had joined David after he arrived in Avalon, though he had initially been left behind when David returned to Earth Two.

Michael looked around at his companions. Each of them had skills and abilities that had brought them to David's attention, but at the moment they were all looking to Michael himself for leadership.

He feared he had none to give, but he had to try. "I don't think this is like any other time he's been to Avalon. He's letting us know that he does have a plan, and that he meant to go to Avalon alone. *If I want to attract bees, I must become a flower.* He's made himself a flower."

"So how do we go after him?" Samuel had his hands on his hips and was gazing down at the raisins, as if by looking he could make them say something different.

"We don't," Michael said flatly. "We have a different mission now."

Mathew had picked up a bun and taken a big bite, which he spoke around. "Which is what exactly?"

Now that the truth was out, he appeared the least affected by what David had done. His faith, as always, was unshakable. That was good as far as it went. Michael himself was far less calm inside, probably because he had a far better idea of what might await David in Avalon. Michael definitely trusted him. He just worried that David had no real idea what he was getting into.

But he had to be confident for his friends. If David was getting himself in trouble in Avalon, Michael still could do nothing about it. "What it has always been. We are David's guards, yes. But really, we're the king's."

"Oh, I understand." Cador's head came up. "He's asking us to trust him, but even more, he is trusting *us*."

Samuel had his arms folded across his chest and was still looking fierce. "What does that mean?"

"Don't you see? He knew Michael would figure out what had happened." Cador pointed at the raisins. "Maybe others of us would have too, given time. But that doesn't matter now. It isn't David we need to protect anymore. We don't have to worry about *him*."

"Then what are we supposed to do?" Venny said. "How is this *him* trusting *us*?"

"He's telling us to protect his family." Constance met Michael's gaze. "Arthur. The baby. Lili." She was normally Lili's bodyguard, and Michael could see her regretting not riding with Ieuan and Darren to the boats. If she had, she would have been with Lili by now.

Constance was still looking intently at her companions. "Is there more we don't know? Is that what we're missing here? Are they in danger?"

Michael thought she was reading too much into a few words, but from the expressions on his friends' faces, he was in the minority. "George is gone." He spoke slowly, thinking it out. "As far as I know he didn't know about our plans beyond what was pertinent to him. He didn't know about the boats. It's clear to me now that David very deliberately kept that information from him, but—"

Constance's eyes were wide and staring. "But what if we're wrong?"

Everyone moved at once.

6

August 2023
Day Three

David

"It's good to see you again, sir." It was Thing One, the shorter of the two men, speaking in an accent that meant he was from New York or New Jersey. It had been his companion who'd called up to George when they were still on the plane, and David was guessing he was from somewhere on the West Coast. "We met a few years ago at Langley."

This greeting was directed to George, of course, not David. Both the federal agents were avoiding eye contact with him, as if they were embarrassed.

For the moment, David didn't mind their disregard. He was still in the process of reevaluating his game plan, to find holes similar to what his interaction with George had revealed. It wasn't a great spot to be in this late in the half, but upon hearing the man's comment, he felt like saying *ah ha!*—since even he knew that the CIA was headquartered outside Washington DC in Langley, Virginia.

"I remember you." George's words came out with a bit of a drawl. David knew him well enough by now to realize he was feeling good about himself—*chuffed* as Michael might say.

"Shall we take this inside?" Thing One asked.

"Lead on."

The two agents turned smartly around, and George took a step after them, heading towards the interior of the hangar. Because he was still holding David's elbow, he hauled him along a few steps before David balked.

"What about Andre?"

George didn't reply and tugged on David to get him moving again. David himself was a large man, 6' 2" and weighing in at around 210—or at least that was what the scale had read a year and a half ago when he'd been poked and prodded by Chad Treadman's people. He dug in his heels and got George to stop.

The others turned back to David, annoyance in their faces, and Thing Two asked, "Who's Andre?"

David's hands were behind his back, so he couldn't spread them wide, but he managed something of a gesture towards the plane with his shoulder. "Back in the plane." He looked at George. "Did you forget about him already?"

Thing Two looked from David to George. "What's he talking about?"

Again, it was David who answered. "You've never heard of Andre Dawson? The man who flew the plane to Earth Two in the first place?"

At the agents' blank expressions, David was mentally pulled up short. They knew nothing about Earth Two or his life there. After a moment's consideration, he supposed that was to be expected. The plane had appeared out of nowhere, and this might not even be a CIA base but one belonging primarily to the National Guard or another agency known by its string of letters: FBI, NSA, ATF. Even CDC. Likely Things One and Two were here for some other purpose and had been diverted from it to deal with David.

Either that or, in distressingly typical fashion, the CIA's disdain for David meant they hadn't bothered to brief their agents on the salient details.

David still wasn't going to leave Andre lying in a heap on the floor. "George knocked him out in order to take over the plane. How about you get him an ambulance?"

Things One and Two looked at each other, and then Thing Two took off at a jog for the plane.

George hummed under his breath. "Always putting everyone else before yourself."

"You should try it some time."

"I didn't forget about him. He's fine." But the look George gave him was full of disillusion.

If George had been one of David's sons, he would have used his Yoda voice and said, *Fail, this is why you always will, hmm hm!*

They left the bright sunlight of the late summer morning and entered the comparative darkness and genuine cool of the airplane hangar. David had never been inside one before, and he swiveled his head, trying to take in everything at once. He didn't intend to escape (yet), but one never knew what knowledge might come in useful later. In particular, in the back corner next to a rollup door, which was larger than one in a home garage, was a regular door with the words EXIT above it. It was a way to leave the hangar without going through the massive openings that abutted the airstrip.

More than anything, the hangar resembled what lay (according to Anna) underneath Chad Treadman's modern castle, except this was above ground. In point of fact, David hadn't known you could build a hangar this big. A 747 would be dwarfed inside. As it was, the hangar was mostly empty, containing three helicopters, a small plane a few feet longer than the one David had just come in on, and a bunch of vehicles: jeeps, sedans, and a personnel carrier.

In the far corner near the little door was also a three-story free-standing office building, which was completely dwarfed by the overall size of the hangar. Ten more similarly-sized buildings could have fit inside—and probably at least six more stories on each.

Since Thing Two hadn't returned, Thing One alone led George and David to the office building's utterly flat and windowless front door, which was the only entrance. The floors above had windows, but they were one-way glass and thus blacked out on this side. David had no doubt the facility was full of cameras and guards, but he didn't see any.

Not that he would know what a modern camera looked like. He imagined by now they were the size of a pinhead.

Thing One opened the door and led them into an anteroom with bare white walls and nothing else except another door right in front of them. He stood perfectly still for a moment, looking above the door to a round object slightly smaller than an old-fashioned light bulb.

Ah ha!

"Where are we going?" David saw no point in being shy and retiring. Worst case, Thing One wouldn't answer.

He didn't and, typically, all George said was, "You'll see."

David grunted to himself. It was no more nor less than he'd expected. These men were doing as they were told. Maybe they believed in their cause. Maybe they didn't really know who he was, and he was fooling himself in thinking that his interview in Wales was something anyone would remember or care about a year and a half later. Who knew what travails the people of Avalon had gone through in his absence? Maybe Chad Treadman no longer cared about Earth Two either.

They should care, though. They all had agency. They all had choices. It was what he had been trying to impress upon the people of Earth Two ever since he arrived. His people didn't necessarily understand either, but they didn't have the benefit of the last seven hundred and twenty-eight years of history either.

David was King of England because the people had chosen him. He was High King of Britain because the people had chosen him. The people in Avalon had a choice too. They didn't have to choose the four horsemen of the apocalypse.

What's more, every one of the people who'd stayed with him in Earth Two, with the exception of George, had stayed because he or she *wanted* to. They all believed in David's mission. They came from all walks of life—from Bronwen, one of the earliest converts, who'd been in Earth Two almost as long as David, to Michael and Livia, the newest additions.

Although several of his companions were MI-5, none until George had been CIA. And maybe that was part of the problem. Those in power were forced to look differently on what David was doing when their own people not only chose to stay with him but advocated for him.

He'd also had the thought that the American intelligence agencies resented, just a little bit, that this American kid from Oregon had become the King of England, and they had no say in the matter and no control over him. There was just enough rivalry between England and the US, and between agencies, for MI-5 to have rubbed the CIA's nose in their superior position a few too many times. More recently, MI-5 had needed to go to the CIA to beg for a return of the information the former director of Five, with the help of Mark Jones, had deleted, and that hadn't helped matters either. If nothing else, MI-5's relative weakness made the CIA think they were coming out on top.

David glanced at George, who was wearing that perpetual smirk David had come to despise. He was one of those people who always thought he was the smartest person in the room. In some people, that conviction arose from a deep sense of insecurity, but David didn't think that was the case with George. He *was* impressive, and he *was* good at his job. Thus, it wasn't so much that his ego was overinflated but that he thought about himself too much. The only benefit of that at the moment was he didn't realize David had been the one calling the shots all along.

Still, despite the less than lukewarm reception, David thought he was safe in assuming that he was a celebrity. Therefore, what they did to him would have to be done in secret. They'd be afraid of him escaping and finding help. Like George with the handcuffs, they would lock him up as securely as they could manage. Already, this was looking like a prison—and not just for David himself.

Finally, deep in the recesses of the building, a buzzer sounded, and Thing One opened the door in front of him. This brought them into a lobby area with a set of stairs directly ahead going up. The lobby was manned (womanned) by a soldier in fatigues, who stood up as the three of them filed through the door. Thing Two was still busy arranging an ambulance for Andre.

So far, the office building was no more exciting than any other industrial office David had ever been in, but he reminded himself that he was dealing with the CIA, and this was just the lobby of their building, located *inside* the biggest airplane hangar in the world. There was more here than met the eye.

So when the woman sent them up the stairs that began behind her desk, he couldn't be surprised to find himself in a much larger room full of computers and technicians. A bank of screens took up one wall, below which a woman in her late thirties or early forties, with short black hair and a stern expression, paced on too high heels that looked uncomfortable to wear. Her face must have communicated something pertinent to Thing One because he made a beeline for her, and thus George and David did too.

She inspected David with a quick up and down that was a little too obvious and maybe a bit too dismissive as well. "This is he?"

David looked at her with careful eyes. She spoke correct English, which wasn't all that common in modern America in David's experience, even in English teachers. At a minimum, she was the boss of the Things and this office. What *this office* actually did, however, was not clear.

Something with computers. His education in Avalon had stopped when he was fourteen. He had spent many hours over the last months poring over the videos, reports, and other media Mark Jones had brought when he'd come. They had tablets and drives full of information. But, at this point, David had been gone so long and was so out of touch with daily life here that he didn't know what he didn't know. The camera above the door was just the beginning.

"It is," Thing One said. "Where do you want him?"

David tried not to laugh at being spoken about as if he himself were a thing instead of a red-blooded American like them. Then again, *thing* was what he'd just dubbed the two men who'd come to greet the plane. There was irony—or hypocrisy anyway.

The woman, whom David decided then and there to call *Heels* until he learned her name, sneered, implying she would have been just as happy to step on him as talk to him, if not for the residue he'd leave on her shoe. David had assumed he'd be disrespected, but this woman was looking at him as if he'd just crawled out of a sewer.

It bowed his head.

For a single moment.

Taking a deep breath, he ran through everything in the plan he'd set for himself, confirming in his own mind that his overall approach remained sound. This was the natural consequence of everything that had gone before. The only way to prevent the CIA from exploiting him, his family, and his world was to face them head on.

On the upside, their thinking had at least progressed to the extent that the truth of who he was could not be denied as it had been so many times before. And if he was real and Earth Two was a real place and George had just spent the last year and a half there, then *of course* a powerful entity like the CIA was going to want to exploit him and his pristine world. Really, given what was at stake, it was remarkable it had taken the CIA as long as it had to reach this point.

Heels tapped a finger to her lower lip as she directed her attention to George. "I understand he's a suicide risk."

George blinked but didn't actually laugh out loud. "That's one way to put it."

Heels nodded to Thing One. "Take him to Interrogation Room B. And don't let him out of your sight." She glowered at the agent. "There will be no screw-ups this time."

This time.

David's thumbs were pricking at the way she hadn't looked directly at him since that initial assessment. She certainly hadn't spoken to him. That said, he hadn't yet decided if he wanted to talk to her anyway. In coming to maturity in a royal court, first his father's and then his own, he'd learned the futility of speaking when his audience wasn't receptive. Right now, to say anything at all in his defense would be a waste of energy and breath. The only reason to do so would be either to prove a point—that he was a functioning adult—or so that later, when the CIA's plans went awry, he could say *I told you so*.

Heels motioned George towards a glass-paneled office behind her, and David allowed Thing One to lead him in the opposite direction, to an elevator. As he reached it, David glanced back to George, who'd stopped too to look at him. George's face was expressionless, and David returned the stony look. It was a little late for regrets—for either of them.

The elevator descended two floors below the ground, dumping them out in a white, utilitarian hallway that smelled like it had been recently painted. The hallway was lined with doors, as it would be, and Thing One took David to the third one along, helpfully labeled with a big B on a plaque at head height. Thing One opened the door with a swipe of his wrist.

Like George a moment ago when Heels had mentioned suicide, David blinked, disbelieving what he'd seen, and then trying not to stare when he realized the man had allowed his employers to insert a chip into his wrist. Now that David thought back, it was how Thing One had opened the elevator too. Back in 2010, chipping people had been the realm of science fiction, and he and his friends had discussed the concept at length. They'd all come down on the side of *no way* for themselves, no matter who wanted to do it. Sure, it might be more convenient and far better for security for the company or government in question, but they'd thought it a massive violation of privacy for the individual.

David's mother and sister had been chased across Oregon the last time they were here. They'd bought disposable phones at a Walmart because Cassie's and Callum's phones were too dangerous to keep. Though David had no phone himself, he understood by now that tracking and surveillance were a way of life for residents of the twenty-first century. To most, the idea that cameras recorded their every move, and the authorities could tap into the GPS on their devices, was so normal as to be unquestioned. They accepted this overstepping as the cost of doing business.

Even with the prevalence of invasive technology, David's Uncle Ted had balked at allowing his auto insurance company to track his son by putting an app on his phone and a device in his vehicle. When his uncle had mentioned this in passing, in reference to the idea that he would really like to have a tracker on Christopher most days, David had thought, *Good on you, Uncle Ted.* But even Uncle Ted's knowledge of these things was quaintly out of date by now, as he too had lived in Earth Two for a year and a half. Things appeared to have evolved since then, since none of his Avalonian companions had mentioned a push by their employers to get everyone chipped. And maybe nobody could get auto insurance now unless they allowed themselves to be tracked.

The interrogation room turned out to be not unlike the one MI-5 had kept him in years ago in Cardiff. David had managed to come down with scarlet fever that time, which forced his transfer to an ambulance and, after shenanigans ensued, ultimately allowed Cassie and Callum to rescue him. That wouldn't be happening this time.

If he did decide things were going south enough that he needed to escape, that everyone was chipped meant he wouldn't be able to open any doorway—not unless he disabled or killed someone in the facility and dug the chip out of his or her wrist. Even then, perhaps there was a mechanism that deactivated the chip once removed from flesh, which would mean he'd have to cut off someone's arm. Or, to escalate, maybe that flesh had to be living.

His only option, then, would be persuasion. This too was as he'd planned, though it would be harder to accomplish if nobody would talk to him.

As David stepped into the interrogation room and looked around at the bare white walls and the shackles attached to the table, he put aside any hope for accommodation or a quick resolution to the current adversarial relationship between him and the CIA.

And acknowledged a plain truth: before things got better, they were likely to get a whole lot worse.

7

August 1295

Day Three

Constance

"What do you think?" Cador slowed his horse as he surveyed the waterline. They were two miles southeast of the monastery, looking to cross the River Seine just downstream from its confluence with the Marne.

"I think the only way across this river is going to be on a bridge," Venny said. "If there's a usable ford, it's going to be farther upstream than we want to ride—and that's if we can even get across the Marne."

"But how are we going to cross even the main bridge? We are not French, and some of us—," here Constance gestured ruefully to herself, "—cannot successfully pretend."

A grim silence settled over the companions, during which time the Seine appeared to rise another two inches. Constance saw now how lucky they'd been to have the boats arrive outside Paris when they had, since what might be a few hours' float down the river could take a day and a half coming up.

They had left Vincennes within an hour of David's own departure. Before, their focus had been entirely on the danger of having him in their company, and how to get him to Rouen without calling undue attention to themselves. While they could attempt to disguise him, they feared the number of people who'd seen his face in Paris. They'd intended either to ride southeast from Vincennes and cross the Seine here, a considerable distance upstream from Paris, or circle around the city to the northeast, following the same road the Jewish refugees had taken in the night.

Once past the city, they would not have boarded riverboats, since theirs were already headed downstream, but continued riding west to Rouen, eighty miles away. They'd assumed they could travel that distance long before the boats, which had twice as far to go and should take four times as long. The original idea had been for anyone who left Paris on horseback to meet the boats in Rouen, which was all the way into Normandy and therefore far enough from Paris to be out of the immediate reach of King Philippe.

Normandy had once been part of the Kingdom of England, but it had been conquered by France nearly a century ago and was now Philippe's gateway to the English Channel through the port of Le Havre at the mouth of the Seine.

Most important of all, Amaury de Montfort was in Rouen. It was he who'd signed the letter that had admitted Rachel, Samuel, and Aaron into Paris. His position as a canon of Rouen's cathedral meant he was responsible for administration of the church and able to participate in the election of a bishop. Even better for their purposes, it gave him enough authority in the city to arrange for the safe passage of the refugees floating down the Seine.

Or so he'd believed. But those arrangements had been made weeks ago, before David had disappeared to parts unknown in a flying chariot.

"You won't have to." Michael's ascension to leadership of their company was for more reasons than just because he was King David's man and friend in a way the rest of them could never be. Over the last few months, they'd seen him become more than he had been, in the same way they'd all, since joining David's company, become more than they'd been. "I'm a nobleman from Sicily still, aren't I? And you are my men—and woman," he amended, throwing out a hand in Constance's direction.

Venny laughed. "Honestly, I'd forgotten that. Other than the Templars and the few of us here, could anyone recognize you as someone else?"

"The queen saw me last night at Vincennes." Michael spoke slowly, thinking hard as each of them was doing in turn to recall the many events of the previous night.

"And I," Venny said, "along with Ieuan and Darren, though the other two should be long gone."

"I doubt she's going to be guarding the bridge across the Seine," Cador said dryly.

"If she is," Matha said, in an equally dry tone, "something really has gone very wrong."

"It is a risk we have to take," Samuel said, not responding to their humor.

"The risk to you is greater than for some." Michael turned to him. "You are Jewish."

"It is no more a risk than I have taken every day I've been in France."

Michael dismounted to pull from his saddlebag a wool cloak in a rich blue, with gold embroidery around its hem. He swung the cloak around his shoulders and, in an instant, became the Sicilian nobleman he'd been pretending to be these last months, never mind the mud on his boots. "Prepare, all of you. We must look the part."

Constance herself was still dressed as she'd been last night, but she had finer clothes in her bags too. Someone had wadded up a Templar cloak and stuffed it on top of her things, another leftover from the events of the night, but underneath was a green dress and matching cloak suitable for riding, both of which Lili had made especially for her. The attire might identify her as fashionable in the English court rather than the French one, but wearing it would make her less conspicuous than trousers. She also managed to tame her hair into a pile on top of her head, prompting an admiring look from her husband.

She wished for the thousandth time since the king had disappeared that she'd ridden to the boats with Ieuan instead of staying behind, admittedly as Lili had requested, saying she could do more good on the road with David, since he had too few men. One more bow might make the difference between success and failure, and Ieuan himself would protect his sister as he always had. Of course, none of them had known David would be leaving them this morning.

Constance harrumphed again, prompting Cador to put out a hand to her. "She'll be fine, if any of us will be. Even had you ridden to Poissy with Darren and Ieuan, none of the boats may have been able to stop long enough for you to board. Those two may be continuing on to Rouen on horseback too."

"I do know that." Constance let out a breath.

"You are here because Lili couldn't be," Cador continued. "Take her encouragement to heart. Maybe she knows something we don't."

"I've never felt so helpless, even when we were imprisoned in Philippe's palace."

"To judge that now would be to stop the story in the middle."

The bridge was fortified, as were many bridges in France. Two great towers rose up on either side of the entrance, with a matching set on the opposite bank. Both a portcullis and a wooden door could block their way across the river if the guards didn't like the look of them. Or, if the guards changed their minds once a traveler rode onto the bridge, all that would be needed to stop them was to drop their portcullis and shout at the men guarding the other side to do the same. Suspects would then be stuck in the middle of the bridge, with no recourse but to surrender or to leap the rail and swim.

The soldiers dropped their pikes while Constance's company was still a dozen yards away, so they slowed their horses to a walk.

Then one of the guards took a step forward, his palm out. "Pardon, my lord. I have been asked to stop everyone who wishes to cross the bridge and turn them back." He leaned this way and that to look past Michael to the faces of his companions. Cador and Constance had ended up directly behind Michael, so the soldier was standing a few feet from her.

As their leader and the nobleman in their party, Michael put his nose into the air, affecting a somewhat haughty attitude, as if speaking to the soldiers who guarded the bridge was beneath him. His other option would have been to be kind and magnanimous, but Constance hadn't noted very many French noblemen with that attitude. "Why would that be? I have business to attend to on the other side of this river."

"My apologies, sir. Orders from Lord Nogaret."

Even as a prisoner, Nogaret's fingers reached into every pie.

Michael bent his gaze intently on the soldier, and his voice deepened. "Your news is old, my friend. Nogaret has been arrested. His orders are no longer in force."

The soldier blinked. "Since when?"

"Since last night. You have not heard as much from your commander?"

"No, my lord. He told us it would be our heads if we let the King of England escape Paris."

"None of us is the King of England," Michael gestured to his companions, every one of whom was suddenly thankful that David wasn't with them. "You must let us pass."

By now, the second guard had walked the full length of the company and back. He nodded at the first guard. "I don't see him."

"It isn't as if we could hide him in our saddle bags." Michael let out a laugh. Nobody else joined him, and when the guards still didn't give way, he spread his hands wide. "My friends, King David is not here. It is absurd to keep us."

"Wait a moment. I know you!" Now that he'd returned to the front of the company, the second guard looked into Michael's face and snapped his fingers. "You're that nobleman from Sicily with the beautiful wife. I was on the wall the other day when you entered the city."

"I am he." Michael answered gravely back, though he didn't give his name nor comment on the guard's rudeness.

"Where's your wife?" The first guard's eyes narrowed, and he looked straight at Constance.

Michael turned in the saddle to look at her too, just for a moment, his eyes assessing, and then he faced front again. "My wife does not ride with me this day."

All of a sudden, both guards relaxed. Their pikes that had been blocking the way came up, and they stepped back, out of the road. "Best of luck to you, my lord."

Constance couldn't see Michael's expression, but he nodded and urged his horse onto the bridge. The others followed immediately behind, not saying a word until they were well clear of the towers on the opposite bank and heading down the road to Rouen.

"What was that about?" Constance finally asked. "Why did they change their minds?"

"*Cariad.*" After a quick glance at the men around them, none of whom would look him in the eye, Cador took it upon himself to explain. "They think you are Michael's mistress."

Constance's mouth fell open. "What?"

"It's all right, boys." Cador put out a hand to the others. "You can laugh. I'm neither angry nor offended."

"I am!" Constance said, to the relieved laughter of her companions.

"Thank you for playing your roles, all of you." Michael slowed his horse so she and Cador could come abreast. "Nogaret was not one to be trifled with, even in his absence, and we might have had to kill them to get across. We couldn't have done this without you."

"Lili was right, my love. You are exactly where you're supposed to be." Cador took Constance's hand and kissed the back of it. "And, as it turns out, King David just might be too."

8

August 2023
Day Three
David

They'd taken his boots.

Of course they had. Though he didn't like it at all, he'd expected nothing less. They knew, as he did, that a man without shoes was a pitiable figure. Maybe David should have been glad they hadn't taken his pants.

First, Thing One had made him sit in the hard plastic chair on the other side of the table from the door. By that time, a soldier in full riot gear and carrying a rifle/machine gun (at this point David didn't know anything about modern weaponry, other than that the weapon shot a lot of rounds) appeared in the doorway in case David tried to get away. Then Thing One attached David's wrists to the shackles. These ran through a hole in the table to a metal ring set into the concrete floor. After that, Thing One had needed to bend awkwardly to remove David's boots. It wasn't easy, as David well knew because at home he needed help from a servant or valet to remove them. Eventually, Thing One wrestled them off, but when he stood, his expression was cold and hard. He knew, as David did, what that had looked like from the other side of the one-way glass or through the cameras set in the corners of the ceiling.

David kept his eyes on Thing One's face and tried to project an aura of matter-of-factness that belied the way Thing One had just humiliated himself at David's feet. "I'm David. What's your name?"

Thing One simply glared, turned on his heel, and left. The guard went with him, and they closed the door behind them. Presumably they were following Heels' decree about not letting him out of their sight by watching him through the aforementioned glass or cameras.

David shifted in the seat, feeling relatively philosophical about his predicament. Though he would have been pleased if Thing One had told him his name, he had expected him not to respond. At this point, it was all about baby steps. David himself had been uncomfortable plenty of times in the last thirteen years. In a way, it was kind of cute they thought what they were doing was intimidating, even if it was still annoying for them to be wasting his time this way. At the very least, he would have also preferred a more comfortable chair and less air-conditioning, since his feet were cold without his boots.

After an hour, a Latina woman with her hair pulled back in a severe bun brought him a bottle of water and a sandwich. He tried to ask her name too, but, like Thing One, she refused to answer. In fact, she acted like he wasn't even there, and she was leaving the sandwich and water in an empty room.

Alone again, he ate and drank, fully cognizant of the fact that his fingerprints would be taken off the bottle, and the sandwich could be filled with sodium pentothal or another drug. In a canter around his conscience, there wasn't anything he knew or could tell them that he minded sharing. They really had only to ask.

Although he could have done without the sheer monotony of being left alone in the room for hours, he wasn't sorry they'd given him time to think. It was sad, really, how little his captors appeared to know what they were doing.

While, as King of England, he rarely had time to read, he'd managed occasionally to appropriate one of Mark Jones' tablets and snatch an hour or two alone late at night. The selection of novels Mark had made available included several where the hero was capable of extracting himself from incredibly dangerous and adversarial situations. Throughout the book, the reader was just waiting for the hero to spring into violent action, take out his attackers with a few clever and emphatic moves, and keep on going until he'd not only disabled or killed all of his opponents but uncovered the treachery of the day in the bargain.

And really, violence was an option for David. At twenty-six, he was as strong and physically powerful as he was ever likely to be. He had spent the last thirteen years ensuring that he could wield a two-pound sword for as long as he needed to. He'd arrived in Earth Two knowing karate and since then had mastered what would be viewed in Avalon as medieval martial arts. He knew how to get an opponent flat on his back and kill him, as quickly and efficiently as possible, with whatever weapon was available, including his own hands.

But violence was not going to solve David's problem with the CIA. It was not possible to kill or disable everyone who wanted to use him as a pawn. He had no power here and no ability to manipulate the circumstances of his capture. He knew a few people in high places, but it wasn't as if he had the president or a general in the army on speed dial.

If he'd been captured unawares, he might have considered some kind of evasive action, but he'd signed up for this. Deliberately. As with most problems, the best way out of this predicament was by using his brain instead of his brawn.

So he waited.

With the sandwich long since consumed, at one point he wadded up the plastic as tightly as he could and threw it against the wall like Steve McQueen in *The Great Escape*, but it wasn't a baseball and didn't bounce back to him. Bored with imagining worst case scenarios, he started singing. He didn't know much in the way of popular music from the last ten years, but he had plenty of repertoire from prior to 2010 and from medieval Wales. Some of his favorites were love ballads written by a Prince of Gwynedd, born in the twelfth century, who was kin to David and with whom he felt kinship, since Hywel had been a prince and a bard too.

Outcasts in Time

Little of Hywel's work survived to the modern age (according to David's mother). The texts of many of his ballads were something else David would have been happy to provide Avalonians. They had only to ask.

A bright fort on a shining slope stands;
A girl, shy and beautiful, plays with the gulls.
Though she thinks of me not,
I will go,
on my white horse,
my soul full of longing;
to seek out the girl whose laughter fills my heart,
to speak of love,
since it has come my way.

Finally, as he finished a song about King Arthur, one he'd forbidden anyone else to sing because of its not-so-subtle reference to David himself, the door opened to reveal another agent, this one sporting a blond crewcut and a blue suit. He wasn't quite a clone of Thing One, but he was close. With him too was a soldier in fatigues, who stayed near the door.

The man, whom David instantly dubbed *Crewcut*, slapped a folder down in front of him. "David, King of England." He sneered.

"I am."

David had been sitting leaned back in the chair with his feet up on the table, and now Crewcut leaned across and shoved at David's legs so his feet dropped to the floor. "You realize you're deluded, don't you? We should send you right now to a mental institution."

David had managed to catch himself before he fell off the chair, and now he straightened. The man's anger was obviously an interview technique, because David had done nothing wrong. Crewcut's attitude was such a stereotype, in fact, that David would have laughed if his wrists hadn't still been chained to the table in front of him. The cuffs were really starting to irritate his skin.

"Why don't you?"

Crewcut glowered for a few seconds before opening the folder in order to show David a grainy image of Anna on a horse inside a room, which David supposed was Westminster Hall in London. "Your sister is wanted for acts of terrorism. Where is she?"

Did this mean MI-5 was cooperating with the CIA? Or did the CIA get that picture from MI-5 a year and a half ago? David was genuinely confused about the point of any of this. They had George. They knew where he'd spent the last year and a half of his life. "You want me to sell out my sister?"

"If you don't tell us what we want to know, we could charge you with aiding and abetting a known terrorist, lock you up, and throw away the key. You would never be heard from again."

David did know that. "I repeat, *why don't you?*"

Crewcut glowered, but David didn't give him anything more—and really, what was there to say? Once David had come to terms with the current political landscape in Avalon, he had accepted the very high possibility that he would experience exactly what he was experiencing now. They'd sent Crewcut in to intimidate, to frighten, to the point of making even David believe he'd done something wrong.

Either that, or they were simply tired of his singing.

9

August 1295

Day Three

Amaury

The gathering of the canons who served Rouen's cathedral was hardly unprecedented, though from Amaury's perspective, it was definitely unwelcome. He had been in a state of nervous anticipation ever since the English boats had poled underneath Rouen's bridge and into the upper portion of the Seine ten days ago. The plan had been for them to come back downriver in two or three days' time, and Amaury had a great deal to do between now and then to ensure they navigated the passage safely.

"Why did the archbishop summon us to council?" He leaned in to whisper to one of his fellow priests. "What's this about?"

"He received a message last night from King Philippe's adviser, Nogaret. It has him very excited."

Amaury tried not to convey his dismay at this news. Nogaret was a wolf—and one who didn't even try to disguise himself in sheep's clothing. Unfortunately, Archbishop Guillaume was cut from the same cloth, and the two men shared more than the same given name. He had risen to his current station at the death of his predecessor, who'd chosen him as his successor, even though Guillaume was neither Norman nor from Rouen and openly disdained the people he was supposed to serve. So far, he'd spent his archbishopric appointing his family members to high positions in the Church. It was perhaps telling that his appointment had been denied initially, until the election of a new pope, who shared his predilection for nepotism.

And really, the rest of the governors of Rouen were hardly better. From the outside, Rouen's government functioned similarly to market towns in England, possessing its own governing body and significant autonomy. On the inside, however, that government was run by an increasingly small number of men who were both wealthy and corrupt, and the archbishop was no exception. In 1291, the people had rioted against them and murdered the city's mayor. King Philippe had sent troops to restore order and revoked Rouen's charter. He'd allowed the people to buy it back only last year.

"Do you know what it—"

But Amaury's companion cut him off with a shushing motion before he could finish his question: Archbishop Guillaume had arrived in all his splendor—gown, staff, and mitre—having apparently decided that the occasion called for the full regalia of his office.

Instead of meeting in the chapter house on the cathedral grounds, they were in the cathedral's nave itself, gathered in a great circle. The archbishop joined them, making the sign of the cross as they all bent their heads before him.

"I have brought you here today," he said in his high, imperious voice, "for a mighty purpose. Today, we continue the great work of our forefathers, to sweep away the sins and failures of prior administrations, and renew the faith of Jesus Christ in Rouen." He brandished a paper his secretary had just handed him. "We have received news that King Philippe, the gracious and most majestic of kings, last night expelled all Jews from Paris. It is Nogaret's suggestion, and my intent, to do the same in Rouen."

As Amaury absorbed his words with as calm an expression as he could muster, the archbishop gazed around at the gathered men. "The edict has already been sent to the castle, and I have returned to Nogaret a pigeon declaring my intent to follow our king's noble course."

Amaury had long suspected Nogaret and the archbishop had a direct means of communication. While he was unhappy with the news, he was glad to see his suspicions confirmed.

"When?" This came from another canon, who seemed to be asking out of curiosity rather than the outrage Amaury was feeling.

"If the Jews do not depart Rouen by tomorrow night, they will be forcibly evicted."

"By whom?" Amaury couldn't help but ask the question. He was not one of Guillaume's favorites, to nobody's surprise, and tried to reserve his objections for the most dire of situations, which in his view this was.

"The Paris Templars did the king's bidding in Paris. Nogaret assures me they will cooperate here as well."

Amaury knew that whatever the Templars had been doing in Paris, it wasn't the king's bidding—or at least not King Philippe's. Early on, he had met with Matthew Norris, the Master of the Paris Temple, and discovered the man was a kindred spirit, focused on the right of things more than his own power. Amaury also knew for a fact that the Paris Temple was acting as the base of operations for King David and his people. The Templars in Rouen, on the other hand, had been in disarray since the death of their previous master. Several were Amaury's friends and had been keeping him apprised of the goings-on there. If electing a master was contentious, the decision to evict Jews from Rouen would be even more so, and none of the current members of the Temple would have the will or ability to coordinate their members in such an action.

None of that could he, or would he, say. "And if the Templars refuse?"

"Then the commander of the castle has assured me of his full cooperation."

There was a moment of silence, during which time the archbishop looked more and more pleased with himself.

After another few heartbeats, Amaury raised his hand again, unable to remain silent. "I would ask that you reconsider."

"Why? Because you have made yourself a champion of the killers of our Holy Savior?" The Archbishop gave a harsh laugh.

"Don't think I am unaware of those letters you wrote and your secret communications with the synagogues."

Amaury kept his expression very still, thankful to his core that the archbishop hadn't mentioned the boats coming down the river. If he'd known about them, Amaury was certain he would have said. "I am simply following the instructions of the pope. *No Christian shall injure their persons, or with violence to take their property, or to change the good customs which they have had until now in whatever region they inhabit.*"

"Are you denying the king is a Christian, Amaury? Or that I am?"

Amaury didn't reply, knowing the peril inherent in answering that question in the affirmative. He kept his back straight and his eyes straight ahead, though he could feel men on both sides pulling away from him, fearing by their proximity to share in his disfavor.

"Pope Alexander is dead." The archbishop's eyes were so narrowed they were barely slits. "You will be dealt with soon enough."

Archbishop Guillaume started to turn away, by the motion declaring the council ended. But then, after a few steps, he turned back. "One more thing. Nogaret also informs me that King Philippe is keeping the King of England in the palace as something of a permanent guest, and he has brought the full force of the French army to bear on Angoulême in Aquitaine." The archbishop allowed himself a real smile as his gaze fell again on Amaury. "We are at war, my friends. Lord Artois commands our men in the field. Nogaret leads the charge in Paris. Rouen will follow, in our own small way." He smiled again, as if to imply self-deprecation. "We will begin by confiscating all English shipping on the Seine."

10

August 2023

Day Three

David

As his interrogator droned on in the same vein as before, David tuned him out, instead staring down at his chained wrists and trying to see his current situation with clear eyes.

Of course they were going to lock him up. They couldn't *not* lock him up. As evidenced by the direction of the interview questions so far, as well as the behavior of various individuals representing MI-5 and the CIA over the years, the threat he represented—to the social order, to the planet, maybe to the very existence of reality—was all they could see. He was, in a very real sense, more powerful and terrifying than an unaccounted-for nuke.

Others would and did see him as a laboratory rat, not quite human, and thus available to be experimented upon. Over the years, he'd encountered every sort of approach, most of which he hadn't seen coming until he was face-to-face with it.

That hadn't been the case today, and he could hardly complain about being on the receiving end of something he'd signed up for and gone into with his eyes wide open. That wasn't to say some new kind of badness wasn't right around the corner. But even if they really were going to send him to a black site that wasn't in Eastern Oregon, lock him up, and throw away the key, it wasn't something he hadn't mentally prepared for. Besides, he knew the way out of that if it came to it: that *suicide risk* discussed earlier.

So far, however, things really weren't that bad. He hadn't been beaten, waterboarded, or starved. He hadn't been blinded by a bright light, and if the current trend held, he wouldn't be subjected to heavy metal music and forced to stay awake all night. They'd fed him a *sandwich*. Ham and cheese with mayo (yay!). From a certain point of view, especially from where he sat in this moment across from this interrogator, the concession was astounding. It was as if he was caught between two opposing forces: one that left him chained to a table and another that fed him.

Maybe they were trying to confuse him into complying with whatever they wanted. This was the bad cop, and the good cop would arrive in a moment. Even so, if that was the case, he still didn't know with what he was supposed to comply. Certainly not these inane questions to which they already knew the answers. Maybe the fact that his interrogator was larger than an ox was meant to overwhelm him with fear. Obviously, nobody here had ever fought for their lives with only their fists as weapons.

Crewcut wound down, pausing his diatribe long enough to take a sip of water from the bottle he'd brought for himself. He'd been listing all the ways David and his family had broken the law over the years, mostly trespassing.

David canted his head. "I thought the CIA wasn't supposed to operate domestically. Don't you care that your agency is running an operation in Oregon and has enlisted the army to help?"

Crewcut narrowed his eyes, swallowed down the latest gulp of water, and then leaned forward with his hands flat on the table and tapping a finger on a new page in the folder, which showed David's eighth-grade school picture, since he hadn't attended high school long enough his first year to get his picture taken. David hadn't knocked him off his perch in the slightest. "Answer me—"

The door behind Crewcut swung open to reveal yet another agent, this one a woman, though not Heels. She could have been twenty years older than David, somewhere in her early forties, slender, with porcelain skin, smooth brown shoulder length hair, and dressed in a dark purple pantsuit. Her brown eyes snapped as she spoke to Crewcut. "Out."

"Yes, ma'am." Crewcut stiffened to attention and left.

A higher authority had arrived.

Or maybe just the *good cop*.

Two more soldiers, one a man and one a woman, also in military fatigues, joined the third who'd endured David's interrogation by staring at the far wall of the room. This new agent snapped her fingers at one of the men. "Get him out of these cuffs."

The soldier hastened to do her bidding, at which point Purple Pantsuit finally spoke directly to David. "I apologize, your highness, for the treatment you have received so far." She put a hand to her heart. "I'm Letitia Johnson, Interim Deputy Director for the Office of Science and Technology. If you will come with me, we have a suite prepared for you."

Then, without waiting for David to reply, she turned on her heel and led the way out of the interrogation room.

Rubbing his wrists, still in his socks, and more than a little wary at this sudden about-face, David followed Letitia down the corridor to the elevator, which they rode upwards one floor. When the doors opened this time, they revealed another long corridor exactly like the first. Except, once they got to the end of it, Letitia opened a plain white metal door to reveal a light, airy apartment. Even more exciting, the apartment had floor-to-ceiling glass windows that took up one wall, on the other side of which was an arboretum.

"This facility's director had the notion that we first needed to establish your credentials, and I regret any discomfort she may have caused you." Letitia gestured down a small corridor, indicating David should precede her. "I hope this suite will be more to your liking."

The apartment's main living area consisted of an open-plan kitchen with an adjacent dining and seating area. Down the hall was a bedroom with a king-sized bed, a walk-in closet, and a bathroom. One wall of the bedroom was also made up of glass windows showing the arboretum.

"Feel free to shower and change, if you like." Letitia checked her watch. "My hope is that we can talk more in an hour. I'll send someone to collect you."

Then she nodded and left, at which point David realized he hadn't spoken a single word the whole time he'd been with her. It hadn't been intentional on his part. Nor was it like him to keep silent. But nothing Letitia had said to him required a response, and she hadn't asked for one.

Huh.

David sat on the end of the bed, not unhappy about the change of venue, but interested all the same in how it had come about. He wasn't an officer in the CIA or a cop, obviously, but he was the father of a six-year-old son, had been the King of England for longer than Arthur had been alive, and had spent considerable time with secret agents, albeit predominantly from MI-5. Thus, his deception barometer that told him when someone was lying was well-developed. That the pricking sensation at the back of his neck was absent today made him think Letitia was telling the truth as she saw it. If so, David genuinely couldn't decide whether or not to be relieved. Once he'd arrived in the interrogation room and sat alone in it for hours, he'd prepared himself for the hostility to last for days or, at worst, to be moved to a black site along the lines of Guantanamo Bay.

He'd known already that Heels had to be the boss of just the local facility and couldn't be the one in charge of the entire project focused on him and his family, if only because George hadn't deferred to her. In truth, George didn't defer to many people (least of all David), but during his conversation over the radio when they'd still been in the air, George had definitely deferred to *someone*. That person might have been Letitia Johnson. Even so, her title as Interim Deputy Director of the Office of Science and Technology, whatever that was, was too low-level to be in charge of a project this huge and expensive. The title sounded made-up to David, but regardless, her director (and her director's director) was still out there.

David urgently wanted to know who Letitia really was, where she'd come from, and why her orders seemed so at odds with those Heels had given. It wasn't as if communication wasn't well-developed in Avalon. Even if Letitia had started the day in Washington DC, she and Heels should have spoken before Letitia's arrival. The fact that this suite was available at all indicated that whoever had ordered it built was prepared for someone like him—maybe even *for* him—to be housed within it.

He stood abruptly, cutting off the train of thought and telling himself he couldn't determine anyone's motivation on such short acquaintance. All he knew for certain was that his personal powers-that-be had dropped him here, in this location, for a reason.

The thought gave him courage and straightened his spine.

And really, he was just happy to be able to use the bathroom.

Rubbing his fingertips along the soft cotton of the deep burgundy towel hanging from the rack, David acknowledged that the facilities were more than comfortable, maybe even kingly, and he didn't mind the idea of sleeping somewhere besides an interrogation room. He also thought a shower might be a good idea.

Leaving the bedroom, he padded down the hall, still in his socks and very aware that he was being watched. He'd already spied bulbous cameras high on the walls of several rooms, including the bathroom. Entering the main room, he went first to open the refrigerator in a casual manner, not displeased to see sandwich-making ingredients, including mayonnaise, and then he sidled over to the door Letitia had closed behind her. David was telegraphing his thoughts by trying to open the door, but he didn't know any other way to determine if it was locked. Those cameras could easily include infrared vision, so turning off the lights while he checked might gain him nothing.

The door handle was a lever, so he put two fingers on it and pressed down. It didn't move.

Then, as if the fact that he was locked in this suite was of no concern to him, he strolled to the windows. It took him only a moment to confirm his earlier suspicion that, while adding a great deal of interest to the room, not to mention light, the windows before him didn't open. Nor was there a doorway or other access to the arboretum.

He was trapped, as if he didn't know that already. A gilded cage was still a cage. Upscale as this suite was and preferable to the sterile interrogation room, he'd merely exchanged one prison for another.

11

August 2023
Day Three
David

David's post-shower surprise was the bedroom's walk-in closet, which offered several changes of clothing that fit him fairly well. That he actually had a choice was something to consider in and of itself. Wearing his medieval clothing again would have been the easy solution—and a tangible reminder to everyone, including himself, that he was a medieval king. But the Avalonians would think it was gross to put back on clothes he'd worn already.

Much of the time he didn't think of himself as an Avalonian anymore, but even *he* would think it was gross—in large part because he knew how long he'd worn his old clothes and what he'd been doing while wearing them. The vomiting incident at Vincennes seemed like a *long* time ago.

He couldn't decide whether he should be comforted or disturbed to find such effort put forth on his behalf. On the one hand, Crewcut's skepticism about Earth Two was entirely feigned, and David wasn't going to waste his or anyone else's time explaining what was real. They knew who he was and didn't need him to tell them.

But, on the other hand, that *they didn't need him to tell them his identity* was, in a way, almost more disturbing. They'd planned for him to be brought here. While he'd been thinking about how he was going to neutralize the CIA for about a year and a half, they'd been planning this moment for *years*. Which meant Letitia had cut short the interrogation, a clearly *pro forma* process, because she was the *good cop*, and because they thought they already knew everything they needed to.

David would have to disagree, but so far he'd been given little chance to do so. The room was nice, but he couldn't allow himself to be lulled into a false sense of security. While in the shower, enjoying the hot water that poured effortlessly from the showerhead, he'd mulled over his options. He had some, even if they were limited in scope. It really was a very rare situation that left a person with no choices at all.

First of all, he could cause enough threat to his life that he would time travel. Although the words *suicide risk* had been mentioned up front, Letitia didn't appear to be taking the fear of it seriously, since she'd left David alone in the apartment. Maybe there were still bits that the CIA didn't entirely believe. Or maybe, if David started doing something destructive, one of the walls in the bathroom would open, and someone would appear within a second or two to prevent him from killing himself. After some consideration, that seemed more likely than not.

He considered throwing a temper tantrum, for the sheer fun of letting loose for once in his life. If he started screaming or ranting, or fighting them the next time he was taken somewhere else, that would elicit a reaction, even if not one he would like. Their best option, whether or not they knew it, might be to sedate him, shove him in the back of a bus or the hold of a plane, and then try to time travel. He had little doubt it would work. All things being equal, it wouldn't be his first choice.

The path of least resistance was to keep on keeping on until he had a compelling reason to make a detour.

Back in the closet, David went through his options one more time. In the end, he rejected the medieval outfit they'd chosen for him because it wasn't quite right for his era. Whoever had put these clothes together may have consulted a historian, but the arrival of David's family in Earth Two had prompted that world's fashion to diverge significantly from that of Avalon's past. David himself insisted on wearing what a historian would view as far too modern trousers—as did some of the women in his court, whether under their dresses or instead of dresses.

So he left that clothing hanging and instead chose the same look Chad Treadman's people had decided upon for his interview in Wales: a dark blue suit with a collared white shirt and black shoes. The fit wasn't bad. He fingered a pair of jeans draped over a hanger, considering again how much effort had been put into having this clothing ready and waiting for him when he came out of the shower.

He didn't know how long he'd been in the interrogation room, but he guessed it was at least five hours, putting the time when Letitia released him at about noon. That meant it was close to one o'clock in the afternoon now. For whatever reason, the time traveling (yeah, yeah *world shifting*), didn't tend to change the time of day, even if technically Oregon was nine time zones earlier than France. David had left Paris in the early morning, and he'd arrived in Eastern Oregon in the early morning too. When he and Anna had left Pennsylvania in 2010 and crashed into 1282 Wales at Cilmeri to save his father's life, it had been the same time of day, dusk, in both places.

He supposed, when one was traveling seven hundred and twenty-eight years into the past (or future), arriving at the same time of day one left was a small matter. And that didn't even get into the way the calendar had shifted several times over the last two thousand years. Some things weren't worth spending energy thinking about. He wasn't in charge of the time traveling, as his captors would soon find out.

Leaving the bedroom, he arrived back in the living area just as the door opened again—without a knock—to reveal Thing Two in the doorway. He looked David up and down in a manner that indicated he was surprised by the clothing, giving David a moment's pang that he'd guessed wrong.

Then the agent gestured out the door. "Sir, if you would come with me."

The *sir* was new, and David was glad to hear it. It gave him a glimmer of hope that Thing Two, if not Thing One, might be won over—and that, as when George had changed clothes, David hadn't guessed wrong about the suit.

"Thank you," David said, though no reply appeared to be required, since Thing Two was already heading down the hallway rather than waiting for David to precede him.

This time, they went up three floors, meaning they were now on the top floor of the building, two above the main lobby where they'd entered and one above the computer facility. This time, Thing Two took him to a conference room.

As in David's suite, one wall was taken up with windows, but rather than an arboretum, these revealed the hot Eastern Oregon day outside.

Which was impossible. They were *inside* an airplane hangar. *Weren't they?*

He eyed the windows, looking for anything—any glitch or waver—that would indicate it was a screen large enough to cause even Chad Treadman envy. But it remained exactly the same, even to the point of a bird flying past, for all intents and purposes a window to the outside world.

Letitia was already in the room, along with numerous other men and women, including the woman from earlier in the day who had ordered David locked up and whose name he still didn't know but continued to refer to in his head as *Heels*. It was lunchtime, and everyone was piling food on their plates from a buffet set against the inner wall. David flashed back to breakfast at the monastery guesthouse. He hoped his friends had found his raisin note. He supposed, if they hadn't, they would still have realized by now that he was gone and wasn't coming back.

Letitia made a gracious gesture in David's direction. "Please, eat."

Had he been younger, he might have dived headfirst into the food, starving and ready to eat everything in sight. But he'd learned a thing or two since he was fourteen about modern food, the most important of which was that it was generally tasteless in comparison to medieval food—and not just in terms of fruits and vegetables. Meat and breads too. That was one reason Chad Treadman had asked David to bring back seeds in the plane. These seeds were currently stashed in a compartment under the couch, presumably now in the hands of the CIA. David also assumed that agents had entered his suite the moment he'd left it and were even now going through his clothing with a fine tooth comb. He couldn't imagine what they'd find, beyond a bit of medieval dirt, though that might excite their scientists for a while.

Thing Two gestured to David that he should take a plate, which David did. The choices before him looked pretty, if nothing else, and he put together his usual sandwich with the thought that it was familiar and most likely to be edible. And then a brownie, which he would eat in honor of all the Avalonians who longed for chocolate and couldn't get it. Sadly, chocolate, unlike coffee, was one New

World food the seeds for which nobody had yet had the opportunity to bring back. David would remedy that this time if he could.

As he was pouring himself a glass of water, Thing Two spoke for the first time since they'd left the suite. "You have a great voice." He kept his own voice low, and as they were the only ones present at the buffet, David didn't think anyone could overhear, especially given the general conversation at the table.

"Thank you."

Thing Two was letting David know he had been observed *and* heard. The comment could have been a calculated piece of statecraft to make David think he was on his side—or even a warning. While David had spotted the cameras in his rooms, he hadn't found any recording devices. He'd assumed they were there, however, even as he let loose in the shower, singing *Fireflies* at the top of his lungs.

"Do you sing yourself?"

"A bit," Thing Two said.

David took that for modesty. "Well, if we get a chance ..." He didn't finish the thought. Nor did Thing Two, who made his way to an empty seat near Thing One.

Only one other seat was available out of the fifteen or so around the table. David still didn't know anyone's name other than Letitia's, and nobody had bothered to introduce him. As he eyed each person in turn, David understood that this was Letitia's real opinion of him, even if her overt manner belied it. Americans loved kings when they were in someone else's country.

He took a bite of the sandwich, wishing the bread tasted like something other than sawdust, and saw the truth for what it was: nobody was paying him any attention, not because they had no respect for him or thought of him as a particularly unintelligent teenager. It was because, for most of them, he wasn't a person at all. His chair might as well have been empty. They didn't want to hear what he had to say, not even Letitia Johnson. They wanted to *use* him.

And it wasn't as if he hadn't signed up for the ride.

David ate enough to satisfy his hunger, all the while taking in his surroundings as he waited for an explanation. Or questions. Or any conversation at all.

But there was nothing. Throughout the meal, he kept glancing up, hoping for a moment to talk, but none of his fellow diners, even Thing Two, would meet his eyes. David felt as awkward as a ninth grader whose friends didn't share his lunch period, and who didn't have the guts to go up to a student he didn't know to ask to eat with him.

This time, however, it wasn't a lack of guts that kept David from talking, so much as curiosity. He'd come here with a plan, which so far the CIA had followed almost to the letter. He'd expected the interrogation room. He'd expected disdain. But he had to give them points for taking their disregard for him to a whole new level.

Most of the people at the table weren't even talking to each other. They were poking at their phones instead. He'd once watched a television show in which phones were required to be surrendered inside a CIA facility, but either the show was wrong or something had changed in the interim. It wasn't as if everything else hadn't.

One of the most difficult changes for his Avalonian companions (Elisa, Ted, and Elen most recently) was the way, upon arrival in Earth Two, their phones had turned into bricks. They could still tell the time, and Elen kept hers charged via the solar array so she could read books on it, but it was no longer the constant source of communication it had once been. Ted, by his own account, had been a complete news junkie, and Elisa's challenge had been her inability to reach her loved ones at will. Like everyone in Avalon, they obsessed about control and the mitigation of risk. Avalon's advances in technology served only to feed the need.

In Earth Two, every time a loved one walked out the door, they might never return. Loss had to be accepted with grace, because what other option was there? David's personal experience as a parent had shown him that love was easy. It was detachment that was hard. And while he himself would love to have been able to call Lili or his mom, if the result was silence around the table, maybe it was just as well he couldn't.

Towards the end of the meal, the woman who'd brought him his sandwich in the interrogation room glanced in his direction, and he caught her eye directly. Instead of giving him a sign that she wanted to communicate, however, she immediately looked away, her shoulders hunched, and didn't look back. He hadn't had much opportunity to read her expression, but he thought she seemed embarrassed—whether by her treatment of him or his behavior he didn't know.

She was younger than the others, as he supposed she would have to be to have reached this level of operations and still have a conscience. Though he didn't know her name, he would remember her, and he saved for later the idea of reaching out to her in some way if he ever saw her again. Rescue wasn't part of his plan currently, but it was nice to know that at least one person in this facility, if not Thing Two as well, might be reconsidering what was coming.

What *was* coming was made a little clearer a minute later when an orderly entered the conference room, went straight to Letitia, and bent to speak to her in a low voice.

Letitia nodded and dismissed him, at which point she looked around the table, though not really at David, who sat at the opposite end, more like she was speaking to the room at large. "The plane is here."

12

August 2023

Day Three

David

As David took his first step outside, a wave of heat hit him that left him gasping. The cooler morning had deceived him into thinking the rest of the day might be as well, and he remembered that summers in Eastern Oregon were, as his mother had been known to say, *hot as blazes*. The humidity was next to nothing as well, making the air and landscape desert dry. It was odd to think he hadn't felt this kind of heat since he was fourteen years old. It just didn't get that hot very often in Britain, even in the height of summer. It was certainly very rarely dry.

There were planes galore in the hangar now, as compared to before, but that still didn't mean it was what you might call *full*. An executive jet was parked next to Chad Treadman's prototype plane, and a third small plane of yet a different design—more like Chad's than the executive jet, though a bit larger—was just taxiing to a stop.

Thirty yards from these smaller planes sat an enormous military cargo plane that hadn't been there when David had arrived. It was surrounded by a ring of heavily armed men in body armor and helmets, as if they were expecting an imminent attack. David started sweating just looking at them—not out of fear but because they had to be cooking hot in all their gear.

Once parked, the door of the recently arrived plane opened and stairs folded down. David had a moment's fear that Chad Treadman himself was going to step through the doorway, proving once and for all that he couldn't be trusted.

But, no. A bevy of people in suits, men and women both, took the steps down from the plane in single file. Amongst them was a gray-haired man of medium height in a dark gray suit, who strode directly to Letitia Johnson. He and she bobbed their heads at one another without shaking hands.

"Sir," Letitia said.

"Letitia."

David felt like saying *ah ha!* again. He imagined there were only a handful of other people Letitia would greet that way. Here was a higher authority.

While the newcomer and Letitia conferred some twenty feet away, everyone else who'd come on the executive plane dispersed quickly, finding counterparts already present, whether in the hangar, in the office building, or near one of the other planes. That left only Thing Two remaining close to David, standing at his right shoulder, presumably to prevent him from running off. In truth, the idea was laughable. It was nice David's hands weren't tied and that they'd fed him lunch, but there was a whole lot of nothing between where he stood and any kind of help. He supposed it paid, however, to be diligent.

Trying to build on what they'd started in the conference room, David took the opportunity to converse again. "What's your name?"

Thing Two blinked, as if startled that David would be so bold as to speak in public, but still he replied (even if rather stiffly), "Tom Baker."

A more English name could not be imagined. One of the things David liked about coming back here was how half the time you couldn't tell someone's background or ancestry by their name.

"Who has just arrived?"

"Charles Makowski, head of Operations."

"All operations, or just those associated with this project?"

Tom pressed his lips together, and for a moment David thought he wasn't going to answer. But then he said, "Office of Special Activities."

David had been the King of England for seven years, so he was well practiced in holding back a mocking snort when presented with new information, and he thought his advisers would be proud of the stone-face he was currently manifesting. *Special Activities* sounded pretty dang ominous.

He met Tom's gaze. "You think he's good at his job, don't you?"

"He wouldn't be where he is if he wasn't."

Competence, in this instance, could be dangerous to David if directed the wrong way, so it was good to be reminded that he shouldn't underestimate anyone here. Everything he had seen so far lent itself to the belief that the CIA had spent a considerable sum of money in pursuit of this *project*. A corollary to that assumption would be that they had put good people on it to spend that money.

"I'm David."

Tom gave a little snort. "I know who you are."

David supposed that shouldn't have been a surprise, even if he hadn't disappeared a year and a half ago in a hail of bullets in front of billions of people watching on their screens.

"Do you know what I'm doing here?"

Tom's eyes narrowed. "Don't you?"

"If I did, would I be asking?"

Tom's chin wrinkled up, and he looked away, not willing, or perhaps not able, to answer that question.

David tried a different tack. "Do you know why Letitia wanted me brought outside?"

Tom glanced at him out of the corner of his eye. "You hot or something?"

"Aren't you?"

For a moment, David thought he had cadged a smile from Tom, but then the agent's chin went up, again not willing to reply and as if CIA agents didn't sweat. David reminded himself that just because he spoke the same American English as these people didn't mean they shared a culture, not anymore, and allowances had to be made (mostly, apparently, by him) for differences in manners and upbringing.

David's questions had been genuine too. He honestly couldn't figure out why he was standing in this heat. It would have been one thing if they'd marched him to the cargo plane they appeared so concerned about. He didn't like the look of it and didn't think it was his ego telling him that it had something to do with him. Standing here waiting and doing nothing but sweating for the last five minutes made him feel like he was in the movie version of *Return of the King* when Gandalf rides out from Minas Tirith against the Nazgul with Pippin in front of him on the horse. It was totally out of character for Gandalf to put Pippin in harm's way for no reason—except that the script writers needed Pippin in the next scene where he is recognized by Faramir.

There were no hobbits here, but it might be that Letitia had brought him outside to orchestrate his first meeting with Charles. By now, they appeared to have finished their initial conversation, because Letitia gestured in David's direction, and Charles strode towards him, Letitia hustling along in his wake.

"So you're David," Charles said without preamble, stopping three paces away and looking David right in the eye. Other than when David had spoken to Tom a moment ago, it was the first time anyone in charge had done that since David had arrived, and he gave Charles points for straightforwardness.

So he replied with a simple, "I am."

"Not what I expected."

To that, no answer was possible and, on further consideration, Charles's first remark hadn't been an actual greeting either. In fact, he was looking at David now similarly to the way Heels had done when he'd first arrived, with a bit of a sneer or as if contemplating a regrettable purchase, rather than as if David were a real person. Truly, the disrespect they were showing him, though not a surprise, was maddening.

Charles now looked at Letitia. "He isn't dressed like I expected him to be."

"His clothes are being laundered. He'll be dressed appropriately when the time comes."

"That time is now." Charles glanced one more time at David, his lip curling, and then returned his attention to Letitia. "Get him ready."

Letitia took a step back, her mouth forming a shape as if to say, "What?"

Charles scoffed under his breath. "Don't tell me you're getting cold feet? If we don't do this now, if we don't get real results, we will run out of time."

"What do you mean *run out of time?*"

"September first is fast approaching." Charles glanced one more time at David, his eyes assessing, before completing the thought. "I have been informed by the director that she will not waste any more money on a project that has gone nowhere."

"But he's here!" Letitia threw out a hand to David. "Standing right there!"

"But can he take us back in time? And once our people arrive in Earth Two, can we fulfill the objectives?"

David was starting to feel genuinely concerned about the way they were having this conversation right in front of him. Once again, he was reminded of a movie, but in this case one that didn't end all that well for the person—meaning him—who was viewed as expendable. Charles didn't appear to be concerned in the slightest about David testifying about what he knew before a Congressional Oversight Committee.

"That gives us three days!" Letitia was visibly horrified.

Charles clapped his hands together once. "Then we'd better get cracking, oughtn't we?"

13

August 1295

Day Three

Amaury

Amaury didn't even take the time to gather his things from the dormitory he shared with his fellow priests. The world was moving on, and he had to move with it. Besides, he had no desire to face questions—or incarceration, for that matter—from his fellow priests or the archbishop. He'd experienced the latter enough for a lifetime, five years in fact, at the hands of King David's predecessor, Edward.

Though catastrophic at the time, it had changed the course of his life.

Many years ago, Amaury's sister, Elinor, had married Llywelyn, the Prince of Wales (at the time). Five years later, she'd died birthing Gwenllian, David's half-sister. Back in 1276, Amaury had been accompanying Elinor to the wedding when King Edward had captured their ship and imprisoned them. Although Edward had eventually released Elinor to marry Llywelyn (once Llywelyn had made his proper obeisance), Edward had kept Amaury in prison until the end of the 1282 war. By the time he was freed, only one member of his family was still alive, his older brother Guy, who himself died in 1288.

One of the conditions of his freedom was that Amaury had to swear never again to return to England unless invited by the king. After Edward died and Wales gained its independence from England, Llywelyn had invited Amaury many times. And once crowned King of England, David had officially revoked the edict. But Amaury had never come, saying that he was called to administer to the people of Normandy, including Jewish ones. In truth, England held only unhappy memories for him, ones he had no wish to revisit.

Amaury himself was a Norman, and although his father had been responsible for pogroms against members of the Jewish faith during his brief reign of England during the Second Baron's War, the Normans as a community had welcomed Jews into their domains in both Normandy and England. Rouen itself was home to the oldest Jewish community in all of France, and it had been Rouen's Jews who'd been instrumental in bringing the plight of their co-religionists in Paris to David's attention in the first place. Amaury was a little ashamed that he hadn't done it first.

Crusaders had led a slaughter of Rouen's Jews in 1096, but shortly thereafter, William Rufus, Normandy's duke and the King of England, had aided in the rebuilding of the community, to the point that, by 1295, it had nearly three thousand members in a city of twenty thousand.

Or there had been, before David (and Amaury) had instigated the effort to spirit them out of the city. To that end, Amaury had befriended or bribed taxmen and dockworkers to ensure the boats coming down the river from Paris would be allowed to stop at Rouen's wharf, in order for the passengers to rest and resupply. The plan had been for them to masquerade as English traders, despite the fact that anyone with eyes would see through the deception from the bank, never mind once they presented their papers. Unfortunately, with the archbishop declaring all English boats and goods forfeit, if not English people themselves, the entire endeavor was now at risk.

Rouen's wharf was located to the west of the bridge because the seafaring ships that sailed upriver from Le Havre were too large to go under it. These ships had to be unloaded and their goods transferred to barges, owned by the good merchants of Rouen, of course, that were then sent upriver to Paris.

Every captain who passed through Rouen traveling upriver or down had to show identification and allow his boat to be inspected, as well as pay a tax, which was the key thing. To ensure compliance, a portcullis blocked the only way through the bridge. While most of the time the portcullis remained raised to river traffic, it could be dropped at a moment's notice if the authorities in Rouen didn't like the look of whoever was coming up or down the river. When the water level was low, an offender floating downstream could easily maneuver to a small landing before the bridge, there to be inspected and taxed, but with the river running as fast as it was, any boat, not just the twenty he knew were on their way, would be in real danger of crashing into the portcullis and bridge footings, capsizing the boats, and throwing everyone on board into the Seine.

And that was before they and all their possessions were confiscated in the name of the archbishop.

Amaury was able to leave the cathedral precincts without being stopped. More people were in the streets than usual, however, and he hugged the wall of a nearby house to avoid the crush.

The City of Rouen lay on the northern bank of the Seine and stretched for three-quarters of a mile along the river. In addition to the fortified bridge with its treacherous portcullis, the city was surrounded by a half-circle of protective wall and two further fortifications: a castle, located to the northwest of the cathedral and incorporated into the city wall; and the Templar commandery, located on the waterfront to the west of the bridge across the Seine. Rouen's old palace, built by the Norman dukes, had been situated right on the River Seine too, in order to guard the west entrance to the city, but the French had destroyed it a century ago when they'd conquered Normandy.

Otherwise, Rouen was not fortified along the Seine itself, since houses and shops lined the riverbank, most with less than a handspan between them. The cathedral precincts were also surrounded by a wall, but that was more to convey to those who entered that this was now the domain of God.

"Excuse me, Father." A man rushed by, followed by a couple wearing yellow badges identifying them as Jews. Their heads were down, and they were walking quickly, which for the moment would be merely against the rain that had started to fall. Given the archbishop's decree, soon it would be out of fear.

They weren't alone in their haste, and Amaury followed them to the speaker's green, located in front of the gatehouse that protected the entrance to the bridge across the Seine. A line of soldiers stood at the bridge's entrance in two concentric rings, separating the large crowd of people from the podium, at which traditionally a speaker would stand to read out edicts from the king, castle, or, in this case, archbishop.

Archbishop Guillaume had said that his edict had already been disseminated to the castle, but he'd implied the Templars didn't yet know. Amaury didn't see any present on the green, even though their commandery was visible to the west from where he stood.

One of the commanders of the city guard stepped into the cleared space between the rings of soldiers and motioned to the town crier that he should begin.

"Silence!" The town crier had achieved his position for a reason, and the crowd settled.

The captain was replaced by another man, this one somewhat elderly and dressed in court clothing, who began to read from a parchment he held in a shaking hand. Amaury knew him as the herald for the administrator at the castle, who wasn't even present, having left Rouen for Paris two months ago and not returned. He spent most of his time there anyway, ostensibly cultivating contacts and resources for the people of Rouen. He probably would not have balked at Archbishop Guillaume's decree. The archbishop had a history of claiming all religious matters were his to decide without input from either the officials at the castle or the board of governors of Rouen, who did little more than fill their own coffers. They would view the sudden availability of Jewish property as a gift to them personally.

All followers of the Jewish religion are to be expelled from Rouen ...

The order set the moment of their expulsion as midnight tomorrow. If they were going to obey, Rouen's Jews needed to start packing immediately.

The uproar was certainly immediate.

Amaury stood in the midst of the crowd, aware of the commander's order for everyone to disperse but not obeying it, realizing he was witnessing the destruction of his city's spirit, something he'd spent the last ten years cultivating and building. As he was jostled by one citizen after another, he found himself on the western edge of the green.

Slipping into a nearby alley, he removed the robes of his office, folded them gently, and left them on an overturned crate. Many churchmen wore nothing but sandals underneath their robes, but Amaury's years in prison had left him unusually sensitive to cold, and he always wore more layers. With the robe put aside, he was dressed in the simple attire of a common man: shirt, overtunic, breeches, and boots.

He would always be a priest and a canon of the cathedral, but he didn't have to live there to serve it or the people of Rouen. Leaving the alley, he returned to the now deserted green and headed west down the street. He had spent his life reinventing himself after setbacks. He knew what he had to do.

14

August 2023
Day Three
David

In another life David might have liked Letitia very much. She reminded him of the secretary at his high school, albeit with a far more 'important' job. He rather thought his high school secretary could have handled being the Deputy Director of the Office of Science and Technology too, since she basically ran the school. As King of England, he had a far better appreciation for the skills required in organizing twelve hundred resentful, rebellious, and occasionally sweet teenagers than he'd had when he'd been one of them.

Today, however, he definitely sensed that Letitia saw him as occupying the rebellious end of the spectrum, which of course wasn't far off from the truth. What she couldn't know, because she hadn't asked, was that he had every intention of cooperating as far as he could for as long as he could. And then they would see.

Charles appeared to be another matter entirely. He was straightforward and competent too, but his dismissal of David was pronounced. It might even be that here was the source of Heels' disdain, and rather than the CIA itself, it was Charles and Letitia who were at odds with how to treat him.

That said, so far both Letitia and Charles shared an approach that didn't include a desire to hear David speak. Given the conversation they'd just had with each other, however, David felt duty bound to at least attempt to get them to listen. "Excuse me, but don't you think it would be a good idea to run what you're planning by me before you do it?"

He had waited to speak until they were back inside and walking up the stairs to the computer center, in part for the pleasure of the air conditioning and also, ideally, because this should be a long conversation. But he'd spoken to their backs since Letitia and Charles had progressed up the stairs in front of him and were currently three steps ahead.

At first, neither replied—nor even acknowledged that he'd spoken, other than a quick turn of Letitia's head towards Charles. David was about to try again when Charles swung around. "Why?"

Charles wasn't looking at him with a glare so much as an aloof, supercilious smile, telegraphing to anyone within sight that he thought David's question absurd. The stairs were open to the lobby until they reached the second floor, so the spot was very public. The lone secretary behind the desk, a man for this shift, kept his head down and typed away at his computer. Everybody else in the lobby had stopped talking as Charles had spoken, so the clickety-clacking of the keys was the only sound in the room.

David was happy to fill the silence that had fallen. If Charles didn't care who knew what they were talking about, he didn't either. "I'm the only one here who's done it. Wouldn't it be a good idea to make sure what you're planning is going to work?"

"Fine." Charles folded his arms across his chest. David had seen that stance often enough among his own people, not to mention his own children, to know that Charles was creating a barrier between them. He was also still above David on the stairs, so even though David was 6' 2" and Charles was 5' 10", Charles loomed over him. "Speak."

"I would have to know first what you're planning."

Charles's upper lip lifted briefly in a sneer, and then Letitia said from beside him, very softly, "It might be a good idea to hear him out. At least then, if things go wrong, you can say you did."

Charles openly scoffed. "I'm disappointed, Letitia. CYA was never your paramount concern." He turned back around and finished his journey up the stairs. Then he walked straight past the computers and technicians into the office David had last seen George entering hours ago. There was no sign of George now, which David thought odd. George should have been first in line to greet Charles when he arrived. They seemed cut from the same cloth.

Heels had been standing near one of the large wall monitors. As they came in, she made a move as if she intended to come over, but Letitia flicked out her fingers in a clear signal to tell her not to. Heels subsided with a visible huff.

The office was large enough for Tom Baker and David to enter after Letitia without crowding her. Tom shut the door behind them.

Charles seated himself behind the desk, rocking back in the chair as if he didn't have a care in the world. For some reason, leaving an underling standing while the boss sat was perceived as intimidating, and that's how David and Charles were arranged now. Charles didn't know, though he had only to ask, that David had just faced down King Philippe and the entire French court, all of whom had wanted his head on a pike, and come out on top. Maybe David was as arrogant as Charles, and he was still underestimating what the CIA might do to him. Then again, he was pretty sure he already knew.

In truth, David was kind of surprised Charles had taken Letitia's advice to talk to him, since his antipathy towards David was so tangible it was almost another person in the room.

"We are going to put you in the cargo plane you saw in the hangar and fly it into a mountain." Charles's words were both bold and matter-of-fact.

David stared at him, almost unable to believe what he had feared they were going to do really *was* what they were going to do.

Charles sniffed. "You're telling me doing that isn't going to cause you to time travel? You told George that it always works."

"Likely it will." David kept his tone even. "Though I was exaggerating for George's benefit. It hasn't always worked. There was that time in France when Philippe and I were shot at on the battlement of Château de Niort and fell into the river below without time traveling."

"We are willing to take that risk."

David wet his lower lip. "We? Are you coming with me?"

"Are you mocking me?" Charles rocked forward in the chair. "You do realize the position you're in, don't you?"

David eased out a breath, slowly and deliberately. This hadn't gone well, but maybe it never could have. He saw now that Charles's animosity towards him wasn't because he saw David as an upstart, juvenile, or an impediment. This was personal.

Still, he had to try, and maybe it was time he took off the gloves a bit himself.

"Do you speak for everyone you're sending with me? You're risking their lives on something you know nothing about and clearly don't understand."

"We understand enough."

"Do you? Is that from George?" David looked around the room. "Where is he, anyway?"

"He's been reassigned." That came from Letitia, who was standing off to one side.

Charles shot her a glare, indicating he would have preferred she hadn't answered.

"What? Why?" David was genuinely aghast. "He was the one person in your entire agency who has been to Earth Two. Why would you sideline him?"

Letitia didn't answer that question, and Charles merely gazed stonily back at David.

The truth rocked David back on his heels. "You don't trust him." He laughed. "He was nothing but a thorn in my side from the first day he arrived. He did everything you asked, but when he gets home, you send him away because you think I've corrupted him." He laughed again.

"It is no concern of yours." Charles's voice was like ice.

David gazed at him, knowing his words were falling on deaf ears, but needing to say them anyway. The moral imperative was clear. Charles *had* to understand how serious this was. They were on a military base, and he appeared to be treating this mission as a military operation, but his dismissal of the danger was more than a little disconcerting. He should have been terrified of something going wrong. *David* was terrified of something going wrong, to the point that his jaw was clenched so tight it was making his back teeth ache, and the sandwich from earlier was sitting in his stomach like a rock.

"Have you explained how many ways this mission could go sideways?"

Charles was undeterred. "They know the risks."

"How could they possibly know the risks when *I* don't?"

"They all volunteered."

David was struck again by Charles's surety. He knew he was right, and there was nothing David could say to change his mind. He had the confidence of a fundamentalist. Still, David felt he had to try one more time. "How do you plan to land the plane? It isn't as if we built an airport outside London."

"That is not your concern."

"It is my concern if I'm going to be on that plane."

Charles waved a hand dismissively. "We have all the data we need for now, and soon we'll have a great deal more. Prepare yourself. You move out in an hour."

Which was how David ended up back in his suite, getting dressed in his old clothes, now freshly laundered and which someone had laid out on the bed. His long-lost boots had been placed on the floor. He had a clear directive to put these clothes on, and he wondered what Charles would do if David refused. Before he'd entered the bedroom, well aware he was being watched by cameras that covered every square foot of the suite, David had strolled to the exit door and casually tried the handle once again. It remained locked from the outside.

As Tom had declined to converse with David on the way back down the elevator and had closed the door in his face, leaving him alone, David could only think that his conversation with Charles had alienated Tom in some way. David had meant it to be more of a warning—as Tom had warned him in the conference room.

But not everyone wanted to hear the truth. As someone famously once said (David's mom would have known who), "It is difficult to get a man to understand something, when his salary depends on his not understanding it." His father had counseled him in the past about not speaking when one didn't have an audience. Tom, like

Charles, was deaf to questions and arguments. Maybe, as with the quote, he couldn't *not* be.

So David got dressed, somewhat defiantly, knowing it was inevitable they would be analyzing his every move. Then he did another circuit of the suite, eyeing the doorframes and the corners of the ceiling, looking for secret doors or two-way windows. If they were there, they were well-disguised, and he didn't see any. So he merely put out both arms and turned slowly on his heel. "I'm ready when you are."

Nothing happened.

Back when he was younger, he'd always wanted to know what was going on. "Run and find out," his mother would say, indulging his need to inquire. It was only in adulthood that he'd realized she shared his proclivities and had sent him to find out so she didn't have to. Becoming the King of England had been the ultimate opportunity to always know what was going on. For all of his previous disparagement of the Avalonian need for control, his last thirteen years in Earth Two had been dominated by his attempt to exert his will over chaotic situations. Likely, he was just as much a hypocrite in this regard as the next man.

But, as Bevyn had told him more than once, *know your strengths.*

Well, he could think on his feet, and he had spent enough time being chased by intelligence agencies to have an inkling of the way they thought. If he was wrong, he might pay for it with his life, but he hadn't been wrong so far. They really were going to put him in that cargo plane.

He walked around his suite again, touching everything, and ended up at the refrigerator. He poured himself a glass of skim milk, which was the only kind they'd given him, and drank it. *Ew.* Thirteen years of real milk had removed any tolerance for this white-colored water he'd drunk as a kid.

Then he sat down on the couch and stared at the plants for a while. He could hear nothing but the sound of his own breathing and the hum of the refrigerator. There was no television or computer screen he recognized. He had nothing to do but think—again—for the second time today. When had that happened since 2010?

He stretched out on the couch, which was long enough to accommodate his full length, thinking Bevyn would be proud of him for following one of his first lessons: soldiers never knew when they would be able to eat or rest, so best to take whatever opportunities presented themselves.

David had already eaten. Now he closed his eyes. And slept.

15

August 2023
Day Three
David

He sat up as the door to his suite opened. He didn't know how much time had passed, but he thought it was more than an hour as it was completely dark in the room. He had thought earlier, as he'd watched the light fade towards late afternoon, that the arboretum was set to mimic the actual rising and setting of the sun, else the plants wouldn't grow properly.

David himself hadn't left on any lights, but Tom at the door said, "Lights."

They came on, as of course they would.

By then, David was on his feet and running a hand through his hair.

"It's time," Tom said, as if by his very presence, and what Charles had said, that wasn't obvious.

David didn't ask for more information, not even to get Tom on his side. For the moment, they were past those concerns. Charles thought he knew what was going to happen, but none of them had any control over the time traveling. The times David had forced the issue had been heart-in-the-throat moments. In a way, the whole point was that he never knew if it was going to work. It was as if Charles had, with great effort, managed to fill a single cup from a stream and now thought he controlled the current.

Tom escorted David outside to a darkened world, confirming David's supposition about the hour. With the setting of the sun, the temperature had dropped too, possibly by as much as twenty degrees.

David was still sweating.

This time, the moment he walked out of the lobby of the office building, a guard of men surrounded him. Though their military bearing gave them away as soldiers, these men were not the ones who'd been guarding the cargo plane earlier, as those men still surrounded it. And rather than wearing modern military gear, someone had spent considerable effort outfitting them in passable medieval clothing. David couldn't see the blades of their swords, since they were in sheaths, but the hilts looked real enough to him. The men were also all relatively light-skinned, six-feet tall, and heavily muscled. They would fit in well in Earth Two, provided they landed in Britain or Europe.

They were also all *men* and indicated that Charles and his minions had given some thought to what was going to happen once they landed. Taking women to the Middle Ages, even in the company of an armed guard, could be fraught with peril if they landed in the wrong place.

But, as usual, nobody had asked him about that possibility, and certainly nobody spoke to him about it now. He was a pawn. Nothing more.

For once, that was fine by him.

They'd learn the error of their ways soon enough.

He hoped.

The thought pulled him up short, and he came to a dead halt at the bottom of the ramp. Because really, it wasn't fine by him at all.

"You need to stop this." He spoke to the world at large, since he had nobody genuinely to talk to.

"Keep moving." This came from the trooper beside him, who grabbed his upper arm and urged him up the ramp a few steps.

David dug in his heels. "It is one thing for me to risk my life every time I travel. It's *my* life. But you are risking yours for something that very well might not work."

It was as if they didn't hear him, and now a second soldier appeared on David's other side. They dragged him into the cargo plane and plopped him into a seat, the last among many down the side of the plane. Each seat faced the center, with the backs to the wall, and had a harness system instead of a regular seatbelt. One of the soldiers strapped David into his without asking, before taking his own seat.

In all, there were twelve soldiers traveling with him. With the addition of David himself, that made thirteen. He wasn't superstitious (much), but time travel was magical enough without adding adverse numerology to the mix.

Towards the front of the plane, stacked containers stretched floor to ceiling. David could well imagine their contents. It made him wonder why they were bothering with the medieval clothing at all, given the rest of what they were bringing.

He tried one more time. "Seriously, guys, this is crazy. Please think about what you're doing."

Nobody responded. Like Charles had said, they had volunteered. And, as with Charles, Letitia, Tom, and whoever else was involved, to express doubt now would be letting down their side. He felt pity for them, in the way they'd been caught up in this tug-of-war between him and the CIA.

Settling further into his seat, he also felt, somewhat strangely, relief. He'd been one hundred percent right (or Chad Treadman had) about what they wanted and that they represented an existential threat to Earth Two. While at one time, David might have assumed that even the CIA would have second thoughts about exploiting a child, that clearly wasn't true anymore, not with the money they'd already sunk into this project.

So for him to be the one experiencing what was happening now was so much better than if George had captured Arthur or Cadell—or worse one of the younger children like Bran, Alexander, or Anna's new baby girl, Rhiannon, born last November. The thought of one of the children strapped into this seat made him want to vomit. David wouldn't perhaps have been so worried about Arthur's physical existence, since he could world shift too when he was in danger, but his emotional state was another matter. He'd handled their sojourn in Paris, including their imprisonment, with a heartening degree of equanimity, but he'd been with his parents the entire time.

And if Arthur or Cadell had been forced to witness the death of one of these men? What kind of impact would that have on a child? What kind of impact was it going to have on David, who by coming here had put what was happening right now in motion?

Then he reminded himself that whatever was happening here had been in motion for a long time. Charles wasn't a rogue agent. These actions had been greenlighted at a high level—maybe even the highest level. Charles had mentioned *the director*.

David himself was determined not to be a victim, which was why he had concocted this loony plan in the first place, but the only one to blame for what was about to happen to any of them was the person or persons in charge. For once, that wasn't him. And when things didn't go according to plan, which David was pretty sure they wouldn't—his personal mission was based on the presumption they wouldn't—he was glad he would be here to help the men who surrounded him.

To that end, as well as because it wasn't in his nature to remain silent, even (or maybe especially) in the face of death, he turned to the man beside him and asked his name. Unfortunately, at the moment he spoke, the plane's engines roared to life, drowning out

David's question. Resigned to silence and whatever was about to happen, he tipped back his head and closed his eyes. The plane taxied down the runway, picked up speed, and, within another minute, was in the air.

David wasn't the only one not talking. If he had to guess, he'd say these men were some kind of special forces, perhaps even the CIA's own paramilitary division. Regardless, he could tell by the way they stared straight ahead, with what some might call their *game face*, that they were tense.

They had every right to be, and because their commander wasn't doing anything about it, David looked to his neighbor one more time. "How long have you been training for this?"

He had to shout. Even then, at first David didn't think the man had heard him. But then he shot David a glance, part skeptical and part resigned. It was as if he was saying, *If I answer will you please shut up?* "I came on six months ago. Sir."

David laughed to himself that his standard for productive conversation had been reduced to eliciting a single, honest sentence.

And that *sir*, quite frankly, was unexpected—and telling to boot. It meant, like Tom, the soldier knew who he was.

"I'm David." He put out his hand.

The man didn't take it. "I know who you are, sir." He cleared his throat. "Sire."

When David left his hand where it was for another few seconds, the man gave a quick shake of his head. "It's against protocol to shake hands."

Oookay. David had no idea why that might be.

Then the man gave a shrug. "I'm Luke O'Malley." He indicated the six men sitting across from them and proceeded to reel off their names in rapid-fire fashion, followed by the other five on David's side of the plane. Each man acknowledged the introduction with a lifted hand or a nod, though Jorge, the man sitting directly across from David, who was the youngest of the bunch at least in appearance, with a buzz cut and a scar near one eye, said, "Hey, man."

"Good to meet you," David said, though he wasn't sure how much of what either he or Luke had said could be heard above the noise of the plane. As the others went back to whatever they'd been contemplating, David turned again to Luke. "Do you know where we're going?"

"The Wallowas."

That wasn't actually the answer David was looking for, but he'd take it for now, and he supposed Charles had no way of determining exactly where they'd come out in Earth Two, if they made it at all. "How can you be sitting here this calmly, knowing the pilot intends to fly this plane, containing you and your fellow soldiers, into a mountain?"

"I'm sitting next to you, aren't I?"

David didn't think that was a reasonable answer. "Do I look calm to you?"

Luke made a motion as if to check his watch, and then grunted when he realized it wasn't on his wrist. "Ten minutes." There was a finality to his tone that indicated he didn't want to talk anymore.

David wasn't fond of shouting anyway, and he settled into his seat, grasping the shoulder straps that kept him constrained. Since everyone else wore them too, he didn't feel like he was being singled out, at least in this instance, and he supposed he should be glad he wasn't still in handcuffs. Tom hadn't put them on him any of the times he'd led him out of the suite, and nobody seemed to think there was a genuine risk of him attacking one of his captors or trying to run away.

The leader of the company was a man named Frank, who was sitting in the row facing David, on the far end closest to the cockpit. He put a hand to his ear and then held up two fingers to everyone.

"Two minutes," Luke said to David out of the corner of his mouth.

David could have guessed that was what Frank meant, but he said *thank you* to Luke anyway for giving him the heads up.

The plane thrummed on. It was uncomfortable not to be able to see outside, and it occurred to David only now—which perhaps was far, far too late—that he'd assumed how *he* felt, the fear in particular, was an integral part of his time traveling. That it was a requirement obviously hadn't occurred to George or anyone else. They assumed it would work because it always did. David wondered again why they hadn't drugged him and flown him into the Wallowas while unconscious on a stretcher. The only reason he could think *not* to do that was because they wanted him awake and functional when they got to Earth Two. On the whole, he'd prefer that as well.

At thirty seconds out, it was a little late to mention any of this. They would find out soon enough what mattered and what didn't.

David's heart started beating a little faster as the tenor of the engines changed, along with the tilt of the plane. They were diving down at such a steep angle the loaded cargo plane couldn't possibly come out of the dive in one piece.

Now it was even more aggravating not to be able to see anything outside, especially after the lights of the plane dimmed in the same instant the plane's engines muffled slightly. These changes lasted a few seconds, and David thought he might have been the only one to notice—since he was the only one looking for them.

Everyone was holding on to their straps and was pressed against the shoulder of their neighbor who was sitting downhill from them. Beside David, Luke's teeth were clenched. Across the aisle, Frank had one hand to his ear piece, listening hard. He didn't say anything, but he was sitting so rigidly that the eyes of every man on David's side of the plane were fixed on him. Jorge, who couldn't really see Frank from his position across from David, had clasped his hands before his face and was praying.

They flew at the steep angle long enough for David to realize there was something very, very wrong. Nobody else in the cargo bay—other than, possibly, Frank—was aware of the exact problem because they'd never time traveled before. But it was taking a terribly long time, if counting in heartbeats, for the nose of the plane to start coming up. It was as if they'd dived into an abyss that kept going into the center of the earth. What's more, the dimming of the lights and the muffling of the engines appeared to toggle on and off … three seconds at a time. Finally, after six instances since the plane first went into a dive, the nose of the plane rose, and they grew level once again. The engines roared.

Likely, only minutes had passed, even if each minute had felt like an hour.

Everyone, even Jorge, looked at Frank, whose expression was like a block of wood. He didn't meet anyone's eyes and kept his gaze straight ahead.

"What's happening?" The question came in a chorus from nearly every soldier.

"Not now." Frank made a slashing motion with one hand.

Fifteen minutes later, the plane's wheels touched down on a surface smooth enough not to jar the plane. Once they taxied to a stop, Frank unbuckled himself and hit the release to open the ramp, which lowered slowly to reveal the same Eastern Oregon night they'd left an hour ago.

They were right back where they'd started.

16

August 2023

Day Three

David

One by one, the soldiers unbuckled their harnesses, rose from their seats, and left the plane. While everyone was a little puzzled, they were also unhurt, and their muted conversations conveyed a skepticism about the entire project. *As if time travel was ever going to be real,* one man, whose name David couldn't remember, said to Luke.

But *something* clearly had happened, given the behavior of the pilot and co-pilot. Their faces were ashen as they passed David, who hurried to follow them down the ramp towards where Charles and Letitia waited in the middle of the hangar. Both men were visibly shaking, and, fortunately for the edification of everyone present, didn't wait for privacy before blurting out their protest.

"We did just as you said!" This was from the captain.

Charles was standing with his arms folded across his chest, seemingly a preferred posture for him. "You couldn't have. If you had, you wouldn't be here."

"That isn't true! We did!" This was the co-pilot speaking now. "We crossed through three seconds of darkness, just like Hanson said, but then—" he broke off, shuddering.

"Then ... what?" Charles dropped his arms, finally genuinely interested.

So was David.

"We were diving, right?" It was the captain's turn again. "Which meant we were still diving when we came out. It was dark, but there were some lights—they looked like fires rather than streetlights—a village—boats on a river maybe—"

"But the ground was *right there!*" The co-pilot interjected. "We couldn't help but hit—"

"—everything went dark again. I pulled on the stick, trying to lift the nose of the plane. It was so slow. Three seconds wasn't enough time—"

"We came out in front of another mountain, or maybe it was the same one."

"It didn't matter." The captain's rapid fire speaking style had slowed, calmer now that he was telling the story. "We crashed into it again."

"And then we were in the darkness again," the co-pilot said.

The captain nodded. "We came out like before, after three seconds, but I couldn't say if it was in the same place or a different place, with so little light to see by. It wasn't as if I could orient us by the stars. There was so little time."

"We were so close to the ground, we hadn't a hope of pulling up." The co-pilot was more settled too. "And then we were back in the Wallowas where we crashed a third time—"

"We time-traveled, but even though I had managed to raise the nose of the plane a few degrees by then, it wasn't enough."

"We went *through* the ground!" The co-pilot shuddered.

The captain put a hand on his companion's arm to calm him. "Once we got back here for the third time I'd lifted the nose of the plane enough that, instead of crashing, I almost scraped the bottom off on a peak."

"So you turned for home." Charles sneered.

The captain scoffed. "I wasn't doing that again. Insanity is doing the same thing over and over again and expecting a different result."

It was definitely something of an emphatic response, as if he was daring Charles to argue with his decision. He *was* the captain of the plane, and it was his right to decide when he could or would not fly.

Charles's eyes were narrowed, his attention fixed on the pilots, but Letitia suddenly seemed to realize that all twelve soldiers who'd ridden in the plane had surrounded them and had been listening intently the whole time—as had David, of course. Letitia spied him through the sea of faces and jerked her head. "Get him back to his room."

Thing One appeared behind David, pulled his hands behind his back, and put the handcuffs on him.

Charles's eyes had snapped to David's face too, and he nodded approvingly at the show of force. When he spoke next, instead of implying anger or disappointment, his voice was a little less strident, more musing than anything else. "We shouldn't have done this the first time in the dark."

"The first time—" The captain appeared genuinely shocked by this conclusion.

Charles waved a hand dismissively, effectively shutting him up. "Not here."

"But—" This was from Luke. Up until now, it seemed he hadn't realized David was a prisoner. "You're the King of—"

"Shut it down, soldier," Frank said. "Not your problem."

David made a rueful face in Luke's direction. He would have told him it was okay, except it wasn't, and Thing One was already pulling him away. Thing Two, who'd been standing outside the circle of men, took David's other arm. Three abreast, they started walking back to the office building in the hangar.

With the way the evening had fallen out, David decided there was no harm in getting confirmation of his suppositions, and, by this point, he somewhat urgently needed to know. "It's personal, isn't it?"

"What's personal?" Thing Two, otherwise known as Tom Baker, asked.

"Charles hates me. Why?"

Neither man replied overtly, though Thing One gripped David's upper arm a little tighter and picked up the pace. It was a little irksome that David still didn't know his name. From the start he'd been more hostile than Tom, and David was still waiting for the opportunity to talk to him like one human being to another.

Once at the door, however, Tom said to Thing One, "I'll take him in. Why don't you see if the director needs anything else."

"Sure." Thing One duly transferred David to Tom's custody.

Tom and David went through the door, just the two of them. After a ten second wait, they were passed through to the lobby. It wasn't until they were in the elevator, headed down to David's suite, that Tom answered David's question. "Director Makowski is more emotional when talking to you than I've ever seen him. He isn't like that usually. He couldn't be and have achieved the position he has. But I guess it has something to do with the death of his brother, Martin, a few years ago. I don't know the whole story."

It was as if Tom had slapped David in the face. "Was his brother a pilot?"

"Yeah. Charles blames your mom for his death. I don't know anything more than that." Tom hadn't asked a question, but his comment definitely ended in a questioning tone.

David deliberated as to whether or not he should fill in the rest of the story, not knowing if this would make things better or worse. Then he decided that telling the truth was definitely better than not in this case. "Ten years ago, Marty was the pilot of the plane that took my mom back to Earth Two. They flew out of Pasco and ended up flying into maybe the very same mountain we just tried to crash through. They both would have died if they hadn't time traveled."

"Tried? That isn't what the pilots said." Tom didn't seem much interested in Marty's story. "They said you did it."

"I couldn't see anything, so I can't tell you one way or the other. The lights dimmed, but that was about it."

Tom's lips pressed together. "I admit, even when you disappeared in front of everyone after that interview, I was skeptical. Time traveling couldn't be real." He paused. "But George Hanson spent the last year and a half somewhere, and I was standing right beside those pilots just now. They say it worked. They believe it worked."

"Yeah," David said. "I suppose I do too."

"But you came back right away. Why?" The elevator doors had opened, but Tom didn't move into the corridor, so David didn't either.

"I time travel when my life is in immediate danger," David said simply.

Tom thought about that for a few seconds, and then his hands went to David's cuffs. There was a *click,* and they came off. He didn't explain, just set off for David's suite without further comment. When he reached the door, he opened it with something of a flourish. "Have a good night, sir. What's left of it."

"Thank you, Tom." David entered the suite.

Tom didn't leave, instead hovering in the doorway. "I'm sorry, sir, but I have to—" He gestured to the handle. "I have my orders."

"I know."

With a further grimace, which was also apologetic, Tom pulled the door closed, once again leaving David alone, but for the cameras.

David turned back to the room and said, "Lights." After they came on, he added, "Dim." They obeyed that order too.

He didn't think much of drinking to relax. He certainly didn't want to be impaired—and thus unprepared—for whatever was coming next. But if they'd left him a bottle of wine he probably would have opened it, if only for the ritual of holding a goblet in his hand. Instead he poured himself a glass of water from a pitcher in the fridge and drank it while leaning a hip against the counter.

Marty was Charles's brother.

What were the odds?

But then, it wasn't about the odds; it looked to him as if Charles had made his own odds. The ten years that had passed since Marty's disappearance were plenty of time for Charles to direct his focus towards David's family, especially if he had already been in the CIA when Marty left. Nobody, David included, had ever asked Marty what his brother did or even if he had a brother. Not that David had ever been given the opportunity. The first time David had met Marty he'd been holding a knife to Anna's throat. And it wasn't as if David's mother had known him before he flew her into the Middle Ages and dumped her at Hadrian's Wall. David had never forgiven Marty for flying away and leaving his mother to her fate.

Regardless, David was glad to know what was really going on. Marty's life and death pretty much explained what was happening here, both in the way Charles was treating David himself and the extent to which he might be unpersuadable as to David's good intentions. Although it wasn't common knowledge in Avalon that Marty had died at the foot of one of Rhuddlan's towers, MI-5 knew, so that meant the CIA—and thus Charles—knew too.

David had certainly affected a lot of people over the years, one way or another. The lives of an entire busload of people had been disrupted by their sojourn in Earth Two after that trip that started in Oregon. To be fair, if the Cardiff bus hadn't ended up in medieval Wales, the passengers likely would have died. Thus, David couldn't, in the end, feel too bad about it.

Marty too would have died, along with David's mother, without her ability to time travel. It was he was who'd lost control of the plane during a storm, not Meg. That he was dead now was also a product of his own actions.

But he was still dead, and it wasn't hard to see that Charles was taking his grief out on David.

17

August 1295

Day Three

Lili

"What is that!" Jacob, the liaison from the Jewish community in Paris, stared in horror and awe as the plane dove towards the ground not a hundred yards from where they stood at the rail of the boat ...

... and disappeared.

"Dafydd. It's Dafydd." Lili's certainty settled over her, even as she hugged their sleeping son to her chest.

She'd heard the plane's engines before she'd seen it burst from the sky above the northern bank. The sun had set hours ago, and the cloud-cover was absolute, but the plane was lit up with lights, so it was impossible to miss. Lili had been standing at the rail of the boat, rocking Alexander to sleep on her shoulder. Amazingly, he'd slept right through the roar—and the subsequent uproar among the passengers on the boat.

They'd been on the river for roughly eighteen hours. The heavy rain that had fallen over the last week farther upriver, and then on and off all day, had turned the water brown. Usually, the Seine's current was slow and lazy, a matter of three or four miles an hour at most. But, for much of that time, they'd been traveling at a rapid clip, up to eight miles an hour in places. It had made it impossible to stop safely, even when hailed at various times by men on the docks of the towns they'd passed.

They had enough water to last until tomorrow, thanks to refilling their supplies from the rain that had fallen over the course of the day. But many people were ill enough from their time in prison, or the hardship of the walk to the river, that the pinched look on Aaron's face had become permanent. He was joined in his efforts by other doctors, among them Rachel's father, Abraham, who'd come with the boats from England expressly for this purpose.

Lili herself had spent many hours moving among the refugees, trying to offer whatever aid she could. Even the two women, a daughter Minna and her mother Esther, whom she'd met in the first hours of their journey, had become unwell, vomiting over the rail the little they could keep down. She hoped it was merely sickness from the rocking of the boat, but she feared their time in captivity had finally caught up with them. All Lili could do was hope that they and everyone else could hang on until they reached Rouen.

For a moment, when Lili had heard the engines, her heart had lifted that Dafydd might be arriving in Chad Treadman's plane and would land in a field nearby. Then, when she'd seen the massive plane coming out of the clouds, she thought it was supplies and people to save them. To her novice eyes, it seemed large enough to hold everyone.

But when the plane disappeared almost as soon as it arrived, her heart sank into her boots.

"That's a U.S. military cargo plane." Ted, Dafydd's uncle from Avalon, appeared next to the rail, which by now was crowded with watchers, who were straining their eyes to see the plane that had already disappeared. "You're sure David's in that thing?"

"Yes."

The word was nearly cut off by the roar of engines coming again, louder and closer than before, if that was even possible. This time, the plane's dive towards the ground wasn't quite as steep, but it nonetheless would have crashed if it hadn't disappeared in the heartbeat before it hit the earth.

"How could this be happening?" Elisa's hands were on her cheeks, and she was weeping silently. She, as well as all the rest of the Avalonians, had run for the prow of the boat. While Lili had never been to Avalon, she'd heard engines before, so it was no surprise they had each in turn recognized the sound as foreign to this world, even those who'd been below decks like Livia or Bronwen.

"What-what-what is happening?" Isabelle, Christopher's new friend, was the third to ask essentially the same question. She wasn't from Avalon and was new to the English court, so had never heard an engine before.

"We don't know." Christopher had his arm around her shoulders. He was looking, along with everyone else, towards the bank.

Lili glanced at the young man, thinking that he and Isabelle had come a long way very quickly—perhaps too quickly—and made a note to herself to treat the young woman as if she belonged in their inner circle, whether or not any of them—they or she—were ready for it.

Then the plane appeared a third time. While its angle as it came out of the void wasn't as steep, it arrived below the cloud cover, so the pilot had even less time to react before the ground rose up to meet the nose. Then it hit—or didn't hit—and was gone yet again.

Lili waited for a long count of ten, holding her breath all the while. When the plane didn't reappear, a general sigh went around everyone in the boat—and maybe all twenty boats. Lili sagged against the rail, near tears. She had flinched every time the plane didn't crash and wanted to vomit from the rush of love and fear she felt for her husband.

Livia put her arm around Lili's shoulder and spoke softly in English, "It's going to be all right. He's all right."

Lili turned to look at her friend, who had to be missing her husband too. The eyes that looked back at her were clear and compassionate—enough to allow Lili herself to take stock of what she felt and what she knew.

"Yes." She breathed the word. "That they disappeared back to Avalon means he's alive."

"And that he didn't return means he's alive there." Livia squeezed her slightly, careful not to wake the sleeping Alexander.

At which point, Elisa turned to them both, tears still on her cheeks. "How can you be sure it was David? It could be Meg. Or Anna. Or one of the children!"

Lili could see the fear in Elisa's eyes. Elisa and Meg hadn't always been as close as they were now, a fact which hadn't been aided by Meg's years in Earth Two and Elisa's refusal to accept the truth about her older sister. But Elisa and Ted's choice to come to Earth Two in Chad Treadman's plane had allowed the sisters to renew their friendship, and, when at home in England, they'd become inseparable. Meg and Llywelyn, along with Math and Anna, were holding the fort in England and Wales while Dafydd and Lili were absent in France. Last any of them had heard, Meg and Anna were where they were supposed to be, but the same could have been said of Dafydd.

"He all but told me he was going back to Avalon," Lili said. "I didn't understand what he was telling me at the time, but I've had this feeling ..."

They all knew that Lili had at times been blessed with the *sight,* which meant their silence was respectful instead of skeptical. But she shook her head. "I haven't *seen* him, so don't think that, but the more I've thought about it, the clearer it has become to me that he believed a confrontation with George and his CIA masters was necessary."

Ieuan ran a hand through his hair. "The plane was parked in a shed at the abbey where he was supposed to spend last night."

Christopher had a fist to his lips, and his expression told Lili he was thinking hard. Now it was Isabelle who put a hand on his shoulder, as she might be the one to do from now on, trying to comfort him.

"What is it, son?" Ted asked.

"Before I left to speak to King Philippe, David told me not to worry about him, no matter what happened or how long it took for him to get to the boats. He told me to look after Arthur and Alexander. They were a big reason he made me come here instead of joining him at the abbey after I talked to the king." Christopher shook his head. "I told him *of course I will,* even though I thought he was overreacting. But now that I think about it, his intensity was even higher than normal for him, and he kept saying *I,* not *we.*"

"With me too." Lili cast her mind back to their conversation two nights earlier, when they'd been in bed at the Paris Temple. "We were discussing how to get me and the boys safely to the English Channel. He wished he had a car."

"Don't we all." Ted very nearly laughed.

Lili had seen the cars in the barn near Llangollen, so she appreciated Ted's fervor. "Then Dafydd said, *The plane would be even better, though, at this point, it's too dangerous to go near in case George has found it and is watching.* And then, *You'll sail or ride for as long as necessary. At least you will have many able companions going with you.*"

Livia, one of those able companions, took in a breath. "You're thinking George found the plane."

"And took Dafydd to Avalon." Ieuan cursed under his breath.

"Yes, but there's more to it than that." Lili cuddled Alexander closer in her arms. "I find it likely that all those hours in captivity at Philippe's palace served only to confirm Dafydd in his opinion that he needed to protect the children at all costs. George *did* take him to Avalon." She looked lovingly around at her friends and family, feeling better now herself though she was quite sure her words weren't going to ease their minds at all. "But more to the point, it was Dafydd who put himself in a position to be taken."

18

August 2023
Day Four
David

*A*re we unhappy yet?

When he was younger, often sitting in the back seat of the car with his sister, Anna, in one of Portland's endless traffic jams, or when whatever trip they were on wasn't going according to plan, his mother would look in the rearview mirror and say those words. It was her way of acknowledging her own irritation and diffusing his and Anna's. Mostly, the ploy worked, though the hardships to which she was attempting to accustom them seemed laughably undifficult in retrospect.

Now, roughly twenty-four hours since he'd arrived in Oregon, Tom collected David from his suite yet again. This time, when David stepped outside into the cool air of another glorious Eastern Oregon morning, Charles was standing near the cargo plane, talking to a pilot. Letitia, meanwhile, had her hands on her hips, staring—or maybe

David could go so far as to say *glaring*—at Charles's back from ten paces away. The tension between them was as palpable as Charles's animosity towards David had been yesterday.

"Are mummy and daddy fighting?" David said out of the corner of his mouth.

Tom snorted laughter, proving himself once again to be amenable to conversation. Ten minutes earlier, when he'd arrived at David's door, he had refused to pull out the handcuffs, and David himself had argued with him, saying that he didn't want Tom to get in trouble with Charles.

"You let me worry about him," Tom had said. Thing One wasn't present. At this point, if David couldn't win him over, he'd just as soon never see him again.

The same troop of men was milling about near the cargo plane's entry ramp. Some were talking, and some were staring at the view. The airport was located above the river valley in which the town nestled, and mountains were visible in the distance, rising above the plain and shadowed by the rising sun behind them. They might even be the ones they'd crashed into last night.

If Tom had become a tentative ally, Luke was another, and he greeted David with a nod and a quick smile. Then he sobered before turning to face Frank, who was just gathering everyone together for their orders.

"We're going in again, same as before." He looked past the others to where Tom and David were standing a foot outside the ring of men. "King David is to ride up front this time, where he can see, in case that makes a difference to the outcome. Luke and I will provide his escort."

King.

Relations had progressed significantly in David's absence.

Once inside the plane, Frank pointed David to a jumpseat located behind the co-pilot. Luke sat in a similar seat across from him, and Frank himself would stand in the doorway, holding on to a strap hanging from the ceiling.

That didn't appear exactly safe to David, but then, he'd ridden in the front of the Cardiff bus as it was driven into a cliff wall, so he could hardly criticize. Besides, given the fiasco of last night, he was genuinely curious—more than outright afraid—as to how this was going to go.

"How exactly do you plan to land this thing with no runway?" He leaned forward to speak to the co-pilot sitting in front of him.

The captain was already talking to the tower and starting to taxi out of the hangar. These men were not the pilots who'd flown the plane last night. To David's mind, flying to an alternative medieval universe was a pretty big ask on short notice, but maybe the project had a whole posse of pilots who'd signed up to time travel, and the two who'd flown last night wouldn't have been asked to fly today regardless. Not that they would have, if asked, David guessed.

"We are trained to land in every condition."

"How about on wet grass?"

This time, the co-pilot turned in his seat as he answered. "Grass?"

"You do realize there are no airstrips in the Middle Ages."

The man faced front again. "There are roads. Good ones. Hanson said so."

David swallowed down a scoff. "Okay. So why does anyone think today is going to go differently from last night?"

"We will not be diving," the co-pilot said, "and this time you're watching."

David was in no way certain that was going to make a difference in the long run and thought the co-pilot's confidence a bit breathtaking. "Sure."

Luke and Frank had watched this exchange with somewhat narrowed eyes. David hadn't asked these questions because he wanted to undermine anyone's confidence in this plan—whatever the plan was exactly—but because he wanted to know for his own sake how bad this was going to get. *Run and find out.*

Now, as the pilot directed the plane down the runway, Frank asked sharply, "What are you thinking, sire?"

David put up both hands. "Nobody seems to care for my opinion."

"I do."

David scratched the top of his head, considering how to say what needed to be said. "I thought from the start that this—" he paused to think again, "—was never going to go the way Charles hoped it would. It probably isn't going to go the way *I* think it will either, but at least I am not blithely trying to land a military cargo plane on an eight-foot-wide, rain-soaked, dirt road. Because, with a few possible exceptions in very specific places in Britain, that's what we're looking at."

Frank pressed his lips together and visibly tightened his grip on the strap above his head.

The trip to the mountains took even less long than David felt it had last night. Then, he'd been sitting in the back of the plane, and now he was watching the peaks come closer. Even in late August, they were topped with snow and higher than David had expected. As they approached their own apocalyptic moment, he saw better how Marty had gotten lost in the storm and crashed his plane—or not crashed it, rather—when he'd taken David's mom to Earth Two.

Following the interstate, they flew over foothills and ridges and then soared over a highland valley of checkerboard fields and small towns. The land rose again, turning first into forested, and then snow-covered, peaks.

The pilot flew down a narrow valley, and, after a brief conversation with someone on the other end of his headset, accelerated the plane towards a mountain straight ahead of them. It looked no different from a dozen nearby mountains, and David didn't know why this one had been chosen as the point of contact, but neither did he think it wouldn't do.

"Oh God." Luke was clutching the straps that held him to his seat. "This is crazy. I can't believe we're doing this."

Frank gripped his strap with both hands. Despite the fact that David had done this a dozen times before—and six times last night apparently—he braced himself with one hand on the back of the co-pilot's seat in front of him.

"We're gonna die." That was Luke again, sounding much younger than the thirty years David pegged him to have achieved.

Frank said, "Get a grip, soldier," but then looked at David. "Are we, sire? Going to die, that is?"

"It hasn't happened so far." David clutched his seat belt too. "Always a first time."

Frank grunted his disbelief.

Yesterday, the men around David had viewed him as a prisoner at worst and a nuisance at best. Today, these two men were behaving more like they were an honor guard for a distinguished colleague. They were calling him *sire*. Though they didn't know it yet, if they were actually going to make it to Earth Two, that's exactly what they would be once they got there.

David was wondering too, in these final moments, what was supposed to happen once they arrived. Charles's face had been stony as he'd dismissed them—dismissed *David*—indicating he had no intention of giving an inch. He seemed to have a real expectation that the men he was sending would continue to keep David imprisoned once they reached Earth Two.

By now, David thought he might know them better than Charles, whom he saw as woefully underestimating the integrity of his subordinates. These men were an elite form of soldier, and they didn't strike David as the type to machine-gun civilians, which was what would be necessary if they were to take over the throne of England, for example. The entire population of Earth Two had experienced war in one fashion or another. Nobody was going to roll over for twelve men, no matter how well-armed or how much firepower they'd loaded into this plane. Eventually, they would run out of bullets.

Truthfully, if Charles really wanted to keep these men in line, he should have come with them. Of course, that would put him in a similar position to Marty, which Charles likely wanted to avoid.

"Look out the window, dammit!" The co-pilot shouted at David.

David supposed that was what he was here for, and now that the mountain was right in front of them, he couldn't look away. His heart was beating fast enough to make his ears pound too. He glanced at Luke, who was staring at the mountain with the same horror as David. While both soldiers wouldn't be here if they didn't have experience with rushes of adrenaline, their bodies couldn't stay calm any more than David's could. And David himself had just done this yesterday at Notre Dame. Lady Jane, the former head of the MI-5, who'd lost her life while protecting David, had developed a theory that stress hormones played a role in his world shifting.

Well, they sure were flooding David now.

"Hang on!" The pilot said.

The mountain loomed.

Luke screamed, not so much in terror but more like the cry of a berserker going into battle.

They hit.

Or rather, they didn't hit, and that utter darkness, which was so complete even sound was muffled, surrounded the plane, as it was prone to do.

One, two, three ...

19

August 2023

Day Four

George

The plane took off with surprising grace, considering its size, and headed east as it had done last night. George watched it go and then put down his binoculars. The sight lines were crap from everywhere around the hangar. Whoever had designed it had known their stuff. The contours of the earth hid the entrance from any road outside the airport, even right up to the fence on the opposite side. In fact, the entrance was hidden from any viewpoint but from within the tower itself. From where George was now, on the road beyond the exterior fence, he was looking at the backside.

He leaned back in his seat, settling in for a wait. If last night was anything to go by, the plane would make its way to the mountains, crash, and be back within the hour. After the plane had returned last night, George had placed a well-timed phone call to Bill Simons, one of the agents who'd met George and David at the plane, and George had heard all about the disastrous time travel attempt in vivid detail.

Yesterday morning, while George was still flying the plane, he'd been patched through to Langley where he'd related the salient details of his arrival. Then, once David had been taken away, George had told a more complete story in the director's office, with a dozen CIA officers joining in remotely. Everyone had listened with gratifying intentness and asked a thousand questions, which George had answered. Afterwards, he had luxuriated in a long, hot shower, eaten a ridiculous amount of food he'd craved for the last year and a half, and basked in the admiration of the other men in the barracks.

But then he'd received his new orders, handed to him by the installation's director, a woman named Charlotte, teetering on too-high heels.

His orders weren't to lead the mission back to Earth Two.

They weren't even to continue as an adviser on the time travel project.

They were for Moscow.

Supposedly, he was being promoted. His only evidence of that was they meant Moscow, Russia, not Moscow, Idaho.

Still, even as they'd dangled that carrot in front of him, he knew better.

He'd stared at Charlotte as she'd laid out his itinerary, which included two days at Langley for further debriefing. He was given keys to a rental car to drive himself to Portland, after which he'd fly coach to Washington D.C.

"Who is going to deal with David?"

Charlotte hesitated, but eventually wilted under his glare. "Letitia Johnson."

"She's coming here?"

"Yes. Among others."

"Who else?"

"Charles Makowski."

Having now talked to Bill, George knew Charlotte's information to be accurate.

At first, George was merely insulted. Objectively, it was appalling to be used and discarded. He'd said something along those lines to Charlotte, who feigned surprise and told him the reason he was being sent to Moscow was because he'd proved himself of such worth they couldn't do without him.

That had sounded plausible right up until the moment George had reconsidered. The more he'd looked at the keys in his hand, the more worried he became. He knew in his gut that something wasn't right about this entire operation. In fact, it had never been right. Fifteen years in the CIA, and then eighteen months in the Middle Ages, meant he'd learned to trust his gut.

Even then, he might still have done exactly as they asked and never been the wiser if Charlotte hadn't thrown a final comment over her shoulder. "Stop by the chip shop on your way out. Langley says you're long overdue."

Chip shop.

That could have been funny if they'd been in England, but she wasn't talking about picking up a greasy, salty packet of fries. He'd saved the stream of profanity for after Charlotte left him, the keys gripped tightly in his hand.

And then he'd left, walked right out the door before anyone noticed, found the rental car, and driven away. It wasn't in his head at that point that he was done with the CIA, only that the conversation about being chipped—or rather, not being chipped— could not be had with Charlotte, who was too low level to have the authority to say he didn't have to do it.

And then they'd ruined everything by sending men after him, presumably to tail him to Portland rather than kill him, but showing again how little they trusted him. That two separate cars had failed to keep up with him showed how far downhill the CIA had gone in the years since he'd joined. Back in the day, he'd met several black ops legends, who'd trained an entire generation of officers, before congressional oversight hamstrung the agency.

George's own trainer, a woman named Paige Blanchard, would have been a legend in her own right if she hadn't died in a mundane car crash on Interstate 95, having been sidelined six months earlier thanks to that same congressional oversight. She'd taught George to be ruthless and never to hesitate. *There* was a woman who could have handled this operation blindfolded, not to mention killed him with her own hands and dumped his body in an abandoned quarry without a backward glance.

It was her training, in fact, that had sent him down the path he was now treading.

The CIA's plan had always been to use David to set up a haven for this world in Earth Two. The information George brought back should have made it clear that, while it could be done, it wouldn't be as easy as his bosses had initially thought. And even George could see that it would be done better with David's cooperation than without it. Instead, they'd locked David up and hadn't even tried to convince him to help. David would do anything to protect his boys, and they'd left him alone for a long time to think.

While David wasn't as smart as he thought he was, he was definitely smarter than Letitia or Charles. Charles was a good officer, on the whole, and had risen in the CIA with rapidity, in large part due to his focus. But he had always had an axe to grind. George supposed, at this point, it was just as well that Paige was dead. If she'd been here, David really would have been in trouble, since she'd been notorious in the agency for a take-no-prisoners attitude and her willingness to do anything to accomplish a mission.

Letitia Johnson, on the other hand, was a flunky and so far down the org chart at Langley that George was surprised they'd let her out of the basement. He'd met her once, but only because he'd found himself lost down there. She was a nobody.

Not anymore, apparently. A lot had changed in the year and a half he'd been gone. Charles and Letitia had cornered David, and it was George's fault for putting both the CIA and David in this position. As George could have predicted, they'd screwed up last night's journey. He was willing to bet dollars to doughnuts (of which he'd eaten six in the last twenty-four hours), they wouldn't be successful today either.

He saw now also that his bosses at the CIA were far less casual about his obedience than Charlotte had implied when she'd given him his new assignment. Maybe she'd expected him to refuse to be chipped. Regardless, the tail cars had appeared within the first mile of leaving the airport. At first, George had settled in for the boring but scenic drive to Portland, but the more he watched them in the rearview mirror, the angrier he'd become. He'd almost wished they'd overtaken him and tried to run him off the road. Instead, they'd sat behind him, not even trying to disguise who they were, taunting him with his lack of power and status.

Rather than put up with that, he'd exited the highway onto a dirt track through the wheat fields and had spent an amusing forty-five minutes kicking up dust in the middle of nowhere before he shook them.

Losing them, in fact, had been one of his finer pieces of tradecraft. It was one thing to shake a tail in a city, with all its stops and turns, alleys, and shopping malls. Losing a team when *the middle of nowhere* was a polite way of describing his location, and the closest parking garage was two hundred miles away, was another thing entirely.

In the end, he'd found his way into an industrial area between the highway and the river, left the rental car on a deserted, half-paved road, and returned to Pendleton in a dusty pickup truck he'd stolen from a Walmart distribution center.

What Charlotte—and her bosses, whoever exactly they were, Letitia or Charles or some nameless bureaucrat at Langley—couldn't know was that he'd been a spy for too long to take anything she told him at face value. He'd given his life to the CIA and his country. It was what had kept him going all that time in Earth Two. He knew he was deceiving people who had tried to be his friends, but he'd believed in the cause. Maybe David was right that Avalon had no right to exploit the resources and isolation of Earth Two. But while he couldn't put that world above his own people, his time in that universe had given him a clearer view of those selfsame people and focused his mind on what was most important: his country. He was a patriot. Which meant he wasn't going to walk away from something that smelled as fishy as what was going on in that hangar just because they'd tried to sideline him.

The men he'd given the slip would have reported back long since. His bosses would know he'd missed his flight, which should be taking off right about now, and eight hours from now he wouldn't be landing in DC. They would try to find him, but he had shed his clothing, his car, and his identity, just as they'd trained him to do. If nothing else, he knew how to live undercover.

In truth, he'd loved the life he'd led. Even being a cop in Chicago had been interesting in its own way, though not so interesting he hadn't been happy to jump ship when the opportunity came.

Working for Chad Treadman had been one of the best jobs he'd had. At least with Chad, he'd been treated with respect.

Too bad, given that he'd abducted David, Chad's job was as much of a lost cause as the CIA's.

Or was it?

George eyed the new burner phone he'd picked up at the local mom and pop gas station that even the briefest survey revealed was doubling as an illegal drug distribution center, given the disturbing number of rattily dressed men who streamed in and out of the lone bathroom.

Chad was here. George knew it. And he would be on high alert, calling in every contact he had to get access to David. Anyone who didn't see the stink coming off what happened last night wasn't paying attention—and Chad would be paying attention.

He accessed the screen on his phone and dialed Chad's emergency number. David hated George now, of that he had no doubt, and didn't trust him. He had no reason to. Chad, however, had trusted George with his life a time or two. Regardless of what George had or had not done, Chad, at least, would listen.

20

August 2023

Day Four

David

"Whoo hoo! We did it!" Frank cheered.

His hand on his chest, Luke was gasping for breath.

The two pilots fist bumped between them as the plane wasn't forced immediately to crash into the earth and soared over a sodden landscape. It was raining, and the clouds were low to the ground, with the plane hardly a thousand feet above the tops of the trees.

The pilots leaned forward slightly, both focused on their instruments and talking rapid-fire to one another through their headsets. After a minute, the co-pilot pushed back one earpiece and glanced behind him. "Where are we, sir?"

David thought at first he was talking to Frank, but when, after a moment, everyone looked at David, he shrugged. "I don't know. I don't arrive at the same place every time. But you know—" He peered first through the front windshield and then out the little window next to his seat. "I'm thinking we may not be in Europe."

The others stared at him.

"Why do you say that?" Frank said.

David made a *look down* motion with his forefinger. "Last I checked, those are palm trees. They don't grow anywhere in Earth Two I've been."

"Christ." Frank looked out the window. "He's right."

"Hmmm." David was looking out his window again. "I see a large body of water. If leaving in the morning means we arrive in the morning, that's the rising sun, and we are flying north. There aren't too many bodies of water that look like that near Britain. Or anywhere else in Europe."

That was an understatement, actually. David should have said, *There aren't any bodies of water that look like that, period.* He was trying to maintain his cool, however, and not throw any of them into a panic so soon after their near-death experience.

The co-pilot was peering out his window too. "Lots of little islands down there."

"That right there is a mangrove swamp," Luke said in a totally flat voice.

"Florida?" Frank's tone was just short of horror.

"Maybe," Luke said. "Or Belize. Kind of looks like Belize, but unless we can fly higher and get a better view of the overall terrain, I can't be sure."

The co-pilot shuddered. "There's lots of bugs down there. I hate bugs."

"How much fuel is in this thing?" David asked, as casually as he could.

It was the captain who answered. "We have a range of two thousand miles, give or take."

David pressed his lips together for a moment and then said what everyone already knew. "It's farther than that across the Atlantic. Just saying."

Nobody spoke a word as the plane flew north, following the coastline, but now a little bit out to sea so they could see it better. David had never been to Central America, but the water, despite the rain, looked pretty and warm. He thought he'd better not say so, in part because he didn't want to interrupt the heavy thinking going on in the cockpit. Eventually everyone would come to the same conclusion he'd already arrived at.

It took a good five minutes, but then the captain said, "We have to try to kill ourselves again."

David didn't outwardly agree with his assessment of the situation, still waiting for the others to catch up. This would work best if everyone was on the same page.

"How, Ben?" Frank asked.

David hadn't known the captain's name until now. Ben removed his headset, since it wasn't connected to anyone outside the plane, and tossed it on the co-pilot's lap. Tentatively, the co-pilot removed his unit too.

"I could dive into the land or the ocean, but it isn't as if this plane has a lot of maneuverability once it's headed down. I hear Jim and Kenneth did that last night, and it didn't turn out great. I think what we just did was better."

Frank took in a long breath through his nose and then finally, *finally*, turned to David. "Sire, we are in your hands. Please tell us what to do."

David didn't acknowledge the honorific or that twenty-four hours was way too long a wait for them to look to him for leadership. "I think Ben is right. As it stands, we can't make Europe, and this world is a much less connected place than Avalon. There's no place to refuel, for starters, and if we put down outside of Europe, we could spend anywhere from months to a lifetime getting back to Britain. I am not personally in favor of that option."

"Me neither," Luke said. "My girlfriend's pregnant."

Frank put a gentle hand on his shoulder. "Congratulations."

It sounded an awful lot like, *I'm sorry you won't live to see your baby born.*

David cleared his throat. "I have a wife and two sons who are at this very moment floating down the River Seine, having escaped the clutches of the King of France, who imprisoned us in Paris. I'd like to see them again too, sooner rather than later."

The others stared at him. They hadn't known about what was going on in his life because they hadn't asked. The location of Lili and the boys had no bearing on their current situation, but it was important for them to keep thinking of David not only as human but as one of them.

Then David added, remembering a long ago middle school geography class, "Southern Mexico has a huge mountain range. One of the mountains is something like eighteen thousand feet, which makes it taller than Mt. Rainier in Washington State. We won't miss it if we get above the clouds—and I suppose even if we ran right into it without seeing it, that would serve our purposes just as well."

What he didn't say was that it didn't matter to him personally what course they chose. He was pretty confident that he himself wasn't going to die—but these men might. David could be thrown from the plane, for example, and travel to Avalon by himself, while these men were stuck in a crashed plane in the middle of the rainforest with no transportation but their feet. If they survived the crash at all, that is.

But since everyone was cooperating and looking pretty cowed while they were doing it, it seemed petty to mention any scenario that had him living and them dying.

For David's part, he would just as soon return to Oregon and continue his battle with the CIA. The sooner their disagreements (to put it mildly) were resolved, the sooner he could focus on the betterment of Earth Two without the constant fear of Avalonian interference. While he wanted to get back to his wife and sons, who really were floating down the River Seine, having come this far, he would rather not defer the confrontation that he'd started.

"How far to the mountain?" Frank looked out the window, as if he could see it from where they were now. Maybe on a clear day he could have.

David shrugged. "Five hundred miles?" He'd never been afraid to acknowledge what he didn't know, even when he was leading men, and wasn't about to start now. "What do you think, Ben?"

The captain sighed. "It could be a little more than that but it isn't a thousand. I know there are smaller mountain ranges between here and there. One of them would work too."

"I don't want to go lower." Frank's jaw was tight. "I don't want to risk any of us surviving here. If we're all going to die, we're going to do it right."

David was glad to agree, though for different reasons. He didn't want to go lower because there were people down there, even now hearing the sound of the plane's engine and looking up to see what was making the strange noise. The sight of a plane crashing into a thousand foot mountain was very different than seeing it as a speck far up in the sky or an unexplained sound above the cloud cover. He would rather not change the course of these peoples' history more than they may already have done, just by appearing here.

"I got it!" Once he'd accepted that they'd world-shifted, the co-pilot had started searching through his stash of paper maps and charts, which airplanes were still required to carry, even a military plane as tricked out as this one. He pointed out the window to a large island in the distance. "It's Belize, like Luke said. That's a caye. And the barrier reef."

"Get me a bearing, Arnaldo." Ben circled the plane once, by which time the co-pilot had set the course. The plane rose above the clouds into the bright sun of a new morning in Earth Two and headed west.

21

August 2023

Day Four

David

David had been right that the mountain was pretty hard to miss, even had the clouds not dissipated farther inland. Leastwise, they didn't miss it, and Ben drove into its snow covered peak with the other men in the cockpit bellowing like madmen, defying every cell in their bodies screaming for Ben to pull up.

During the several hours it took to fly there, David and Frank went to speak to the men in the back. Even though Frank had said he would do the talking, he'd wanted David there. So David had stood behind him and a little to his left, legs spread and his hands behind his back, listening with the others as Frank explained what had happened and what they'd decided to do about it.

Several of the dozen men weren't entirely of European descent, and one of them, Daniel, was a member of the Yakama Nation.

"We could stay for a while. I'd like to see what it was like; I speak Yakama and a little Sahaptin."

Two men, who said they were Latino, nodded their agreement. "It would be nice to see the country when we were the ones who ran it."

"We have reason to think that wouldn't be a good idea." Frank gestured that David should approach.

Understanding now that Frank had wanted him there so he could bear the brunt of the objections, David took one step forward. "I hear what you're saying. Please believe me that I do. But we have to look at the practicality of it. There is no place on this entire continent we could land safely. There are no actual roads. I don't know if you realize, but the New World never utilized the wheel, so even the roads that do exist are narrower than in Europe."

"And you're sure we can't make it to England?" Jorge asked.

"It isn't me. It's simple math." David tipped his head to Frank, who nodded too. "If you've been briefed on this plane's capabilities, you yourself know that our range is around two thousand miles. That could get us into the middle of the Atlantic if we fly northeast or northern California if we fly northwest. But even if we successfully landed the plane in the desert or ditched in the ocean and swam to shore, it's still a long walk to Yakima."

"What about horses?" This was from a red-headed man named Chet, who spoke with an accent David thought meant he was from Texas or Oklahoma. "I learned to ride when I was three."

It was Daniel who answered, shaking his head before Chet had finished speaking. "There are no horses here in 1295. Same way there's no wagons."

The news was unwelcome, and the others slumped in their seats, at which point Daniel looked directly at David. "Can you get us home?"

Before David could reply, another man who hadn't said anything up until now, let out a snort. "He isn't going to help us. Why would he? He's our prisoner. Which means, even if he says he'll help us, we can't trust him."

David turned his gaze on him. "What's your name?"

"Brad Furtwangler."

"You have a point, Brad. I do have no reason to help you, other than the fact that I am not interested in seeing another man die on my watch." He looked around at the men assembled. "How many of you saw my interview, whether live or afterwards?"

Every hand went up.

"Then you know more about me than I know about you. But to my eyes, you are doing as you were ordered to by Charles, and we all know what he thinks of me."

"Not much." This was from Chet, and everybody laughed, though the laughter ended quickly and a little sheepishly.

David nodded. "I am well aware that I am your prisoner. You can do with me as you wish. You can trust me or not. But if any of you watched that interview and saw something you could believe in, then believe me when I tell you the plan we've come up with has the best chance of getting not only me home safely, but all of you as well."

Brad grunted. "I saw the interview. No way he should have asked that question about killing people."

There were murmurs of agreement all around. Oddly enough, though David had been fighting battles since he was fourteen, he had never felt much in the way of camaraderie with other soldiers, mostly because of differences in rank and his own social inadequacies. Now as the King of England, his ability to relate to others was even more limited. But he was the same age as most of these men, and king or not, for a moment it felt like they viewed him as one of them.

Daniel transferred his gaze to Frank. "Can I see what's out there?"

Frank tipped his head towards the cockpit. "Come on up. The clouds are dissipating so you should be able to see something. We'll go below the clouds again if we have to." Then he looked generally at the others. "Anyone who wants to see what the world looks like is welcome."

The rest of the men made their way to the front a few at a time, watched for several minutes and then returned, quieter than when they'd arrived. David could only agree with what he saw in their faces: after the initial excitement wore off, they were left with the enormity of what faced them here.

By the time they were approaching the mountain, everyone had returned to their seats, strapped themselves in, and were bracing themselves for death and/or time travel. This time, as Ben drove the plane into the mountain, after the first glance to evaluate the trajectory, David didn't bother to look and instead kept his eyes closed and his forehead pressed to the back of Arnaldo's seat. He didn't need to see what was happening to know it was happening.

The darkness came and went, evident even through David's closed eyes by the change in the light and the muffling of the plane's engines. Regardless, he'd have known they had entered the three seconds of darkness because the men around him stopped screaming, stunned, as always, into silence.

As they came out into the blue skies of Eastern Oregon, he felt some relief to know that the arc of his destiny wasn't yet complete, and that God, or the powers-that-be, or some ancient spirit of Merlin hiding in a cave in Snowdonia, still had a plan for him.

And yet, the burden of that responsibility bowed his shoulders and, for a moment, made him press his forehead a little harder into the back of the seat.

He'd saved his father. He'd saved Wales. He'd become King of England and eventually High King of Britain. And still, it wasn't enough.

With great power comes great responsibility, yada, yada, yada. He'd been told that every day of his life since he was fourteen years old and suddenly discovered he was the true son of the Prince of Wales and heir to the throne. At the time, the future had stretched before him in one vast, exciting expanse. He'd reveled in his responsibilities.

And then he'd fought them.

And then he'd accepted them.

And today, he found himself simply tired.

That was the real reason he'd closed his eyes as they'd passed through the mountain, to come out once again in sunny Oregon, circling above the little airport. Straightening again in his seat and meeting Luke's jubilant eyes with more somber ones of his own, Lili's voice echoed inside his head, as often was the case when he was needing advice, if the voice wasn't his mother's or Callum's: *with some problems, the only way through them is* through *them.*

The plane taxied to a halt, and Letitia came out to meet it. Charles was nowhere to be seen, but, of course, Ben had been talking through his headset since they arrived a few minutes ago, so everyone on the ground already knew the outline of what had happened.

David unbuckled his seatbelt and headed towards the back of the plane and the ramp that would take him out of the cargo bay and into the airplane hangar. The other men joined him, rising to their feet with grins on their faces at having survived, patting his back and thanking him as he passed. In that moment, he found inspiration in the words of another English king, from the only Shakespeare play he'd actually read: "Once more unto the breach, my friends."

22

August 1295
Day Four
Lili

"What is it, Ieuan?" Lili moved to stand beside her brother, who was deep in conversation with Amaury de Montfort's steward.

"We have a situation, sis," Ieuan said in Welsh. "It's looking like things could get ugly."

That was a phrase he'd learned from the Avalonians, no surprise since he was married to one.

The boats had made their first concerted effort to stop at Pont-de-l'Arche (Bridge of the Arch) where there was a Templar commandery and massive fortifications on both ends of the bridge across the Seine. But not only had the dock at the commandery been washed away, the bridge was gone as well, having collapsed into the middle of the river. They were lucky the current had slowed a bit by then, because otherwise their boats might have crashed into the fallen pieces. As it was, they had a narrow gap to shoot through, which had given them all some white-knuckle moments.

By road, it was nearly seventy miles from Poissy, the town where they'd collected Christopher, Ieuan, and Darren, to Rouen, their current destination. The distance was more than twice that on the river. Even with the slowing current, they'd made the journey in record time and could be in Rouen before nightfall.

From the look on Ieuan's face, maybe she shouldn't have been as happy about that as she'd been a moment ago.

They'd finally managed to stop here, just before Elbeuf. The holding was ancient, founded originally by one Richard the Fearless, who'd been the grandson of the Viking chief, Rollo, who himself had founded Normandy.

Thus, not only was Amaury a supporter of what Dafydd was trying to accomplish in France, but the residents of the area were of Norman descent, and thus possibly less hostile towards English traders, which the boat passengers were pretending to be. A side channel flowing into the Seine had given them the opportunity for a safe harbor, and they'd managed to escape the main current and arrive at the dock without too much trouble.

She'd disembarked to stand alongside many of her fellow passengers, happy beyond measure to be on solid ground for just a moment to stretch her legs. Unfortunately, many passengers remained too ill to rise, Minna and her mother, Esther, among them. Regardless of the bad news Ieuan had to impart, their arrival in Rouen couldn't happen soon enough.

"Just tell me, Ieuan. Best to hear it all at once."

Ieuan still looked reluctant, but he gestured to Amaury's man. "Tell her, please."

"We have rumors of unrest in Rouen. It seems the people have taken to the streets and been met by soldiers from the castle."

Lili took in a breath. "Do we think it's true?"

"We don't know. One person tells another, who tells another, who told me an edict was read out in the city yesterday. There appears to be a plan to confiscate all English shipping. They know about King Philippe's attack on Aquitaine."

Lili's stomach dropped into her boots. "But not the result?"

"No."

"And nothing about Jews?"

"Not that anyone said."

"Where is Amaury?"

"I have not seen my lord since your boats came up the river a week ago."

Lili made a face. "But Amaury still has a plan to get us through the bridge's portcullis, right?"

"So he said, but I am concerned that the assumptions we made before you left about your journey might not hold true any longer. And, as we know, as Rouen goes, so goes Normandy."

It was some comfort that the steward was claiming them, saying *we* like they were all in this together. Though Lili herself had never met Amaury, he was one of the heroes of this mission and had not only thrown himself into Dafydd's project with enthusiasm and passion but had been instrumental in organizing the Rouen portion of the Underground Railroad that had brought Jews safely across France to the English Channel.

Lili had never seen a railroad other than in images on one of Mark Jones's devices, but never mind. She knew what it was and what it did. Not everything that came from Avalon was of benefit to her world, and she wasn't sorry Dafydd had decided to skip over (as he said) burning coal and polluting the skies in favor of powering machines with sun, wind, and water. But not only did a *railroad* provide a means of transporting a great number of people quickly, the very word itself conjured in the imagination a mighty force—almost a weapon, in truth.

In short, there were few men as righteous as Dafydd, but Amaury seemed to be one of them.

Ieuan grunted. "Does the rumor say if the edict is directed specifically at us? Do they know we're coming?"

The steward shook his head again. "It isn't clear, my lord. The man to whom I spoke said his nephew had heard this from his neighbor, who'd spent the night in the city itself."

In other words, the news was hearsay. Three citizens confronting a single soldier could be blown up into civil war if the news of it passed through enough people. Still, they couldn't dismiss it. Rumor often contained a grain of truth. And the news about the edict was very specific. It certainly sounded as if it was directed at them.

"We need to know more." Lili had her hands on her hips as she considered their options. "Do you have enough good horses for us to send riders ahead to Rouen?"

"I-I-I have five, my lady." The steward stuttered a bit, perhaps surprised that she was taking charge. He shouldn't have been. She was the Queen of England. In Dafydd's absence, whether from a boat on the River Seine or from a throne in Westminster, she, not Ieuan, was in charge, even if he was Dafydd's close friend and Lili's brother.

"Good. We'll take them all with gratitude."

"What are you thinking?" Ieuan asked her in Welsh.

She faced him, sure in this and that they had to do *something*. "What if we sent Christopher and his friends to Rouen? It's what? Ten miles by road?"

"A little more."

"Then they could be there in a little more than an hour, while it will take us at least four, five if we dawdle here for a bit."

"They have been disguising themselves as French for some time now." Ieuan's eyes narrowed as he thought. "They would have to be quick to get in and out and back to the boats to warn us of anything untoward before our arrival in the city."

"We need them to try, Ieuan. While the last thing I want is to unload everyone and walk around Rouen, we will do it if we have to."

"Many wouldn't make it."

"Many won't make it either way," she said crisply. "That isn't the point. We are on the river at all because Amaury de Montfort assured that as long as we paid the appropriate tax, nobody in Rouen was going to look at us twice. But all that could now be changed. They have the power to bar the river against us. *Confiscate English shipping.*" She shook her head. "It is a little early for the governors in Rouen to have received word of the expulsion from Paris, and certainly too soon for the news that English trading boats are transporting Paris's Jews to the English Channel." She frowned as she looked at her brother. Earlier they had wanted to get to Rouen as quickly as possible. Now, she was wondering if they should get there at all.

"Unless someone sent a pigeon. Nogaret."

Nogaret. Lili wanted to spit. "He still didn't know about the boats."

"I would send Isabelle with them." Ieuan spoke tentatively, which wasn't usual for him.

She brushed aside his hesitation. "I would too. Christopher and his friends are excellent at what they do, but Isabelle has spent the last year in the French court. She can speak French like a Parisian, and she is the daughter of the current master of the Paris Temple. She has standing in France in a way the others do not."

And then at Ieuan's surprised look, Lili spread her hands wide. "Did you think I would object to her inclusion?"

"I was afraid you would want to go in her stead."

Lili laughed. "I have no such ambition, brother."

"You fought at Skipton."

"I did, but I am not in a position at the moment where it makes any kind of sense to indulge my desire to investigate. I have two sons who spent the last week under enormous stress, and five hundred refugees who look to me for leadership." Because she knew that to him she would always be that little girl who demanded he teach her to shoot, she kept her tone light, no more than teasing. "Only Dafydd can sometimes be in two places at once."

While they'd been talking, Jacob, the Jewish liaison, approached. He was quick-witted and didn't need the implications explained to him once outlined. "If this rumor of unrest and confrontations between the citizens and the castle is true, it could be only a matter of time before they turn on their Jewish neighbors. They've done it before. We have many family members in Rouen."

We to Jacob didn't mean everyone in the boats. It meant *his* people, the Jewish refugees.

Jacob had started out somewhat combative, unsure of both Dafydd and his reception in the English court, and it seemed in this moment that some of his uncertainty remained. There was a hint of a question in his tone, as if he couldn't quite believe in Lili and Ieuan's sincerity, despite the fact that they were responsible not only for spiriting the entire Jewish community of Paris out of the city but had brought an armada, captained for the most part by English people, to do it.

"We will help them too, if we can." Lili put out a hand, trying to reassure him.

"Of course, we will," Ieuan said.

Jacob nodded, mollified for now. Lili supposed she couldn't blame him for assuming the worst and wondering how far Dafydd's beneficence would stretch. Jewish people had endured a millennium of persecution at the hands of Christians. That history wasn't going to be swept away in a few days.

Even with what they'd promised Jacob, however, she didn't know what they could really do. Their boats were full. And, on top of the fact that most of the people they were carrying were Jewish, their whole disguise was based on the fact that they were *English*, even if the rest of the passengers, herself included, were not.

So she spoke her mind to Jacob and her brother. "If the good people of Rouen want to bar our boats from continuing to the sea, so be it. They will find, as King Philippe did, that God is not on their side."

Ieuan gazed at her with something of an unreadable expression, before turning again to Jacob. "I expected some opposition before now, but I think the current has moved us along too quickly to allow any force to come to bear against us."

Jacob's eyes narrowed. "You said nothing about those concerns to me."

"I said nothing about them to anybody." Ieuan spoke more gently than he could have. "These last hours I have watched the eastern bank, hoping at any moment to see King Dafydd and his men riding towards us."

"Or, at the very least, King Dafydd's men," Lili said softly.

Ieuan put a hand on her shoulder. "We will know soon enough where he is."

After the cargo plane had disappeared the third time, Lili had tried to get some sleep, lying on a pallet with Arthur and Alexander—

and weeping soft tears of despair. When necessary, she could be strong for her boys, and for everyone else, but the thought of Dafydd having to die over and over again at the behest of people who should love him brought a grief to her heart she couldn't suppress another moment. She knew he loved her and their sons more than life itself. It was why he'd gone to Avalon. But sometimes it was hard to be the one who loved him.

To disguise her emotions and be even more reassuring, Lili smiled at Jacob. "We've already done the impossible. We mustn't lose faith now."

But once Jacob had departed, she looked at her brother, and allowed some of that despair she'd felt earlier to show. "What *can* we do if the king's forces try to stop us?"

Ieuan looked towards the bank, his expression pensive. "I don't know."

23

August 1295

Day Four

Christopher

"*Something* is happening in this city," William pointed to the way the citizens of Rouen rushed past them with their heads down. "They look fearful to me."

"I would be fearful too if I were English," Huw said, and then added under his breath, "which I am not."

"Let's ask someone." As usual, Isabelle was up for taking the direct approach. Without waiting for any of the others to agree, she leaned down to a woman hurrying by. "*Un moment?*"

The woman glanced up, but even though Isabelle was obviously nobility, she didn't stop. "*Pardon, demoiselle.*" And she was past them, heading for the gate.

"Well, we're here now." William straightened his shoulders. "I'm down with finding out what we can." It was he, of all Christopher's friends, who'd taken to American slang most easily and incorporated it into his vocabulary at every opportunity. "We will deal with whatever else comes our way when it comes."

"As we do," Christopher said.

William and Christopher were only repeating words they'd heard David say time and again. It was an affirmation of sorts. They were missing David, all of them, and Christopher got a cold feeling in his stomach every time he thought about the way the cargo plane had arrived and disappeared three times. Lili was sure it was David on the plane. If so, he was going through hell right about now at the hands of the CIA. All the more reason for Christopher and his friends to safeguard what was happening here.

Christopher put out a hand to Isabelle, who grasped it briefly in her own. They'd known each other for all of three days, the entirety of which had been under significant duress. He couldn't say that whatever was going on between them would last, but he sure wanted to find out if it could.

The five of them reached the bridge across the moat that protected the city walls, Isabelle and Christopher in the lead, as would be the case with an escort for a noblewoman. They had been intending to affect as casual and oblivious an attitude as possible, cantering through the gate without stopping as was normal for nobility, but the barbican was blocked by a line of wagons and people. In single file, men and women hurried by the wagons that were stopped in the road. Up ahead, most of the people were being waved through into the city, but the wagons were being inspected thoroughly.

It was as if the guards were looking for something.

Or *someone*.

Isabelle had the same thought in the same moment as Christopher. "They're looking for King David!"

That froze all of them in their tracks, until Christopher gave a shake of his head and a laugh. "He isn't here, so they won't find him, and we don't need to worry."

The tension eased a bit in the others too, and Christopher turned in the saddle to look at William. "Are we using vinegar or honey?"

"Oh vinegar. Definitely vinegar." William grinned. "Let me do it while you stay beside Isabelle. You couldn't intimidate a lamb. And you're a terrible liar."

Urging his horse forward, William cantered the last few yards past the wagons that were holding up the line. Isabelle followed with her nose in the air, while the others endeavored to look like seasoned warriors, which they actually were, even though they were young. Before they could pass through the gatehouse, however, two guards stepped right in front of William's horse, moving so quickly that the horse startled and reared.

William was an expert horseman and held on, but he didn't have to pretend to be angry and lashed out with his tongue. "Fools! You could have killed me!"

Pressing themselves against the stones of the barbican, other travelers hastened to get out of the way of the horse's dancing hooves.

"Sorry, my lord," said one of the guards, this one tall with red hair.

"What were you thinking?"

"Orders from the archbishop, my lord."

"You had orders to frighten my horse?"

The red-headed man plucked at his forelock and bowed. "No, my lord. Sorry, my lord. We have orders to stop everyone entering the city."

"Who are you looking for?"

"Jews and Englishmen, my lord."

Not David. Worse.

"Do I look like a Jew to you?" William's voice rose, and his sneer was impressive. "Or an Englishman?"

"No, my lord." All the guards looked suitably chastened.

William continued to look down his nose with disdain and feigned ignorance. "Why is this a problem in the first place? Thousands of Jews live in Rouen already. And Rouen trades daily with the English."

The second guard, shorter and pudgier than his companion, spoke for the first time. "Archbishop Guillaume has decreed that Rouen is to follow Paris's lead. All Jews are banished from the city."

Worse and worse. Christopher found himself frozen to the saddle. That Amaury's steward hadn't known about this second edict testified to how little those reporting the news of Rouen to him cared about Jews.

"So then why are you looking for Englishmen?" William asked.

"King Philippe has declared war on Aquitaine and its English allies. We will no longer allow English traders on the Seine nor in our midst."

As if spurred by the terrible news, the urgency of the people hurrying past seemed to have increased. Their heads remained down, and their shoulder's hunched, as if any moment fearing an arrow in the back.

"The archbishop himself is overseeing this?" Recovering somewhat, Christopher did his best to mimic William's accent, which he realized (with some astonishment, since he'd never thought about it before) was for all intents and purposes the same as that of the red-headed guard. Of course Christopher had noticed that the Normans in David's court spoke French with a different accent from Parisians, but it hadn't occurred to him before what that *meant*.

"He has enlisted the aid of the king's men." The pudgy guard was still talking. "We will be evicting all Jews tonight." He looked as if this would be the major achievement of his life.

Christopher had never thought to witness such a momentous day in history. Others might have thrilled to the experience, but all he felt was sick—and angry. He couldn't have lived for years in David's court and not know that King Edward had finished off England's pogroms against the Jewish community by expelling them in 1290. David had put a stop to all that in England, and they were here in

France in the first place to change history for the better for France's Jewish population.

But despite their best efforts, the worst was happening anyway, eleven years too soon. That was probably their fault, at least in part. Because they'd tried to help, they'd accelerated the timeline.

Still, as David had said more times than Christopher could count, this wasn't the same world as Avalon. You couldn't go back and change a history that was already established, only work with one that was progressing along its own natural lines. The French king had been persecuting his Jewish citizens long before David started interfering. That Philippe had been doing so was *why* David had interfered.

"Are there that many soldiers of the king stationed in Rouen?" William asked.

"They are Jews." The man spat on the ground. "We have enough men."

Christopher didn't want to believe him. His mom or Livia would know the numbers more exactly, but Rouen had a castle and ten gates, each of which would normally be guarded at most by a half-dozen men per shift. More likely two. That ten were on this gate meant it was all-hands-on-deck. If the king had four hundred men in Rouen, Christopher would be surprised. More likely, he had half that number. And even if Rouen's governor had been here, which he wasn't, he was an ineffectual prig, appointed as a political favor rather than because he was a competent leader. Rouen was a plum position, and men wanted a leadership position here because it was a way to get rich.

And then the guard added, "And if we don't, the Templars will assist us."

Christopher struggled to keep the horror he was feeling out of his face.

"Where are Rouen's Jews—or any Jews—supposed to go?" This was from Robbie, who by now had approached.

"We don't care. Just so long as they're gone!" This was from the second guard again. "We will march them into the sea if we have to."

Robbie's eyes narrowed. "You are not from Rouen."

"Paris, my lord." He straightened his shoulders, looking more confident in his duty by the second, and fixed his gaze on Robbie. "Your name, my lord?"

Robbie put his own nose into the air. "Robert Bruce, heir to the Earldom of Carrick. You'll note that is in Scotland. I have business with the Templars myself." He then made a casual gesture with one hand. "These are my companions. I assume you can take my word that none of them are what you're looking for and need not trouble us further."

"No, my lord. Of course not, my lord." The guard backed down, well aware of the capriciousness of high lords, some of whom wouldn't be above reporting him to his superiors if he wasn't appropriately respectful. "Apologies for the delay, my lord."

"Very well." Robbie led the way into the city, all of them heaving a sigh at the close call they'd just had.

"Good of you to name drop the Templars instead of Amaury," Christopher said.

Robbie nodded in acknowledgement. "I figured if the Templars are evicting Jews, they, at least, are still in favor."

"The Templars here would only do that if they didn't know what really happened last night," Isabelle said from behind Christopher, albeit again in an undertone.

The city streets were as busy as the gatehouse, such that Christopher had to follow directly behind Robbie, so as not to run anyone over. This hour should have been the height of commerce, with everyone buying supplies for dinner or their livelihood, but nobody was stopping, and most of the shops and market stalls were closed.

Lili's commission for them had seemed manageable when she'd sent them off, but Rouen was a much larger city than Christopher had anticipated, even knowing in advance its population, the entirety of which seemed to be currently on the streets. As they'd been talking to the guards, he'd become worried that their task was too big.

Now, he was certain of it.

24

August 2023

Day Four

David

David sat up with a start. He'd fallen asleep on the couch again. Without Lili, the bed seemed too big, and sleeping in it implied he was letting down his guard in a way sleeping on the couch did not. The arboretum lights were on, indicating it was still daytime. He checked the time on the clock on the microwave: 4:06. He'd spent hours alone, while Charles and whomever he'd decided to consult (not David, obviously) decided what to do next.

David had been dreaming of dying and had woken up right before he'd hit the ground after a long fall off a cliff. It had been the dream, rather than a noise or a step outside his door, that had woken him. He threw up an arm to cover his eyes and allowed his pulse to settle. One would have thought that, having time traveled nine times in the last two days, he'd be getting used to it, even in his dreams.

He didn't fear the accumulated total, as if he were a cat and after nine lives he'd run out of them and die on the tenth. By his count, the transition to Avalon with George had been his twelfth passage through the void, so he was really at twenty. He figured if his DNA was going to be rearranged by his world shifting it would have happened already.

But what had really brought him out of his deep sleep was the sudden realization that he wasn't as alone as he'd been thinking he was when he went to sleep. *He'd time traveled nine times.* That meant anyone paying attention to the flashes as he went in and out of this universe would know he was here and, what's more, would know where he was right now.

Chad Treadman would know.

MI-5 would know.

Back in the planning stages of this mission, he'd assumed they would be keeping tabs on him. But once he'd arrived in Avalon, he'd had so much to think about and honestly had felt so isolated, knowing how fully he was going it alone, it hadn't been at the forefront of his mind.

As a billionaire who'd made his money primarily in tech, but also by buying up other companies of every kind and stripe, Chad Treadman had placed at David's disposal anything he needed to make the transitions between worlds smoother. When David had arrived in Avalon last time, Chad had hired Michael instantly as David's bodyguard. It had been Michael (and Livia, from MI-5), who'd driven through the night to pick up Cadell in Llanberis and then protected him afterwards. It was on Chad's plane that George had flown from medieval Paris to modern Oregon. George, in fact, had originally been Chad's right-hand man.

Clearly, that had been a disastrous hiring mistake—and also a surprising one, given how thoroughly Chad must have vetted him. That the CIA had managed to fool even Chad was an indication of how deep George's cover had been. David could only think that Charles, if he really was the one in charge, wanted David's family punished very, very badly, and he'd put all the resources the United States government would give him to ensure it.

That the CIA was racing against Chad and MI-5, as well as a financial clock, could also be behind Charles's urgency. While September 1st, when funding would be cut off, was two days away, he must also be worried that Chad's organization, and maybe MI-5 itself, would make a move to interfere. Charles would also know that they knew David was here.

Furthermore, now that David was seeing the situation more clearly, he understood why he hadn't so far set foot outside the airplane hangar. Charles couldn't disguise the *flash* that ripped open a door from one universe to another; he couldn't prevent Chad from tracking his plane's GPS, at least initially until they disabled it; but he could shield David from watching eyes. The real consideration for David now was where Chad was, or MI-5 was, and what they were planning to do about his presence in Oregon—if anything.

While MI-5 wasn't supposed to be operating outside of Britain, neither was the CIA supposed to be operating inside the US.

They both had external resources to draw upon, however. If Director-General Philips thought the urgency was great enough, he could ask MI-6 for help. Five had done so in the past specifically because of David. In turn, the CIA was already piggybacking on the military. The cooperation of the National Guard might also be giving the CIA some cover if Charles or his bosses ever had to face real oversight.

Chad's commitment to helping David and his family had been great up until now, and David had no doubt he was here. Chad was American for starters, so it would be nothing for him to take over one of the nicer hotels David had seen on the hill by the highway, or even buy himself an entire estate like he'd done in Wales. While it was true that he had all the money in the world (nearly literally), he would also be devoting his *time* to this endeavor, which was a far more valuable commodity to someone like Chad. Even with all those possibilities, David very much didn't want any of these people to rescue him. To be rescued would, in fact, ruin his plans.

There would be plenty of time to get Chad's seeds to him when this was over.

But the time crunch meant David needed to accelerate the situation with the CIA, and Charles in particular. Although up until now David had disciplined himself to a wait-and-see attitude, with Chad and Five breathing down his neck as well as Charles, David needed to push Charles to act. These five hours, or however many he'd been stuck inside this room, were long enough.

David swung his feet to the floor, too restless now to lie still. Maybe there'd been a noise in the corridor too, which had sparked the ending of the dream, because now a knock came at the door, and it opened. The knock was politeness only, since David himself had no ability to open the door, but it was yet another step towards civility on the part of Tom Baker, who stood again in the doorway.

"They want you." His expression was very dour.

David didn't say *good*, even though that's what he was thinking. Instead, he made a joke. "Too bad we never had a chance to sing."

Tom took him seriously. "Yes, sir," he said, and then led him back to the conference room where David found Charles standing with his arms folded across his chest, staring out the window at the sunny day. Letitia was the only other person in the room, and she nodded that Tom should leave David alone with them.

Tom obeyed, closing the door behind David, who stood three paces into the room.

After a moment's pause, during which nobody said anything, since both Letitia and David were waiting for Charles to speak, he finally said without turning around, "The only reason you're here is because Letitia insisted."

While these words were the first Charles had spoken to David since yesterday, as before, they were really directed at Letitia, who took them as her cue to continue the thought. "We are concerned about the extent to which you are not cooperating with what we're doing here."

Charles spoke again, still to the window, before David could question the very notion of *cooperating* when he was a prisoner. "If you don't mend your ways, we can make this much more unpleasant than it has been up until now."

This wasn't a conversation so much as an ambush. In other words, nothing new. "I believe you."

Charles swung around. "Is that all you have to say? You stand there, sneering—" He broke off and looked back to the window, his fists clenched at his sides. The sun was bright enough that David couldn't see a reflection in the glass—if that's what it was rather than a computer screen—but from his words, not to mention the set of his shoulders, Charles was furious. It seemed credible to think it was a permanent condition.

David hadn't actually been sneering either, though maybe he should have been, if things were to progress along the lines he'd decided they needed to. Then again, Charles was doing a perfectly adequate job of escalating their relationship all on his own, seeing in David what he wanted to see without any assistance from David himself.

Letitia glanced at Charles and then looked back to David. "So you'll help?"

David spread his hands wide. "I don't even know what that means."

Letitia tsked through her teeth. "What do *you* want?"

At Letitia's question, Charles swung around, implying to David she was going off script.

He hastened to answer before Charles could cut him off. "To go home. And, if I'm honest, to no longer suffer the interference of your organization."

"Suffer?" Charles glared at him. "You little—" His color was high but he managed not to curse at David. "You're lying. You want to go home so *you* can exploit what's there. What gives you the right to decide what goes on in Earth Two more than anyone else?" Charles had adopted the name for the medieval world—Earth Two— Chad had come up with, perhaps a product of George's debrief.

David wet his lips. He could try to defuse Charles's wrath in the hopes it was even possible and Charles was capable of cooperating, but all evidence indicated it wasn't going to work. He was angry and grieving and a long way from ready to negotiate.

So instead, David told the truth because nothing that had happened up until now said that stopping would be of benefit to any of them. "I'm not lying, and I resent your accusation that I am, based on no knowledge of me or my people. I don't think I have to remind you that I am the King of England. The people of England *chose* me as their king. So, yes, I do get to decide what happens there."

If Charles had been angry before, now he was apoplectic. "The *people*." He didn't actually spit on the ground, but came close. "Why *you*?"

This is going well. The mocking thought passed through David's head, but really, it *was* going well. He needed to know what he was dealing with, and Charles needed to say what he was thinking. It wasn't as if David hadn't heard worse many times, most recently a few days ago in Philippe's palace on the Seine. David knew something of grief, after living in Earth Two for as long as he had, even if he hadn't lost a sibling.

So David answered. "I have said before, and I will say to you both, that I don't control the time traveling."

"Then who does?"

The angrier Charles got, the calmer David felt himself becoming—though, from the looks, his calmness was only making Charles more irate. "I do not know."

Charles snorted his skepticism. "You're lying again."

"Charles—" That was Letitia, trying to intervene, to the point of calling Charles by his given name instead of *sir*.

Charles glared at her. "Shut up, Letitia. He has never told us the truth, and you know it."

David had, in fact, done nothing but tell the truth, so he took in a breath and elaborated. He wasn't going to reach Charles, but convincing Letitia might lead to calmer heads later, when David needed them. "The CIA was a participant in the studies we did back when Lady Jane was the head of MI-5. It was your organization that returned to them the information they needed when I arrived here in 2022. You still have all of that, I assume. What does it tell you?"

Charles continued to glare, but Letitia, who was closer to David and whose face was slightly turned away from Charles, looked thoughtful.

David tried again. "Do you think my parents *wanted* to land in that resort's pool near Aberystwyth? Do you think my sister *meant* to trespass inside Westminster Hall and be arrested as a terrorist? Do you think I had anything to do with the way she and I arrived at

Cilmeri and saved my father's life thirteen years ago? I was fourteen years old.

"I'm sorry for your loss, Charles, but whatever it is that makes my family time travel—whatever *this* is—you must accept that I don't control it, and whoever or whatever does control it has a mind of their own. You need to believe me."

"I don't *need* to do anything, particularly what you say."

"He is right, Charles," Letitia said softly, though with only the three of them in the room, nobody else was listening. "He really is telling the truth. He doesn't control it."

"Then *we* will." Charles strode to a box on the table and pressed a button. "He's ready. Take him."

The door behind David burst open, and he swung around a half-second before he was engulfed by four fully kitted out (as Callum would say) military personnel. They weren't larger men than he was, but they were certainly more threatening, given their armor and gear.

"No, Charles! We said—"

But there was no gainsaying Charles, certainly not by Letitia.

The soldiers forced David out of the conference room and into the elevator, held him rigidly while inside, and then frog-marched him towards the cargo plane.

None of the men who'd gone with David the first two times were in sight—nor on the cargo plane when he reached it, which was empty except for the five of them. Instead of going through the cargo hold, they entered this time through a door in the side. He couldn't see or hear the pilots. Maybe they were Ben and Arnaldo or the two pilots from the first failed mission, but he had no way of knowing. David himself would have refused this assignment, and he was thinking, even from his brief acquaintance, that they all would have too.

None of these men talked to him or gave any indication they saw him as anything other than a package to be delivered. Each man wore goggles, and one of them strapped a similar pair around David's head. That was the extent of the interaction. Another soldier buckled David into his seat, and the plane took off.

David tried to speak to the man beside him, as he'd done with Luke that first day, but he stared stonily ahead and didn't respond.

They'd been sitting for hardly five minutes when the leader motioned that everyone was to stand. He got David up too and strapped a harness on him that went around his waist and over his shoulders, to which he attached with a carabiner one end of a very long black rope, with the other end connected to himself. Then he arranged for similar lengths of rope between himself and the other three men, who'd spent that time putting on parachutes and adjusting them so they fit.

David tugged on the rope, the length of which pooled on the floor of the plane between him and the others. "What are we doing?"

Nobody replied. Then the leader slammed his fist into the button that opened the cargo ramp, which began to descend. He walked down it, pulling David along with him, followed by the other men. Then two of them grasped David by the harness and hauled him to the edge of the ramp.

They were going to throw him out of the airplane without a parachute.

"You can't be serious!"

David gaped at the ground. It was full daylight still, and he could clearly see the yellow stubble of the harvested fields two thousand feet below him. He did the calculations in his head: a body falling two thousand feet would reach a velocity of two hundred miles an hour before it hit the ground, provided no other forces were acting on it. There was going to be some wind, but nobody was surviving that fall. David tried to take a step back, shocked at the lengths Charles was going, and yet somehow not surprised either. But the men around him prevented him from backing away from the edge.

Maybe even more amazing was that Charles had found four men to throw him out of the plane and follow after him.

And then, as they set themselves to jump, David realized the significance of the ropes. The one between him and the leader wasn't two thousand feet long, but it was long enough that if David hit the ground and died without time traveling, the four men would have time to pull their chutes and live.

Nice.

The leader made a motion with his arm, indicating it was time to go. He didn't speak, however, not surprising given the noise of the plane with the ramp down. With the goggles, David couldn't see into his eyes. Who he was, and what he thought about what he was doing, was a total mystery. For all intents and purposes, he was soulless, and David was suddenly so angry that for a moment he believed the man really didn't have a soul.

Then the anger was replaced by fear as they threw him out of the plane.

He'd never skydived before. He hadn't even been on a roller coaster since he was thirteen.

Falling out of a plane was like nothing David had ever experienced.

At first he tumbled, and he tried to right himself by spreading his arms and legs to make himself a bigger surface area, like he'd seen on TV. After a few seconds of that, when it became clear he couldn't get it right and with the panic reaching epic proportions, he made himself a pencil instead, arms at his sides and feet together, like he was jumping into a lake and headed for the bottom.

His calculations had also told him that his fall would take all of twenty seconds, and even for someone who'd been time traveling for half his life, it was both the longest and shortest twenty seconds he'd ever experienced. He focused on breathing and not passing out. At first he squeezed his eyes shut, and then, as the last moments of his life blew by him, he opened his eyes in time to see the ground coming up to meet him.

Everything went dark, and it was as if he'd been suspended not only in time but in space. All that momentum was as nothing. Every law of physics, except the one they hadn't discovered which allowed world-shifting, was violated. He might as well not have ever been falling at all. It was a physical impossibility to eliminate all that momentum between one heartbeat and the next, but—

One, two, three ...

25

August 1295

Day Four

Isabelle

Huw took the lead now, having remembered the way through Rouen best of all of them from a map of the city he'd studied back at the Paris Temple. He'd also come up the Seine most recently and seen both commandery and cathedral from the river. On the whole, Isabelle was fortunate to have had her presence accepted by Christopher's friends. It couldn't be easy for them to see Christopher pulling away from them towards her. She hoped, over time, they'd understand that she had no desire to take him away from them and, in fact, hoped for the opposite. Christopher was unlike any man she'd ever met, and she had no desire to change him in any way.

She'd imagined herself in love before, as all girls did at one time or another, fancying themselves swept into the arms of a man of legendary talents, a Lancelot or Galahad from the legends of Arthur. This was different. This felt different.

But what was strange too about it, beyond how her heart raced a bit whenever they were together, was that Christopher genuinely *was* a man out of the Arthurian legends. King David was the return of Arthur. Christopher was the Hero of Westminster. And yet, so human too.

What's more, and even more oddly, he appeared to want to be with *her*.

The very thought made her toss her head. She didn't *want* to feel this way. It made her insides uncomfortable. It would definitely be easier if she didn't care for him. Some of the other girls at the palace would have insisted that she show him nothing but disdain, because that was how a man knew a girl liked him. Isabelle had tried it once, however, and the man in question had never spoken to her again. With that, Isabelle had resolved never to be anything other than herself.

She had been to Rouen on her own journey to Paris many months ago and had some familiarity with the place, as well as the ability to read a map. Although her father hadn't understood girls at all, once he'd been saddled with one, he had insisted she was educated as befitted the daughter of a Templar Master.

Up ahead of them, at the intersection of multiple streets, was a small gathering space in the shape of a triangle, where perhaps a building used to be. It wasn't the speaker's green, located in front of the bridge across the Seine, but it was being used for the same purpose. A man wearing a peasant's cap was standing on an overturned crate, gesticulating above his head and haranguing those listening. His clothing was common, but his argument was not.

"What right does the king or his men have to tell us—" here he pounded his hand to his chest, "—what goes on in our city?" He spoke with an accent not far off from Isabelle's own, when she wasn't putting on a Parisian one. She'd learned French in England, where she'd been born and raised, so it was no surprise she spoke similarly to Christopher and his friends when she wanted to.

One of the townspeople attempted to shout him down. "He's the king!"

"But is he *our* king?" The man roared back. "When has Philippe le Bel ever been *our* king?"

"The Jews—" This came from someone else, but again the man on the crate overrode him.

"Are you that much of a fool, Emile? This isn't about Jews!" He snapped his fingers. "Philippe expels the Jews from Paris, and the archbishop expels them from Rouen, so they can take their wealth, and so we will turn on our neighbors instead of our rulers!"

"What about the English?" Again someone else in the crowd spoke up.

"The English?" The man roared back. "England is our greatest trading partner! English silver flows through our streets! The archbishop wants it flowing through his fingers instead! Philippe and all who aid him are our real foe. You want to cut off trade because Philippe fears a man who loves freedom more than his own crown?

What will Rouen be when two of our greatest sources of wealth—the Jews and the English—are gone?"

Beside Isabelle, Christopher murmured, "I can hear David saying, *I would have preferred he appealed to his audience's humanity, but I suppose I won't argue if he's on our side.*" As he spoke, he even affected David's tone and diction.

Before meeting Christopher, Isabelle had given no thought ever to the fate of Jews in England or France. If she thought about them at all, it was to gawk at their hair and clothing. The yellow badges they were forced to wear made her uncomfortable to see, but she had accepted, as did everyone, the idea that Jews shouldn't be able to move about within society unidentified.

And yet, she hadn't needed much of Bronwen's long lecture on the nature of humanity to embrace the idea of personal freedom and responsibility. She'd already memorized what Bronwen had quoted to her: *We hold these truths to be self-evident, that all men—* and women, Bronwen had amended—*are created equal, that they are endowed by their Creator with certain unalienable rights, that among these are life, liberty and the pursuit of happiness.*

The words were, to take a phrase from William de Bohun, *mind-blowing*. When he'd used the word, he'd made a motion with his hands and a sound with his mouth reminiscent of ... well, she didn't know what. He called it *an explosion*. She'd also had to ask Bronwen why she'd needed to add *women* to the quote, at which point Bronwen had snorted and told her that, even in Avalon, it had taken far too long for men to see women as their equals.

It was oddly comforting, actually, to know that these Avalonians had not arrived in the world fully developed, like Athena from the head of Zeus, but had learned over time. It gave her hope that the people here—men and women—could learn too.

And here in Rouen, she could see the first stirrings of this idea that Bronwen had so boldly stated, in that the speaker's words had resulted in general muttering among his listeners but no outright disagreement.

Then the speaker swung his arm to point towards the castle, which could be seen in the far distance, a moment of afternoon sun glinting off its tallest tower. "This isn't about Jews or English traders! It's about Paris telling Rouen what's best for Normandy!"

"Normandy for Normans!" The call came from somewhere in the back of the crowd where a man had thrown his fist into the air. He repeated the phrase a second time, after which other men around him took up the cry.

The speaker joined in. "Normandy for Normans! Normandy for Normans!"

Then the ally pushed through the crowd and leapt onto the box beside the first speaker, who moved aside to give him room. This second man was tall and thin, with hair so blonde it was white. Above the chanting, he shouted in the same resonant voice as before. "Paris is a hundred miles from here!"

"More like eighty miles to the Louvre, but whatever," William murmured in English. "I'm guessing he's a plant."

A plant? Isabelle didn't have any idea how the newcomer resembled a plant, except maybe a white willow in the winter without its leaves.

"I think so too, but I'm not arguing either if he wants to make our case for us. It's fascinating the way they've pivoted, from the archbishop declaring Jews expelled and English goods forfeit, to defying the king." Then Christopher must have seen her continued quizzical look and guessed correctly what she hadn't understood, because he explained: "*A plant* is someone in the crowd who pretends to be persuaded but was really a friend all along. He's *planted* there in advance."

Her eyes widened as she saw what he meant. These Avalonians were so clever with words. She had never heard anyone use *plant* that way before, but it made perfect sense once she understood.

Christopher's mouth twisted into a rueful smile. "Again, I'm a little concerned about exactly who these people mean by *Normans*, but I suppose our priority needs to be freedom first and worrying about exactly who is free later."

"I want to know when the archbishop decided to expel all Jews from Rouen," Robbie said. "How did Rouen learn of what happened in Paris so soon?"

"A pigeon, clearly," William said. "The question before us now is what else was in that message."

"I'm worried we are in over our heads with this," Christopher said.

As she'd noted from the moment she'd met him, Christopher's ability to admit not only ignorance but uncertainty and fear was astounding. His friends, on the other hand, appeared to think nothing of it, and his comment in no way diminished his standing with them. In fact, it seemed to enhance it, which was something she had mulled over long and hard during the walk from the Paris Temple to the boats, coming to the conclusion that admitting weakness and ignorance when one was uncertain or didn't know something gave more credence to one's words and actions when one did.

The blond man stuck a finger in the air to keep the attention of his audience. "What power should a king with no notion of our people, our history, have over us? Why should he have a say in the course of our country?"

The initial speaker, who may or may not have been his friend, also pointed a finger at the sky. "Aquitaine votes for its own parliament in a fortnight. How is it that we have none? Why are they so privileged?"

"Because David is the Duke of Aquitaine," It was Huw murmuring now, "and he rules there."

Nobody could have heard his words except the few of them, but a woman in the crowd shouted much the same thing anyway: "Because our king is Philippe, not David, who should be our duke too! What right has Philippe to deny we are Norman and say instead that we must be French!" She looked around at the people with her. "We will never be French!"

"You go girl," William said.

It was again a phrase Isabelle had never heard before, but she could see William's pride in Normandy swelling before her eyes. She had been taught that questioning the power of kings was dangerous—but none of the men around her blinked at this foray into treason.

More people in the crowd started shaking their fists at the sky, and there were enough of them now that they'd started to draw the attention of the authorities. Two guards ran past where Isabelle and her companions had stopped, and they were joined by five more soldiers coming from the opposite direction.

William sprang to life. "We need to move before they cut off our way to the cathedral!"

"And we should be on foot!" Christopher dismounted in a fluid motion and reached up to Isabelle to help her off her horse. "It would be better if we don't call more attention to ourselves than we already have."

Isabelle dropped to the ground right in front of an inn whose proprietor had been peering out his gate at the speakers. She put out her hand before he could pull the gate all the way closed. "Wait!"

The innkeeper hesitated, keeping the gate open a crack and peering at her with one blue eye.

She hurriedly continued, "What is happening?"

The man opened the door enough to see her with both eyes. "You heard them! It isn't safe in the street." He didn't offer to admit them. The man's fear was palpable and served to emphasize to Isabelle the danger and urgency of their mission.

Isabelle didn't ask for sanctuary either. Hiding in an inn was not the mission.

"What about the Jews?" William pressed forward. "They are truly banished from Rouen?"

"So says the archbishop! But I think Pierre is right. They are of Normandy too."

Isabelle guessed that Pierre was one of the speakers.

Then the innkeeper's face screwed up as if he was daring them to censure him. "My son learned to figure and do sums from a Jew."

"What of the Templars?" Isabelle asked.

"What of them?" The innkeeper's lip lifted. "They say they cannot take sides, that they are not subject to the laws of the country in which they live, but who evicted the Jews from Paris, I ask? The Templars! They are servants of the king and will be no help to us."

It was a terrific subversion of traditional prejudices, unless you had been counting on the Templars to help you to be surreptitious. Really, as the rabble-rousers in the streets had shown, what the people of Rouen hated most was Paris. The Templars were merely a convenient target—for once more so than Jews.

While she was glad she hadn't identified herself, either to the guards at the gate or to this innkeeper, she still had to fight against her compulsion to set the record straight. David had been adamant that if the Templars in France weren't to be expelled along with the Jews, the French king could not know they had been escorting them out of Paris on David's behalf, not evicting them at the behest of King Philippe.

Then the innkeeper was hailed by someone behind him, an older woman with a large bust, who waved her kerchief at him. With apologies, he shut the gate, and Isabelle heard the bar drop to lock it.

"What do we do now?" She turned to Christopher.

"Nothing has changed. We should go to the cathedral as we originally planned."

By the time they put a row of buildings between themselves and the green, a dozen more soldiers had surrounded the townspeople on it. Then a bell at a nearby church started tolling, and the sound was picked up by others. In short order, the whole city was filled with bells.

The bell in the cathedral directly in front of them was the last to toll, drowning out all others, though maybe that was only because they had finally reached it. As they approached the perimeter, like the proprietor of the inn a moment before, a priest was closing the gate and didn't stop even though he had to have seen them coming.

"Wait!" Christopher said in French. "Please let us in."

This bar also dropped with a thud. "No admittance this late in the day," came the reply, shouted over the thick door that separated them from the cathedral grounds. The wall was higher than Christopher's head, but not by much, and the man's words could clearly be heard over it.

His excuse was also absurd, and everybody knew it.

"Do you know what's happening out here?" Isabelle pressed a hand to the stiff oak door. "Are you truly going to deny safe haven to your own people?"

"The grounds are closed by order of the Archbishop of Rouen." Now a different voice called to them, more confident than the first. Neither man's accent sounded Norman to Isabelle, which might go a long way to explaining the fear and retreat.

"Wait! Please!" Christopher pounded on the door with his fist. "Can you at least let Amaury de Montfort know that he has visitors at the gate? We would speak with him."

"Canon Montfort is not here."

That was momentarily befuddling, and Christopher looked at Isabelle before gathering himself again. "Can you tell us where we might find him?"

"He has estates outside the city. Perhaps you should try there."

The news was disappointing to say the least.

"When did you last see him?" Isabelle asked, putting all the urgency in her heart into the question. They knew, of course, that Amaury wasn't on his estates outside the city, or at least not the ones along the Seine.

But no reply came, and when Isabelle put her ear to the door, she thought she could hear footfalls walking away.

Stepping back, she cast around despairingly at the men in front of her, all of whom were looking as disconcerted as she felt.

"The wall isn't that high," William said. "We could climb it."

"To what end?" Robbie said. "We don't actually want asylum. We want Amaury." The five of them had crowded close, each holding the reins of his or her horse. "Do we believe the gatekeeper that he isn't inside?"

Even William, that hardened Marcher lord, looked affronted. "Why would a priest lie?"

Isabelle was more prosaic. Her eyes had been opened to many things since she'd met Christopher, and a lying priest would be *small potatoes*, as she'd heard William say, compared to the enormity of what she had learned was possible. "He wanted to get rid of us, and that was a good way to do it."

"How far to the Templar commandery from here?" Christopher looked at her.

"It's down a ways." She didn't ask why he was asking. "There are two, one is a smaller outpost on the northern side of the city, but we'd want the main commandery on the Seine." She paused, hesitating.

Being uncertain wasn't much like her, and Christopher knew it. "What is it?"

"My father warned me that Rouen's Templars might not welcome us. The old master died and, last he heard, the brothers were still disputing among themselves for who was best suited to lead them. As I recall, there were several candidates. My father expressed his preference, which, he confessed to me, may have made things worse, since the knights resented his interference." She shrugged.

"Likely they've chosen by now, but I don't know who he is. He may resent my father too, especially if he wasn't my father's choice."

Christopher's face told her he didn't like the sound of that, which was of course why she had been reluctant to speak of it.

"What are you thinking?" William asked Christopher.

"I'm worried that Amaury may have been imprisoned or sidelined in some other way."

Huw grimaced. "I've been worried about that too. He knew we were coming. Why isn't he here?"

"Maybe we need to make what Robbie said at the city gate true. We really do have business with the Templars." Christopher swept his gaze around his friends. "Likely they know only what the archbishop has told them: that the Templars were the ones who did Philippe's bidding in Paris. That's why the innkeeper was so disparaging of them."

Isabelle gave a sharp nod. "Maybe they won't let me in, but I am still my father's daughter, and I agree it would be worse not to try."

"I wish James Stewart were here," Robbie said, all of a sudden. "He would know what to do."

"Unfortunately, he is not here, so it's up to us." Christopher spoke past gritted teeth. "We do know one thing for sure. The Master of the Temple could still be a friend. The Archbishop of Rouen definitely is not."

26

August 2023

Day Four

David

David had decided that he liked the idea of being controlled by the ancient Welsh wizard, Merlin, or Myrddin as he was known in Wales, hiding in a cave in Snowdonia, waiting for the moment he could bring about Welsh independence. By traveling to Earth Two with his sister, David had done exactly that. As a result, David felt like Myrddin owed him one.

The next second, as he came out of the void between worlds, he got the favor he desperately needed, thudding to earth with both feet as if he'd fallen two feet instead of two thousand.

But that was the extent of the favor—maybe. David straightened in time to see a horseman galloping towards him, his sword out and a moment later sweeping down to remove David's head—

One, two, three ...

27

August 1295

Day Four

Christopher

That the Archbishop of Rouen would close the gates of his cathedral to his own parishioners wasn't as much of a surprise to Christopher as to his friends. They'd been raised not to question the precepts of the Church, where, in Christopher's time, most of his friends had never darkened the door of one. But Christopher had been in the room when his Aunt Meg had given David an earful about Archbishop Guillaume and the little she thought of his stewardship.

But even if his friends had not expected what had happened, they all had known that Amaury's outlook was not to be taken as the general attitude of the church in Rouen towards David, Jews, or the idea of Normandy's independence.

They could see the castle from the cathedral, and even from this distance it was impossible to miss the men running back and forth on the battlement. While they'd been talking to the cathedral's gatekeeper, the cathedral bell had stopped tolling. Now, the castle bell rang across the whole city with a deep *bong, bong, bong*. Leading their horses and having traveled another hundred feet, they reached a broad avenue they couldn't avoid crossing, though to do so would expose them to the contingent of soldiers that even now were marching down it towards the river. The king's faction might not have many men, but whoever was in charge was making the most of those he did have.

"What are you waiting for?" said Huw. "If we are to reach the commandery, we have to cross the street now!"

"We do," Christopher gave a quick shake of his head, "but not all of us can go. You and Robbie need to get back to the boats. If some of us don't leave now, none of us may be leaving at all."

"What are you going to do?" Robbie said, thankfully not arguing with what he also had to realize was the only proper course. "What if the Templars won't admit you any more than the archbishop would?"

"We have to try," Christopher said.

"The Templars need to know what really happened in Paris. We need to give them a chance to decide which side they're on." Isabelle's jaw was set and her expression grim. "They'll let us in."

Christopher wasn't so sure, but he didn't say so because his friends didn't need to know he had a secret weapon: the password into the commandery, one of the deepest, darkest secrets of the Templar world. Years ago, David had been told the phrase *et mortuus est in Golgotha* by Nicholas de Carew, who happened to be the brother of the master of the London Temple. Knowing the password had saved David's life and the life of King Philippe. It was intended for use as a last resort, and only by Templars, which David was not. Nor was Christopher. David had nonetheless whispered the words to him before Christopher had gone to the palace to speak to Philippe and David had left for Vincennes.

But then later, in the few moments Christopher was at the Paris Temple, between when he returned from the palace and when he set off to meet the boats at Poissy, Matthew Norris had pulled him aside. Being an astute father and observer of men, he'd seen what was happening between Christopher and Isabelle. It wasn't as if either of them had tried to hide the fact that they liked each other.

But this was the Middle Ages, and Isabelle's father was letting his daughter out of his sight under great duress.

"You will take care of her."

It hadn't been a question. He was handing his daughter off to Christopher, one man to another.

"Yes."

And then Master Norris had given Christopher the password and made him swear on his soul that he would use it to protect Isabelle.

Because of that trust, Christopher wasn't going to repeat the password out loud to his three friends and merely said to Robbie, "You may have the more dangerous road in the end."

"Damn you, Christopher, for making sense." In a moment, both Robbie and Huw were mounted and off at a gallop, heedless of the people in the streets, some of whom had to throw themselves out of the way to avoid the horses' hooves.

"They will be fine," William said, as they watched their friends go. "They will fulfill the mission."

"Meanwhile, our mission has changed." Christopher turned to his two remaining friends. "Those boats are coming, hell and high water notwithstanding. It's up to us to make sure they get through that portcullis in one piece."

28

August 2023

Day Four

David

He'd had enough time before the blade sliced off his head to shift his weight. Thus, he'd been falling backwards in advance of the sword, which meant when he arrived back in Avalon, he was lying flat on his back in the stubble of a harvested wheat field, staring up at a glorious blue sky. A few contrails headed northwest, indicating a plane had flown towards Seattle and its international airport. Portland had a large airport too, but this contrail didn't go that way.

    Above him also were the four men who'd flown with him to Earth Two and back, coming down hard since they'd pulled their parachutes relatively close to the ground. If they'd really wanted to do damage in Earth Two without David's moderating influence, the leader should have cut the rope that connected him to David while they were in Earth Two, and all four would have stayed. Admittedly, their sojourn in Earth Two had been a matter of five seconds at most, and since David had instantly been killed (or almost killed), they'd had minimal time to react.

David decided this particular observation would remain his secret, in case Charles had the idea to try this little stunt again. He shuddered to think what would have happened if the sword heading towards his head had cut through the rope that bound the men to him.

Letting these men loose in his world was a nightmare of epic proportions. They were only four men, but he was fully cognizant of what a few people had accomplished in Earth Two in thirteen years. Obviously, many more people than just his mother, sister, and David himself had come to Avalon in that time, but everyone's intentions had been honorable, with the exception of a mere handful. And yet, that handful had caused an outsized amount of damage and was half the reason he was enduring all of this in the first place.

The soldiers each touched down, staggering in turn by the force of the landing. One man rolled in a manner David had been taught in karate. Another kept his feet but then vomited into the stubble.

Neither of these was the leader, whose name David still didn't know, and who paused a moment to collect himself.

Then he marched over to David. "Get up!"

David let out a laughing breath, because, at this point, *what else was there to do*? Did the man think David was going to lie in the field forever? Maybe he should have. But he didn't.

Instead, he pushed himself to a sitting position before accepting the man's hand and allowing himself to be hauled to his feet. As soon as David was upright, the leader started walking him in the direction of the airport a quarter of a mile away. By the time they'd gone two hundred yards, upwards of fourteen military trucks were converging on them, following the dirt road from the airport. The five men reached the edge of the field at nearly the same moment the first truck did. It had large enough tires that the driver could have crossed the field to reach them if he'd needed to.

The driver turned out to be Luke, and he didn't stir from his position in the driver's seat as David approached, keeping both hands gripped around the wheel and his eyes straight ahead. Once the group leader sat David in one of the rear seats, the rest of the soldiers dispersed to several other trucks, and they moved off as one, back to the airport.

Luke pulled the truck into the hangar and parked near where the cargo plane was just taxiing to a stop. As David got out—or rather, was hauled out by the group leader—Charles was standing in the middle of the concrete floor, halfway between the truck and the office building. Letitia was just coming out the door, though she was stopped by a soldier with a clipboard, who had been hurrying to catch up to her. The group leader marched up to Charles and, in a fairly loud voice, told him what had happened.

The rest of the men had arrived by now too, and they clustered around David, making him feel less like a prisoner and more like one of them. By accident or design, Luke ended up on one side of

David, along with several other men from the trip to Belize, who'd either been driving the trucks or milling about the hangar. It wasn't the first time it occurred to him that he'd seen a fraction of the spaces within the office building, and that it also had to contain barracks, a mess hall, and other facilities for these men when they weren't on duty.

The leader's tone was matter-of-fact. "The horseman swung his sword to decapitate the subject, but as promised, he didn't die. Instead of dying, we returned here. Sir." He straightened to attention.

Luke cursed fluently under his breath, ending with, "Sorry, man."

"Yeah, me too."

The soldier's description of David's near-death experiences—both being thrown out of the plane and the barely averted decapitation—had been disturbingly clinical. David didn't think he was ever going to stop seeing the sword swinging towards his head.

Charles grunted, disappointed, but there was no surprise in him to see them back so quickly. By this point, failure was becoming a habit. Or, at least, David hoped it was. "Where were you?"

"No idea, sir. I didn't recognize the terrain."

"Woods? Desert?"

"Woods."

Charles pointed at the man to David's left, not Luke. "Hold him still."

The soldier moved instantly to obey, though Luke said, "Hey!"

"Get away from him, O'Malley!" The commander ordered.

"It's okay, Luke," David said, in an undertone. "Do as they say. This isn't worth losing your job or rank over."

"Isn't it?"

But then Frank was there too, and a look passed between the two of them that prompted Luke to step several paces away.

Charles held out his hand to one of the soldiers who'd gone with David most recently. "Give me your side arm."

The soldier hesitated.

"Now, soldier!"

The soldier obeyed his command, surrendering his pistol.

Letitia had finished with the documents she'd been waylaid to sign and now approached close enough to ask, "What are you doing, Charles?"

Rather than answer, Charles pointed the gun directly at David's chest. And fired.

29

August 1295

Day Four

Lili

"I apologize, my lady, for not speaking to you sooner, but there's more you should know. About Rouen, I mean." The captain stood in front of Lili, working his hands nervously on the brim of his hat.

The boats were back underway, heading down the Seine. They'd taken their time at Amaury's dock, refilling their water and replenishing their food stocks. Amaury's steward had been nothing but helpful throughout. They could have stayed longer, even overnight, but they were torn between fear of what lay ahead and that which they knew lay behind.

"What is it, Renauld?"

The captain's mouth worked, and at first no sound came out. It was as if he didn't know how to say what he had come to her to say, or perhaps didn't know if he should.

"Just tell us, man," Ieuan said. "Can it be worse than what we fear?"

"Not worse." The captain took in a breath. "This is Normandy. We crossed the border some time back."

"We do know that," Lili said, keeping her tone even. "Go on."

The captain seemed to finally realize he was destroying his hat and fitted it back on his head. "If the people here—in Elbeuf or Rouen—really know about the attack on Aquitaine, and even more if they heard of the defeat of the French forces there, they might not ... mind."

It took a moment for Lili to understand what the captain was telling them, and since the captain had reverted again to stutters and hums, she suggested, "The people of Normandy might support my husband against the French crown?"

The captain's expression turned to one of relief. "Yes, madam."

"To the point of disobeying the edicts of the archbishop?" Ieuan asked. "To the point of challenging soldiers from the castle and those who rule over them?"

"Maybe." The captain was back to being reluctant, but she could tell that the real answer could be *yes*.

Lili suppressed her impulse to laugh—not at the man's sincerity, but in surprise. Over the years as Queen of England she had learned to control that instinctive response. And while she had been genuinely surprised, she didn't want the captain to think she was mocking him or questioning what he'd told them.

"This would be because of my husband's example? His leadership?"

"Yes, madam. They aren't doing it *for* him, you understand? It would be for themselves."

"What do they even know of England?" Lili said. "There's no one alive today who hasn't lived the entirety of his life as part of France."

"Aquitaine votes on its own Parliament in a fortnight. The people here are asking themselves why Aquitaine and not Normandy? Why can't they have a Parliament too? Where is their self-rule?"

"That will never happen under Philippe of France," Ieuan said. "It is because the French crown invaded Normandy a century ago and wrested it from English rule that they are in this predicament in the first place."

"They know." The captain had finally found his courage, and spoke flatly, his words an assertion of fact that could not be contested. "Some do blame you for not defending them."

"Why would you be reluctant to tell us about this?" Ieuan asked.

The man blinked. "Because to speak of rebellion against the crown is treason!"

Unlike virtually everyone else in their armada, their boat's captain was a native of Normandy, hired because he knew the Seine like the back of his hand (or so he said). None wanted to risk sailing in unknown waters, even on a river, without a guide. From the evidence so far, he had been speaking the truth and had guided them down the Seine as he'd promised, under adverse conditions, to say the least. The rest of their boats, whose captains were native to England, though many had traversed the Seine in the past, had followed safely in his wake.

So she simply bent her head in acknowledgement of the effort he'd made to enlighten them. "Thank you."

Ieuan dismissed him and then turned to her, a light in his eyes that hadn't been there before. "They know. He said *they know*."

Lili kept a tight grip on her rising excitement. "Talking about treason is a long way from actually committing it."

Ieuan dimmed a little. "And it's a significant leap to go from resenting Philippe's rule to seeing a better future with Dafydd as king—or maybe with no king at all."

"Dafydd would be fine with that too," Lili said, "except Normandy would be well advised to join the CSB for protection, alliance, and as a defense against Philippe."

"Dafydd will not start a war, even for Normandy." Ieuan was thinking hard. "He might join one already started, however."

"The French crown was desperate to annex Normandy a hundred years ago because of its long coastline and many ports on the English Channel and the Atlantic Ocean. They acquired Aigues-Mortes on the Mediterranean for the same reason." Lili looked towards where she knew Rouen lay, though she couldn't see it from here. "Philippe won't be giving up a single yard of Normandy without a fight."

30

August 1295

Day Four

David

This time, the void was replaced by high seas. David and the man who'd been holding him dropped from three feet above the surface, as if falling from a boat, even though there was no boat, and they hadn't been falling. David came up sputtering, having inadvertently swallowed a disgustingly large gulp.

Judging from the salt in the water, he was in the middle of an ocean. In his surprise to find himself wet, David's companion had at first tightened his grip on David's harness, which was still around his body, but a second later was forced to let go as they were overcome by a massive wave neither of them had seen coming before it hit them.

It still seemed to be daytime, but dark clouds covered the sky from horizon to horizon, and he couldn't tell where the sun was. Lightning flashed, illuminating the water as David bobbed up for a second time. Already, his arms and legs felt stiff and heavy, weighed down by his boots, which he couldn't get off by himself, not while trying to stay afloat. The water wasn't freezing, so he wouldn't immediately die of hypothermia, but he wasn't exactly swimming in bathwater either. From the temperature, he doubted he was anywhere close to Britain. More likely, he was in the Gulf of Mexico again or the Aegean Sea near Greece.

While he'd felt anger and then panic when he'd been thrown out of the plane, the fear now was different. He'd never drowned before. He really didn't want to drown this time.

David knew he should be taking easy breaths, maybe floating on his back, but the amount of clothing and gear he wore made it difficult to move his arms, and he felt more weighted down with every heartbeat. Another huge wave swamped him, and he went under for the third time in the twenty-three seconds he'd been here.

With his head above the surface again, he treaded water the best he could while turning in place, looking for the man who'd come with him. In his heart, David knew he was gone, drowned in less than a minute, which before right this moment David wouldn't have thought possible. Panic used up all the oxygen in the body incredibly quickly, as David's own body testified. Panic and fear were so thick in his own mouth he could taste them. He didn't want to drown. He didn't want to die again. He didn't want any of this—

Why me? Oh God, why me?

As the thought rose screaming to the forefront of David's mind, the prow of a sailing vessel, one not unlike those made in his own shipyards on the Thames, crested the next wave that was rolling above him and came down the other side, straight at his head—

31

August 1295

Day Four

Christopher

They made it across the street without being stopped, leading the horses because to be seen riding them would make them a target. It made Robbie and Huw a target too, but they were trying to be recognized as noblemen, in hopes it would get them out of the city as quickly as possible. What still wasn't clear to Christopher was *how* his friends were supposed to get the information they'd learned to those on the boat. He supposed, as had happened every time they'd been confronted with a puzzle, Huw and Robbie were smart enough that they would figure it out when they got there.

People continued to pour out of their houses and fill the streets, maybe still in response to the bells from the churches, as well as the heavy bonging from the castle. If Christopher had been inside a house, he would have wanted to know what was going on in the city too.

But it made it harder to get where they wanted to go. He put out a hand in front of him to help weave his way through the people. Most were heading in the opposite direction, towards the cathedral, so Christopher and his friends were sailing against this particular current. Good luck getting inside the cathedral walls when they got there.

David had spoken of his not-so-secret hope that one day the former Norman duchies of Brittany and Normandy could be reunited with England—or rather, united with the CSB—just like Aquitaine had been. Among David's advisers, there'd been a bit of debate as to whether David should bring Aquitaine into the CSB on his own as duke, or if, once elected, Aquitaine's parliament should vote if they wanted to join the CSB in the first place. On the one hand, if democracy was really in the offing, they needed to be able to make real decisions that affected their future. Bronwen had argued that if David was going to give up power in Aquitaine, he had to really do it—and that meant not making such a momentous decision for the people. On the other hand, Aunt Meg's point, which had carried the day, had been that people needed to learn to walk before they could run, and Aquitaine's ability to even have a parliament was conditional on being part of the CSB. Without its protection, Aquitaine would be swallowed up by France.

In the end, Aquitaine had joined the CSB with David as its duke, a position he would retain for now, even after a prime minister was elected, and it was under that structure they were voting for a parliament. Establishing a new government, to no one's surprise, was complicated.

"Left, Christopher," Isabelle said from behind him.

Equality of men and women aside, Christopher and William (without having to discuss it) were keeping her positioned between them. If she were in the rear, it would be too easy for her to become separated from them in the middle of what could very well turn into a riot. But it was because size had no relationship to intelligence, and because he trusted her, that Christopher obeyed her command, which was really a suggestion, since that's the way it already was between them. This particular alley seemed cleaner, wider, and held fewer people than some of the others they'd passed. For a brief stint, they were able to lope along beside their horses.

But when they came out the other side, they were surrounded by more people than ever. Masses of them were gathering on a nearby green in front of the bridge that crossed the Seine, and, within the space of a few seconds, Christopher and his friends found themselves surrounded by irate citizens. Many had their fists in the air and were shouting at soldiers who were trying to control them, but who suddenly seemed to realize they were badly outnumbered and were backing into a more defensive position in front of the bridge's two towers. As the crowd pressed close, a finely dressed man in a deep blue robe and wearing a large hat was being guarded by three soldiers. It looked to Christopher as if he might have just finished speaking, and it was his words that had incited the crowd.

With one hand, Christopher kept a tight grip on the reins of his horse and held Isabelle's hand in the other, glad she gave no sign of wanting to let go. The crowd was seething more and more every second. Like Christopher and his friends, some people were trying to escape the crowd, while many more citizens continued to pour into the space before the gate. The chanting, *Normandy for Normans! Normandy for Normans!* was so loud that Christopher could barely hear himself think.

The three of them finally extricated themselves from the western edge of the crowd, at which point Christopher boosted Isabelle onto the back of her horse, as he should have done ten minutes earlier, to protect her from the onslaught.

Meanwhile, the troops Christopher had seen leaving the castle gate earlier had arrived at the green to enforce order. Pikes in hand, they blocked the street that led back into the city. The only free path was the way they wanted to go anyway, down the street that ran along the river towards the commandery, which was recognizable from far away by its banners showing a red cross on a white background.

Above Christopher, from her perch on the horse, Isabelle gave a moan of relief. If nothing else, the commandery's towers would give them a vantage point by which to overlook the river, so they could see the boats coming down it when they came. Even if that didn't happen until dark, Christopher's binoculars, which he carried in his pack, had night vision capabilities.

They hurried up to the commandery's wicket gate and pounded on the door. After a somewhat tense pause, a six-inch square window opened at chin height, forcing Christopher to scrunch down a bit to see through it, and a man poked out his nose at them. "Who goes there?"

Christopher was never going to get over being pleased to hear that phrase.

Before he could answer with either the truth or the Golgotha phrase, Isabelle, who'd dismounted, stepped closer. "Isabelle Norris, daughter of Matthew Norris, the Master of the Paris Temple."

The Templar stared at her, eyes narrowed. "You have no business here. Brother Norris is not our master." Just calling him *brother* instead of *master* showed his disrespect.

He was in the act of closing the little window, when a voice came from behind him, farther within the commandery. "Let them in, Raymond. We do not turn away Templars, nor daughters of Templars."

"She is a woman!"

"As Master Norris's daughter, she would be." The other Templar's tone remained dry. "Let them in. As you well know, Grand Master Molay has temporarily relaxed the prohibition against women in a commandery."

Obviously irked, the Templar slammed the window shut, and there was a moment's pause when they didn't know which one of the two Templars had won the argument. But then the bar was pulled back and the entire gate before them opened, necessary to admit their horses as well as the three of them. Christopher breathed a sigh of relief as they found themselves in a courtyard paved in white stones, with darker, reddish stones forming a massive cross in the center. He'd spent much of the last three months in the vicinity of the Paris Temple, and he was pretty sure he was falling in love with the daughter of a Templar master. He was never going to look upon that red cross with anything but positive feelings.

The Templar knight who faced them was one of the more intimidating Christopher had encountered—and that included Isabelle's father. He was fifty if he was a day, but had a full head of dark brown hair shot through with gray. Christopher had spent three years in Earth Two, so he thought he was used to feeling out of place. And yet, he had never felt more like a foreigner than in this moment, facing a knight with a presence that could not be denied. The Templar looked as if he was ready to take on the crowd outside, the commander at the castle, the archbishop, and King Philippe all at the same time.

"How could you allow Master Norris's daughter to roam the streets of Rouen at this hour?" the knight said to him as his opening salvo, the dry tone forgotten.

It wasn't really a question either. It also wasn't a particularly late hour. And while there were a great many possible answers, Christopher gave the only one that, after some consideration, he could: "Isabelle is her own woman, and she is here for the same reason William and I are." He squared his shoulders. "We are King David's men." He didn't bother to add, *of England* to David's title. By now, all of Europe knew there was only one *David*.

William added, "We heard there was unrest in Rouen, and we came here to discover if the rumor was true. Even now twenty boats of Jewish refugees are floating down the Seine. They should be here in a few hours."

The knight did not give way, though he didn't look quite as angry as before either. "But Master Norris's daughter—"

"I am more than his daughter." In interrupting the Templar, Isabelle had more guts than Christopher, but her color was high, and there was no stopping her. "I am here because there was a chance I could be needed. You let us in because of who I am, didn't you?"

The Templar still hadn't moved any part of his body, not even to shake his head at her impertinence. "The word in the streets to which my brother here was reacting is that the Templars did the king's bidding last night."

"My father did nothing wrong!" Shy and retiring, Isabelle wasn't, and the pride in her voice was unmistakable. "If Jews were to be evicted, better it was done by the Templars than King Philippe's men!"

"It is not for a Templar Master to put the orders of the king before that of God." The gatekeeper's sour look remained fixed to his face as he crossed himself at the mention of God.

"Philippe does not control my father." Isabelle enunciated each word and wasn't giving a single inch.

"That's not—" This was from the gatekeeper again.

"That's enough, Raymond." The knight cut him off and finally did move, making a gesture in the gatekeeper's direction. "Return to your station. I will handle this."

The gatekeeper obeyed, though not without a last, searing look at the three of them.

Something was going on here, undercurrents Christopher wasn't able to read. He had grown used to the deference directed his way by virtue of being the king's cousin. The Templar had to have heard the Norman French in William's voice, as well as noted the quality of their clothing. That they had horses at all should have told him they were noblemen, but the mention of Master Norris had put everything else aside.

Unless they'd guessed wrong.

By this point, Christopher thought it was just as well they hadn't had to use the secret password. It was, as Denethor had said in the *Return of the King,* for *the uttermost end of need.*

Even as Christopher was still trying to figure out what was happening here, William took it upon himself to stride right up to the knight, who was now alone in the courtyard but for them. "We have come from Master Norris, and we can answer any accusations directed his way. He is an honorable man."

"I am not arguing with you," the Templar said, back to the same mild tone he'd used earlier. "You'll have to forgive Raymond his prejudices. He is partisan, though not in the way you think." For a moment, the Templar's eyes actually appeared to twinkle. "I hear Normandy in your voice, my lord. Who might you be?"

William's head was up, defiant. "William de Bohun, heir to the Earldom of Hereford. My father is Constable of England."

"And you?" He fixed Christopher with what he could only think of as a beady eye.

The man was a knight in the Templar order. He already knew Isabelle's and William's identities. Christopher couldn't see lying to him about his own, not if he wanted his help, which he did. "I am Christopher, cousin to King David."

"The Hero of Westminster."

"Yes, sir."

The Templar's only reply to that was another quick scan of their faces.

"We passed through half the city to get here," Christopher said, thinking that the man hadn't believed him. "The unrest is spreading. We need to speak to the master of this commandery. Our mission is urgent."

"Of that I have no doubt. You mistake my questions." As the Templar spoke, he snapped his fingers once. Christopher hadn't noticed anyone watching, but at the Templar's summons, two young men dashed from the stables. They were dressed in brown robes, indicating they weren't knights or sergeants, but servants. He had seen men and boys dressed just like them in Paris. It was convenient to outsiders that the Templars were color-coded.

"So—" Isabelle was as confused as Christopher.

The Templar surveyed them, and the twinkle in his eye was back. "I merely needed to be sure of your identities."

William's expression was as intent as Christopher had ever seen it. "We aren't here because we are taking sides in any fight. We are doing what is right, and we are hoping the Templars in Rouen will too."

The Templar knight put up a hand to quell William's fervor, at the same time settling back on his heels with an air of satisfaction that tempered some of the steel in his spine. "I am not interested in battle, my young friends. I had hope when Isabelle called out her name that you were truly allies, but the risk of being wrong, of allowing a snake into our midst in this moment, was too high not to ask questions and evaluate answers."

Again, his searching eyes went to each of their faces, one at a time. It was as if he was waiting for a sign that he wasn't being deceived.

Christopher saw that the time had come. "*Et mortuus—*"

The Templar's eyes snapped back to Christopher's face with a suddenness that cut off the rest of the password. While Isabelle and William looked on, bewildered, he bent his head in a slight bow in Christopher's direction. "You must understand that it is my responsibility to be sure of whomever I have allowed entry into this commandery, especially when we are pressed on all sides to step outside our usual realm of action. I am well aware that you would not expect to find me here in this hour. But you have, and I must give thanks to God that He, as always, has arranged things as they should be. Even in, and perhaps especially in, the darkest hours, He has purpose, and

I am grateful that I could be given even a slight glimpse into His mysteries."

He put a hand to his chest and finally introduced himself. "I am Amaury de Montfort, master of the Rouen Commandery. We will help in any way we can."

32

Date: Unknown

Place: Unknown

David

Being suspended in the void was like nothing David had ever experienced anywhere on any earth. He was surrounded by ... nothing.

Nothing to see. Nothing to smell. Nothing to hear.

The void was always more suffocating when he traveled without a vehicle, outside and alone. In those few seconds, he understood completely how sensory deprivation could drive a man mad. The darkness pressed on him from every side, filling his being and convincing him he was never going to escape. But as always, it was only a few seconds before—

33

August 1295

Day Four

Michael

"Where are we exactly?" Rhys dismounted with a certain amount of stiffness Michael himself was feeling.

"The Templar Commandery at Pont-de-l'Arche," Michael said, though its claim to fame, a good bridge across the Seine, appeared to be no longer.

Hundreds of brooks, streams, and rivers emptied into the Seine before it reached the English Channel. Up until now, Michael's plan had been to cross here rather than travel any farther on this side of the river on the way to Rouen. Now they had no choice but to continue as they'd been and hope that Rouen's bridge was still intact. Or rather, he would hope for it unless its destruction would ensure their boats made it past the city without being stopped.

Years ago, when Gilbert de Clare had tried to take the throne, David had ridden across France in record time. He'd been able to do it because he'd called upon the Templars for help. In fact, that journey marked the beginning of his close relationship with the Templars, which had paid off all these years later in Paris.

When he'd been in danger, disguised as a Templar, David had used the Templar system of commanderies and outposts to ride more than three hundred miles in two days. Michael just wanted to change horses one time. They had ridden all the way here on the horses they'd started with at Vincennes. By this point, a full day and a half later, they were lucky that any of the horses were able to put one hoof in front of the other.

Again, when David had traveled across France, he'd done it with a document of safe passage given to him by the master of the La Rochelle commandery. Master Villiers had also given him Henri, one of his Templar knights, who'd become a friend. Michael and his companions didn't have either paper or friends, not even a message of safe passage from Matthew Norris at the Paris Temple. Michael knew there was a secret password that would ensure safe entry into any commandery, since David had been freer with the knowledge of it than the Templars would probably have liked, but Michael hadn't been so blessed with what it actually was.

The Templars would also be able to tell them if the boats had already passed by their position. To get to Rouen, they would have had to. Or they were still coming. Either way, Michael would have more information after talking to these Templars than he had right now.

Cador looked up at the battlement above the gatehouse. "It's less inviting than some."

"If they have horses, it doesn't matter what the place looks like." Venny dismounted and began to lead his horse towards the main gate.

In the medieval world, when approaching an unfamiliar stronghold and one at which one's company was not expected, especially when that company served the English king and this was France, dismounting was a good idea.

To tell the truth, Michael's horse was doing better than he was. A healthy horse could travel ten miles in an hour with little trouble, as long as it didn't need to maintain that pace longer than an hour. It could walk for days, and they'd been managing something in between a walk and a canter to cover the seventy miles by road it had taken to get to this point. But a man like Michael, who hadn't ever sat on a horse before coming to Earth Two, couldn't maintain his seat for hour after hour without eventually being unable to sit anymore. It had become very clear to him very quickly during this ride that his months in Paris had made him soft—at least for riding long distances.

Venny lifted his chin to call up to the battlement, "We would speak to your master!"

Up until now, they'd eschewed contact with anyone. Castles dotted the countryside, as did villages and towns, but Michael had avoided all of them out of fear they'd be stopped if someone learned who they were. Admittedly, they'd spent these last weeks in Paris pretending to be other than they were, and none of the French had ever learned otherwise. But they'd gone about in twos and threes. The eight of them together made a company and a different matter entirely.

The Templar guarding the gate peered down at them in response to Venny's hail and then disappeared from sight.

They waited, but nothing happened.

Matha frowned. "Are they going to let us in?"

The wait was long enough that Michael was preparing to turn away—or try again with a password he made up on the spot—when the great gate creaked open, revealing a courtyard already full of men and horses in full Templar regalia. At the head was a man as much the vision of a medieval knight as Michael had ever thought to see, and he'd been living with Templars since June. Michael couldn't see anything of his face because it was blocked by a bucket metal helmet with the characteristic red cross on the side and, in his case, a red plume.

At the sight of the eight of them standing in the road before the gate, the knight rode forward a few yards. Then he took off his helmet.

Michael laughed to see who he was, and the Templar laughed with him.

He wasn't David, which would have been a fantastic result. But the sight of Henri, the selfsame Templar about whom Michael had just been thinking, was enough to cause him to cheer out loud. Four other Templars from the Paris commandery rode with him, including Gerard, whom Michael had found so competent during the course of their mission in Paris.

Henri leaned forward to rest his forearms on the pommel of his saddle. "While the sight of you is an unforeseen pleasure, my friend, I am somewhat dismayed by the fewness of your number and the speed at which you must have traveled to reach this point at this hour. You were at the monastery near Vincennes two nights ago with King David, were you not?"

"We were." Michael looked past him to Gerard, who'd moved closer too. "You are wondering about our speed, but how is it that you are here as well? You had just as far to ride as we did in what I would have thought was less time!"

"Ah, we had more time, in fact, since we started earlier."

"How—"

Henri grinned. "It was a very busy night, I admit! But as you may recall, I was not among those who drank the tainted wine at Vincennes, and I left shortly after you did in order to be among those who shadowed the refugees on their journey down the Seine. Others, Gerard among them, of course, had already kept an eye on them until they reached the boats, to ensure they came to no harm."

Michael found himself gaping at Henri, who was looking very pleased with himself.

"Since then, many of us have carried on through day and night, following their progress from the bank."

Venny had been listening intently to their conversation and seemed much less surprised than Michael at what he was hearing. "So they've passed this point already?"

"According to the master here, they passed by earlier today, heading for Rouen. This commandery had orders to give them refuge if they were able to stop, but with the destruction of our dock as well as the bridge, it was impossible."

Henri paused and lowered his voice. "The king is not with you?"

"He is not." Michael bent his head. "King David has returned to Avalon." He barely breathed the words.

Henri's laughter of earlier gave way to lines of worry.

"Was he ... forced?" Gerard asked the question as if it was eating him up inside. And then at Michael's surprised look, he added, "You forget that young Christopher came to the Temple when he learned of George's plan for Prince Arthur and told everyone assembled. It wasn't a secret to be kept, and my brothers didn't. George took King David in Arthur's stead?"

"Or David went in Arthur's stead."

"Which is a different matter entirely." Henri straightened in the saddle, comprehension in his face.

But Gerard blinked his surprise. "Why would he do that?"

"To save Arthur. And, I suspect, to save all of us." Henri gave a knowing nod.

Michael nodded back, sure of that, if nothing else. At a minimum, it made David's silence easier to forgive. "With this knowledge, you will understand that we ride in haste and with some desperation."

Henri looked Michael up and down and then at his companions. "You came here looking not for me but for food and fresh horses?"

"Yes, my friend." And because Henri was a high ranking knight, Michael thought to observe a little formality. "It is an imposition I hope can be forgiven. I am not King David, but our need is just as great."

"I would be disappointed if you hadn't come." Henri waved a hand at the men behind him. Several scrambled to do his bidding, and an older sergeant, not dressed for battle, ran to take the horse Michael had been riding. "As it is, we feel ourselves woefully behind. From the Paris Temple, we followed the north bank of the Seine, thinking to reach this commandery simply by crossing here at Pont-de-l'Arche. Instead, we arrived to find the bridge washed away, forcing us to double back many miles to find another bridge."

Gerard anticipated Michael's next question, which would have been *why did you leave the boats unattended?* "If we are to help the people on the Seine, we need more men. Others went on to Rouen without us."

"Did King David know Master Norris intended to send you to follow the boats?" Michael almost held his breath as he asked this question.

"Of course, though the king tried to talk him out of it. He had worked so hard to keep his alliance with the Templars hidden, and he didn't want anything to jeopardize the standing of the Paris Temple with the king. But Master Norris couldn't abide the thought of so many vulnerable women and children, not to mention his own daughter, sailing down the Seine with no defense. He sent the men he could spare, and more he couldn't, as escort."

Michael tried not to feel a little put out at how much David hadn't told him. He understood why he hadn't, and understood even more how careful David had felt he had to be. But it hurt a little.

Then again, Michael was pretty sure David hadn't told Lili what he was planning either. As king, it was his prerogative, but he hoped Lili gave him an earful about it when he returned.

If he returned.

Michael ruthlessly suppressed the thought. They were all here, doing what needed to be done, because of David. Michael, like all his friends from Avalon, had come to care very deeply about the fate of this world. It had become *his* world now. And for that reason, he couldn't be sorry Master Norris had done an end run around David. Michael's wife was sailing down the Seine too.

They all had new horses by now, and the rest of the companions had mounted. Mathew was munching on a bun, and he wasn't the only one who was feeling better about this mission than they had at any time since they'd left Vincennes.

Henri had a final word: "You should know before going on that there is trouble in Rouen."

The tension in Michael's neck and shoulders returned in full. "What kind of trouble?"

"We heard that the people of Normandy are rising. *Normandy for Normans*, one traveler told us. Another, a merchant, said the archbishop sought to have Jews evicted from Rouen as they had been from Paris."

"English traders too," Gerard said heavily.

Michael stared at his friends, horrified. "But that means—"

"Yes," Henri said.

Michael moved his gaze to the other Templar knights and sergeants behind them. "What do they think about all this?"

Henri tossed his head in a manner Michael thought of as very French. "They know what went on in Paris. They know Master Norris serves Grand Master Molay and God alone. The Templar Order will not be a party to injustice nor stand by as it is perpetrated on others."

Michael put his hand on the neck of Henri's horse. "King David would not want you to risk the Order."

"But he is not here, is he?" Henri's face suddenly blossomed into a smile. "Leave Templar business to Templars, my friend. We owe allegiance to no king, and we will make our own decisions about what is right."

Michael gave way. "Thank you, Henri. If he were here, David would thank you for all you've done."

"I do not need thanks, nor does Master Norris. Now, are you ready to join me and my brothers?" Then Henri hesitated, before adding with a laugh, "Or maybe, it is we who are again joining you!"

34

August 2023
Day Four
David

David appeared in the airplane hangar in much the same position as when he'd left Earth Two. He'd been treading water, which meant he ended up on one knee on the concrete, with a hand to the ground, soaking wet and alone.

Myrddin had dropped him twenty-five feet from where he'd left, so he was outside the circle of men, off to one side and able to take in the scene with a single glance.

Charles was still standing where David had last seen him, and the gun was still out. Now, however it was pointed at Frank, who stood a few feet in front of him, closer than David had been, pleading with him to give it up.

Behind Frank and beyond where David had been standing, a soldier lay on the ground, his blood seeping across the concrete floor.

David knew instantly what had happened: the soldier had been standing behind David when Charles had fired. David had time traveled to avoid the bullet, so it had hit the soldier instead. He'd simply been in the wrong place at the wrong time. Several men were working on him, trying to save his life. A soldier with a medical kit burst from the office building, followed by three other men, one with a stretcher, and ran towards the action.

David had been gone for maybe a minute, and that minute had been long enough to change everything. The anger and fear in the air was so thick David could have cut it with a knife.

Charles's lips were bloodless, but he still wasn't giving up the gun and, by now, a ring of soldiers not working on their fallen comrade had pulled their weapons too. All of them were pointed at Charles.

"Give me the gun, sir." Frank held out his hand, palm up.

"Everyone put their weapons down." Letitia made a broad motion with both hands. "You don't want to do this."

None of them had yet noted David's return.

Things were coming to a head, and while David didn't want to upend what he'd worked so hard to achieve and wasn't quite ready to leave for good, if Charles was going to shoot anyone, it should be him again. So he strode across the hangar floor, finally drawing everyone's attention, including that of Charles, whose already wide eyes dilated further in shock. Of course, that didn't stop him from turning the gun on David instead of Frank.

David didn't stop moving, passing between two soldiers and entering the circle of men. "Go ahead. Shoot me again."

Charles hesitated, giving David the last two strides to reach him.

Then, as Callum had taught, David ripped the gun from Charles's hand before he could pull the trigger and turned it on him. He had learned over the years that hesitation was the surest way to lose a fight. Even better was never to fight at all.

Raising his hands, Charles took two steps back to see his own gun pointing at him.

All the soldiers now pivoted to point their weapons at David. Meanwhile, the fallen soldier had been loaded onto a stretcher by medics, who were keeping a wary eye on David and Charles, but otherwise were moving without urgency, indicating the man was already dead. He must have been by the amount of blood underneath him.

So David ignored them too and laughed without humor. "This man just killed a fellow soldier before your eyes, and another just drowned before mine. I'm done with this. Send me home." And then, because the anger was fading, replaced by further resolve, he added, "Go ahead. Make my day."

The shock of murdering one of his own soldiers had been great, but Charles hadn't achieved his position as the director of a branch of the CIA without being quick on his feet. He saw what was happening. "Don't shoot him. That's just what he wants."

Nobody moved. They didn't shoot him, but they also didn't lower their guns.

"Where's Josh?" A soldier David didn't recognize, younger than anyone else here, advanced out of the ring of soldiers. "You're saying he drowned?"

The grief in the man's face and voice at the question he'd asked, and the answer he already knew, swept away David's anger entirely, replacing it, for the most part, with pity. "Yes."

"He can't be gone! He was just here!" The soldier sighted his weapon, the little red light aimed at David's heart.

"I'm sorry."

"If I shot you right now could you bring him back?"

Everybody froze, waiting for David's answer, even the men by the stretcher. It felt to David almost as if he was in the void again, with the silence pressing on his ears and his pounding heart the only thing he could hear. "It doesn't work that way."

"What doesn't? You're just saying that because you want to change history for yourself, but you won't do it for anyone else!"

"I know that's what you've been told, but what we've been doing isn't time travel." David enunciated each word clearly in a voice loud enough to carry to everyone in the hangar. "We say *time travel* as a shorthand, but I am not traveling to a time in our history. Earth Two is a different world that, for whatever reason, has a present day that's only reached 1295. I can't go back to an earlier time before your friend was dead. I'm sorry. Time travel isn't real. None of us can change the past. Only the future."

The man stared at David for a count of five. Then his face crumpled and the red dot trembled on David's chest.

Luke had not been armed in the first place, and now he put himself between David and the soldier. "Put it away, Chris. There's been enough killing today." And then he said to David over his shoulder, "You too, sire. We know you're not going to shoot anyone."

He was right, of course. Instantly, David straightened, putting his arms out and loosening the pistol in his hand so he held the grip with only a finger and thumb. A soldier behind him relieved him of it a second later and pinioned both hands behind his back. His willingness to arrest David rather than Charles implied he was one of the anonymous men who'd thrown David out of the plane.

David, however, had more to say, and he would keep speaking until they muzzled him. With Charles, that wasn't out of the question. "Aren't you done with this yet? How many more men have to die before it's enough? You have the power to stop what's happening here. Each of you can choose not to listen to him anymore." He jerked his head to indicate Charles.

More silence.

David now looked towards Charles, who was the one who should be in handcuffs but so far was not. The space around him *had* widened, as if nobody wanted to be contaminated by him but didn't know what to do with him. "You have crashed a plane into a mountain an absurd number of times, thrown me out of an airplane, and shot me. Each time I didn't stay in Earth Two and ended up back here. What does that tell you?"

Charles didn't answer.

But Letitia, who was standing by Frank, said, "What does it tell *you*?"

David scoffed. "People had to die before you thought to ask?" Maybe it wasn't the smartest thing to say, to mock her, but this had been something of a rough day, and he couldn't help himself. "I should have shot myself and rid myself of all of you."

From behind him, Luke said softly, "That isn't something you'd do either, sire."

David took in a breath and let it out. "Maybe it would be easier if it were."

"Why are you listening to him?" Charles looked to be recovering, and he motioned with his head towards the leader of the group of four, who'd thrown David out of the plane. "Get him back inside!"

The man eyed David speculatively and then looked at Charles. "I think I won't." He flicked out a finger, and all of a sudden David's hands were free.

Charles advanced on the leader. "That's an order, soldier!"

"I threw a fellow American and soldier out of a plane. You *killed* one of my men before our eyes, and King David tells us the man you forced to time travel with him is dead too."

Charles was still glaring. "This is war, son. Men die."

"I've been to war, and this is not it," the man shot back. "This is over, for all of us."

"You are right. King David is right." Letitia finally stepped in with some real force. It looked to David as if she'd been waiting until she saw which way the wind was blowing before making a decision.

But he supposed that, in this case, late was better than never. Her gaze swept around the room, ending up at David. "King David is right. We cannot do this anymore."

35

August 1295

Day Four

Isabelle

"This is good news!" William was looking at Amaury with something like awe in his face.

But Christopher asked with characteristic bluntness, "Since when?"

Amaury's mouth twitched, threatening a real smile and abandoning the mask of severity. "You would not have known of it since I took orders yesterday and was immediately elected master of this commandery."

"Just like that?" Isabelle was close to shedding tears of relief at having such a capable ally. They'd needed friends, and they'd found one. But still, she'd had to ask.

"It has long been my dream to combine my love for God with justice." Amaury's countenance brightened even more. "This commandery had been in disarray since the death of the last master, who spoke to me many times of following in his footsteps. Until yesterday I had refused, thinking my destiny lay elsewhere." His mouth twisted into a wry smile. "That my estates have become the property of the Templars may have had some influence on their decision to accept me. I will have to inform my steward of the change of ownership. I'm not sure he will be pleased."

"We talked to your steward," Christopher said. "He hadn't heard from you."

"I sent a message to him not an hour ago. You are earlier than I expected. I thought I had more time."

"Well, we're here now," Christopher said. "It's the portcullis. The boats—"

"Are on their way, sooner than I hoped as well." Amaury gave a sharp nod and gestured towards the keep behind him. "Our plans will have to be accelerated. Best that the last holdouts hear it from you."

The three of them trooped across the courtyard after Amaury, with Christopher regaling him with a more complete explanation of what had gone on in Paris and their journey to this point, and Isabelle and William following close behind.

William's expression had turned pensive again. "I don't like the feeling in the city. It's like the night before a battle."

Isabelle glanced at him, seeing a real willingness to talk to her and wanting to encourage it. "I hear the two of you fought together at Tara."

"And at Skipton. Huw and Robbie were there too, along with Henri and Thomas, two of the Templars you met in Paris."

"Would you tell me of it?"

William looked at her quizzically. "You mean Christopher hasn't?"

"He won't talk to me about war. None of you will. I know what I know only because everybody does."

William hesitated. "I don't know that I'm the one you should be asking."

Isabelle's eyes narrowed. "Whyever not?"

"I would hate to speak out of turn if Christopher himself hasn't said." William canted his head. "You do realize he's the best of us, don't you?"

"He was heroic, wasn't he?" Isabelle's breath caught in her throat.

"Of course he was." William snorted. "He doesn't know how to be anything else. Why do you think I'm here? Why do you think my father, who at one time was a regent of England and later tried to ensure that I ascended to the throne, supports David so staunchly?" Now he swept out a hand. "Don't get me wrong. This isn't about being perfect. Nobody is perfect, and everybody falters sometimes, or loses faith, or fails. Even David makes mistakes, and Christopher is not David. There's nobody like David. But not even David is a better man."

They'd reached the door to the keep, beyond which Christopher and Amaury had already disappeared, when suddenly a shout came from the rampart above them and a great puff of smoke billowed into the air to the northeast of their position.

"It's started." Christopher hastened back to the doorway to look for himself. "Whatever *it* is."

"Come inside, all of you." Amaury motioned them into the keep and then led the way with long strides. Isabelle, who was the shortest of all of them, hustled to keep up. "I fear for the people of Normandy. My own father led a rebellion against the King of England and died in the process."

"My father fought with yours," William said, "and he lost his father too, at Evesham ... but your father did not have King David on his side."

Amaury stopped in the act of pushing open a door to reveal a large reception area full of Templars. It was both familiar to Isabelle and daunting. "Why do you think I'm helping him?"

As Amaury entered, his Templar brothers turned to look, nodding their heads or bowing slightly at the waist. Respect was evident in their faces, even if the old gatekeeper was uncertain of his new master, and Amaury had implied that his estates had been a deciding factor in his election. Nobody was looking askance at Isabelle either. Maybe it was just that kind of day.

Amaury gestured that William, Christopher, and Isabelle should fully enter the room and stand to one side, while he took his place in the center of the ring of men.

A man with a bushy brown beard, though that described fully half of the Templars present, was the first to speak. "What are our orders, brother?"

Amaury gestured towards where Isabelle and her friends were standing. "Emissaries from Paris have arrived with news. The flotilla of boats with the Jewish refugees from Paris could be in Rouen within the hour. We will continue what Master Norris and Grand Master Molay started."

"Which is what? You are asking us to help the archbishop evict our Jews from Rouen as Master Norris did in Paris?" This came from an older man, who looked more shocked than sneering.

"You know why he did what he did," Amaury said before Isabelle could step in to defend her father. In truth, he didn't need defending. "No, brother, you misunderstand. We will not be evicting Jews. Or stopping those on the river. Like our brethren in Paris, we will be taking to the streets to protect them."

"I bring word from Paris!"

The door to the great hall opened, and none other than Thomas Hartley strode inside, accompanied by two sergeants.

At the sight of him, Christopher gave a loud *whoop* and ran to embrace him.

Isabelle herself had been raised with affection from her aunt and uncle, but Christopher was more likely to touch the people around him than virtually anyone she had ever met. He touched her all the time, not that she was complaining, but it was yet another way he was different from all others.

For Thomas's part, he accepted Christopher's hug with aplomb and even returned it. Then he looked past Christopher to Amaury. "Your gatekeeper had a great deal to say about the goings on here in the last hour."

Amaury gave a little grunt. "My apologies."

Thomas grinned. "I made sure he knew I was completely in favor of all of it."

Then he bent over Isabelle's hand. "Your father will be very pleased to learn you are well. I will be sure to tell him when next I see him." As he straightened he glanced at Christopher. "Though he might not be happy you brought her into Rouen in the middle of a riot!"

"Queen Lili sent her," Christopher said, turning serious in an instant.

Thomas bobbed his head. "Of course." He glanced at Isabelle. "I would never question her judgment."

"Well, I would." Another one of the older Templars had been staring at Isabelle, and now he harrumphed. "I don't take to these changes."

Isabelle moved closer to Christopher, and he made a motion as if to put an arm around her, but then stopped himself, replying to the Templar instead, "If I may speak, friend, change is the way of the world, and we are fortunate that what your master is asking of you in that regard—what I believe Thomas has come also to ask of you—is entirely in keeping with the Templar motto."

"*Non nobis, Domine, non nobis, sed Nomini tuo da gloriam,*" Isabelle quoted. "Not unto us, O Lord, not unto us, but unto thy Name give glory."

After shooting an approving look at Isabelle, Amaury swept out a hand to encompass his brothers. "The Templar Order was formed to protect pilgrims on the road to Jerusalem. These pilgrims included Muslims and Jews. Grand Master Molay considered his efforts to aid King David an extension of that duty."

One of the Templars raised a hand. "What about the commotion in the streets calling to free Normandy from France?"

"Many of us will feel a partisan pull in that regard, but that is not what we are here for. We will certainly not intervene on the side of King Philippe or his archbishop."

William raised a hand too. "I am not a Templar, nor could I ever take orders as I am my father's heir. But if you will grant me permission to stand amongst you, I would join my sword with yours."

"It is granted," Amaury said immediately, prompting Thomas to grin and stick out his arm to William, who grasped it.

"What about you?" Amaury looked at Christopher.

"I cannot."

Isabelle nudged him. "Do not stay behind on my account! I cannot fight, but I would not stop you from doing so!"

She could tell that her words had been overheard by many, including Amaury, and that Christopher's refusal had surprised them.

Christopher looked apologetic but nonetheless remained steadfast. "I am King David's cousin, known to many as the Hero of Westminster. If it became common knowledge that I marched with Templars in Rouen, any hope my cousin might have of maintaining his fragile peace with France would be lost. He has worked so hard to keep the connection between the English court, Templars, and Jews a secret. His role in the departure of Jews from Paris—or the ongoing movement of all France's Jews to England and Aquitaine—has not been discovered by King Philippe. Perhaps with all of you aware of the connection, any hope of continued secrecy is already lost, but I cannot be the one who ensured it." To punctuate his comment, he reached out a hand and grasped Isabelle's. "No matter how satisfying I might find it to join you, I must decline."

As the others turned away to discuss their preparations, Isabelle and Christopher retreated behind a pillar.

"Are you sure?" she said. "You may not be a Templar, but these men are your brothers."

Christopher still shook his head. "I don't need to stand beside my brothers to fight with them."

36

August 2023

Day Four

David

"You're just going to roll over for him? He killed my brother." Charles clenched his hands into fists as he'd done in the conference room earlier that day, though it seemed like yet another lifetime ago to David since those soldiers had hauled him from the room. He'd died four more times since then.

Mummy and daddy *were* fighting, but everyone but Charles could see that his position had become untenable. Two men were dead, effectively by his hand. Nobody was taking his orders anymore, even if he ostensibly was still the boss here.

"*He* did not, Charles, as you well know," Letitia said. "Your brother's plane was caught in a storm, and because he was with David's mother, he didn't die on the mountain, but lived another few years."

"He died—"

"Because he tried to abduct David's sister. You know this. I read the same reports you did."

If Charles hadn't already killed two people in pursuit of his revenge, David would have felt for him. But there was a point where sympathy had to give way to hard reality.

Charles was staring straight ahead, jaw tightly clenched like his fists, at first looking past David, and then his eyes shifted to meet David's. It was hard to give up an idea once established, especially one as potent and emotional as this mission to destroy David's family and Earth Two in the process. "What happened to Petrofsky?"

"Josh, you mean?" He glanced to where the young soldier was standing with his head down, as dejected as David had ever seen another human being. "You mean the man you told to hold me while you shot me and sent me back to Earth Two?"

David wasn't Charles's father, but he had been behaving like a vengeful nine-year-old, and he needed to face what he'd wrought. David feared that none of the men and women around him and beneath him in the hierarchy could, in the end, make him really see the truth.

Charles didn't move. "Yes. I mean him."

"We were dropped into the middle of an ocean, in the middle of a storm. The waves were twenty feet above my head. I don't know if he could swim, but even if he could, he let go of me within the first few seconds. After we were swamped by a giant wave, he slipped beneath the surface."

"How did you get back?"

"A sailing boat crested the next wave and drove straight into my head."

Charles passed a hand in front of his face, then turned slowly to look one by one at each of the men who encircled them.

None of them were looking at him because their eyes were on Letitia.

She made a motion with her hand to Frank. "Do your duty, soldier."

Frank pulled Charles's hands behind his back and cuffed them.

Then Letitia spoke to David without actually looking directly at him. Some habits were hard to break. "You are free to go."

David didn't move. "I would prefer not to go anywhere."

Letitia swung her head up to look him full in the face. "What did you say?"

At long last, David had her full attention. "While your plans to take me back to Earth Two and exploit it didn't work out, maybe you couldn't help but notice that every time you thought the mission had failed I was brought right back here, to this hangar. Why would that be when I could go anywhere in the world? *Why here?*"

Letitia herself didn't answer, so at first there was no response from anyone, even though the soldiers remained close and listening. And then Tom Baker, who was holding one of Charles's upper arms said, "Because you were meant to."

"Yes. I was meant to." David returned his gaze to Letitia, since she was now the one in charge. "Have you asked yourself why, when

George flew the plane here, we weren't dropped into the UK, at Chad Treadman's compound specifically? I could have returned to any place on the planet, especially this last time after Josh died when I was all by myself. Instead, I came back here. Heck, if I'd been dropped close to Britain, I could have swum to shore and didn't have to come back at all."

Charles tried to take a step forward, but Frank and Tom pulled him back. "Are you saying you chose to come—"

"I didn't *choose* anything." David cut him off. "I told you I don't control it—whatever *it* is. But I think I do understand it, just a little bit. More than you, anyway. You could force me to time travel a hundred times, a thousand times, and it would *never* do your bidding and keep coming up with creative ways to repel and deflect you. Earth Two has rejected you and your ideals. That door is closed, no matter how hard and often you pound on it to be let in."

Charles's expression remained incredulous. David swiveled on his heel in order to cast his gaze around at everyone else. "I didn't come here because George made me. Once I knew he was going to try to abduct me, I let him take me."

"Why?" This was Luke, speaking out of turn, but there was no rank among them in this moment. "Why put yourself through this?"

"Because I figured you lot would do exactly what you did do. Any person—any organization—that could conceive a plan to kidnap my six-year-old son in order to ride him back and forth from Avalon to Earth Two had to be dealt with head on."

"What—what did you say?" Frank looked from David to Charles, where his eyes stopped, glaring.

"That was the original plan," David said flatly. "It was all arranged ... until I put a stop to it." He swallowed at the thought of what might have been, but anger wouldn't get him where he needed to go. And he took some comfort in the horror in the faces around him. Even if Arthur had been the one abducted, these men would have been hard-pressed to go along with what Charles had wanted. "And now, *you* all need to put a stop to this, once and for all. I am not a tool in anyone's arsenal, and Earth Two is not your playground, retreat, or safety net for the disaster you've made of this world. When I agreed to that interview a year and a half ago, I did so because it was time people knew about me. Knew *me*. But it was a publicity stunt. The man you saw there isn't who I am. *This* is. You need to make sure everyone knows it."

"What are you proposing?" Letitia said.

"I never intended not to help you. I simply objected to your scheming to abduct my son."

Letitia looked down at the ground. "That wasn't my idea."

"Still, the order was given. Charles was allowed to give it. This mission was green-lighted at the highest levels."

"It was," Letitia said softly, "for the greater good."

"Then this has become more than about negotiating with you or Charles. You have bosses, who will need to be convinced as well." He was looking hard at Letitia, whose eyes weren't meeting his. "So, I am going to go now. By the time we meet next, you need to have written up everything you planned and everything that has happened here over the last two days. You need to send it to every intelligence agency on the planet, and then to every news agency on the planet. And then you need to let the families of those two dead soldiers know exactly how and why they died."

"And if we don't?"

"I will." David turned away from her to the men around him. "If I walked out of here right now, would any of you stop me?"

"No, sire," Frank said.

"It will mean Charles's career," Letitia said softly. "Jailtime."

"He killed two people." David turned back to her. "He held the fate of an entire universe in his hands, and *this* is what he chose to do with it."

David had been King of England long enough to have had to chastise underlings when it became necessary. Even then, he avoided letting loose the royal temper because he found it had limited efficacy in the long run.

So now he canted his head. "But what he did here doesn't have to be a model for what happens next. Our relationship doesn't have to be adversarial. I never wanted that. If the CIA is capable of learning from its mistakes, legion as they may be, it could choose to be my ally. I don't even mind if it ropes in MI-5 to spread some of the love around." He gestured broadly. "What went on here needs never to happen again. You few can ensure it."

Luke said under his breath, "The few, the proud…" It was audible enough that several of the men looked as if they'd been slapped.

"If we do as you say, then what?" Charles was almost back to his former self, ready to fight again. In another hour, this would become all David's fault.

David held out his hand. "If someone has a phone I can borrow, I have friends I need to call."

37

August 1295

Day Four

Lili

That her brother hadn't known what he was going to do if they were attacked on the river—and that he'd admitted it—was such an unusual situation that Lili almost didn't know how to deal with it. Dafydd had been known to admit ignorance at times; Ieuan would too, but not so often and not under such potentially dire circumstances.

She could hear Dafydd's voice in her head saying, *Good! He's learning to let go.*

Then again, Ieuan had said those words in Welsh, for her ears alone. And from that moment on, he'd stood in the prow of the boat, bow at the ready, watching both banks in earnest for signs of French troops. He was ready … but for what, they couldn't yet say. Her fingers itched for her bow too, and she wondered if she should retrieve it from the hold. It wasn't doing her any good down there.

Up ahead, somewhere, was the City of Rouen. Their initial escape from Paris had been under the cover of darkness, and by the time the sun had risen yesterday, they'd already been on the water for four hours. They hadn't been able to properly disguise their presence during daylight hours yesterday and today, not with twenty boats and five hundred people cruising down the Seine. Once the sun set tonight, however, they could be less of a presence again, especially if they ran, as they had the previous night, with few lights.

Furthermore, as the afternoon had worn on, clouds had thickened above their heads. It was going to rain again.

Before that could happen, Huw and Robbie appeared on the right bank of the river, which at the moment was to the east because of the way the Seine wended through the countryside, and the boats were sailing directly north.

It was a relief to know the young men had returned, though her next thought was to wonder where William, Isabelle, and Christopher were.

The river had broadened in this location, but it was still moving along at a rapid clip, so the two young men on the bank had to urge their horses into a canter in order to keep up.

Ieuan cupped his hands around his mouth. "We see you! What's happening?"

Lili moved to stand beside her brother and leaned over the rail, trying to get as close as possible to them, even another few inches, in order to better hear their shouts.

"The steward was right! There is unrest in the city!" Huw was the one shouting, but in the process of calling to them, he hadn't focused enough attention on where he was going and almost ran into a tree. His horse avoided it at the last moment, with an assist from Robbie, who grabbed the horse's bridle.

Lili mimicked her brother, cupping her hands around her mouth. "Where are the others?"

"Still in Rouen! They will try to ensure you can get past the bridge. The order is to confiscate all English shipping!"

Ieuan swung around to call back to the captain in the stern. "Can we stop the boat?"

"You know better than that, my lord! We're in the middle of the current. If we couldn't stop at Pont-de-l'Arche, we can't stop here!"

Ieuan rubbed his chin. "Will we be able to dock at Rouen?"

The captain blinked. "We have to dock, regardless of what faces us. They have a bridge, which, if it isn't washed out, can be navigated by a single boat at a time and not at our current pace. And that's if they don't close the portcullis against us. Even with it open, we could capsize if we don't position ourselves exactly right."

Aaron, their longtime friend and companion, approached with Jacob, and both men stood at the rail too. "Even if the authorities didn't require us to stop at Rouen to pay the tax, my lord, we *have* to stop, and not for the reasons the captain stated. One of the former prisoners has already died. We have many more at death's door, both in this boat and in the others. They need more than we can give them on the water."

Huw and Robbie were struggling to keep up, less because of the speed of the boats on the river than because of the ruggedness of the terrain on the bank. This time it was Robbie who tried again to speak to them while on a clearer, straight stretch. "There's more you need to know! The archbishop has expelled all Jews from Rouen. They are to be evicted from their homes by tonight."

Either the captain had maneuvered them closer or Robbie had extra breath that made his voice carry to all who were listening in Lili's boat—and maybe all the boats. If it wasn't against Lili's nature, she would have cursed, wishing that Robbie had kept that piece of information to himself for just a little longer.

In response, Jacob exclaimed out loud, "Rouen is home to as many of us as Paris. More perhaps!"

Lili put out a calming hand. "We know, Jacob. We said already we would help them, and we will."

"How?"

Ieuan turned on him, suddenly irate and unable to moderate his tone. "Are you really asking me that now, after all that's happened and all that we've done?"

Jacob's expression was fierce. "I can see now that a few thousand Jews were all very well and good, since England can use us for our education and wealth, but you will balk at taking on a country full of people."

Ieuan was no less furious. "You ungrateful—"

Jacob overrode him. "You helped us because you wanted a place to hide the queen and her boys, so they could escape from Paris amongst us with nobody the wiser!"

"You must realize how absurd that sounds!" Ieuan's jaw was bulging. "Instead of taking heart that Dafydd entrusted you with his wife, you instead think it was all a ruse to get her out of the city? You think we did *all* this so boats of Jewish refugees were the last place Philippe would look for her?"

From the expression on Jacob's face, he hadn't quite reached that point in his conclusions, but now that Ieuan had spoken, he was willing to believe it was true.

Ieuan saw it too. "And what happens when we get to Rouen, and she's discovered among you by the king's men? All our good work is for nothing, and the people of France turn on you more than they already have."

"Philippe has already expelled us from Paris! We have lost everything!"

"Those orders came from Nogaret," Ieuan said in an icy tone. "He is in a cell because of Dafydd."

Bronwen had become aware of the commotion by now and joined their little group at the prow of the boat. She put a hand on her husband's chest, understanding, as Lili did, how unwelcome this news was, but not for the reasons Jacob was accusing them of. She got Ieuan to back off, which likely he was about to do anyway, and focus instead on the whereabouts of Huw and Robbie on the bank.

Once her husband was subdued, Bronwen turned to face Jacob and spoke English, which was one of his many languages, but one understood by few others in the boat. "I realize you're scared, but by becoming the official liaison between the English court and your people, you put yourself forward as an example. It is time for you to accept that mantle of leadership and control your emotions. Like you, we have just heard this news. We do not have a plan as yet as to what we are going to do about it or how exactly we can help. We *will* have a plan if we take some time to think. I would assume you will want to be part of that consultation. We will not abandon you. We are literally in the same boat as you! In the interim, your people need you to be confident and secure. So get your attitude right and go liaise."

Jacob's mouth opened and closed like a fish. It was gratifying, really, how Bronwen had cut through the anger and fear and gone straight to what mattered most. At the Paris synagogue, Jacob had initially been defensive and angry, with a large chip on his shoulder. But by the time he'd arrived at the Paris Temple, his anger had turned to a somewhat joyous acceptance as he realized Dafydd meant what he said—and that they all meant what they said.

But Jewish people had been abused and exploited for far too long not to need repeated affirmations that their faith was not misplaced. Her own people, who'd spent generations mistrusting English, had needed similar help. The Irish and Scots too. That was one reason Dafydd had created the Confederated States of Britain in the first place. He knew, as did all those who had embraced his vision, that a single moment of perceived intolerance or injustice, unintentional as it would be, could destroy everything he'd spent thirteen years building.

His record with the Jewish community, however, was unmarred, and Jacob would remember it if he allowed himself to think for a moment instead of panicking.

Then Ieuan tugged on Lili's arm. "Huw and Robbie have something more to say."

They all went to the rail. While Huw had fallen behind the boats, perhaps because he was on a slower horse, Robbie had been riding with increasing desperation, and Lili's eyes were good enough that she could see the relief on his face when he finally caught their attention again. The rush of the water beneath the boat was very loud, and it was all Lili could do to hear his next words.

"You didn't let us finish! The people of Rouen have risen *against* King Philippe and the archbishop, not their Jewish neighbors! They want their freedom and to vote for their own parliament like Aquitaine! *Normandy for Normans* they are saying. They are talking about joining *us*!"

Those who did understand Robbie's English translated furiously for those who didn't, prompting half of the people on the boat to rush to the rail. They moved so quickly, in fact, that they threatened to swamp the boat. Jacob was one of them, and he stood openmouthed, stunned to the point of being unable to find a reply. To be fair, his surprise was shared by many—including Lili herself, even having heard something of this already from their boat's captain.

Ieuan gave Robbie a thumbs up, which was an American gesture but one Robbie knew, and he fell back with Huw, finally stymied by the terrain along the bank. His last words were, "We'll meet you in Rouen!"

At that point, Jacob managed to articulate what he was truly thinking: "I don't believe it."

Lili herself was pleased that her faith had not been misplaced. "The world is not always terrible."

"Such has not been my experience." Then Jacob's eyes tracked to Ieuan, who'd pulled his bow from his back and strung it in a few quick movements. While he'd nocked the arrow, he hadn't yet pulled the string to his ear but was watching the sky to the north.

"What is it, my lord?"

Rather than answering, Ieuan pointed the arrow at the sky and loosed it, followed immediately by another and then one more, released even before the first hit the bird at which he'd been aiming and fell to earth out of sight. In the distance, Huw and Robbie noted the arrows and the aftermath, and urged their horses towards where it, and then a second bird, had fallen.

"Those were pigeons?" Jacob's eyes moved between the sky and where the birds had disappeared behind some trees.

"Flying east." Ieuan continued to scan the sky, looking for more, even as he added. "If Robbie and Huw are right, we cannot let news of what is happening in Rouen reach Paris. Every day of delay means more time for Normandy to find its feet on its own."

Jacob said tentatively, "I have heard that pigeons are often sent in threes."

He had hardly finished speaking when in a smooth motion Ieuan nocked and loosed another arrow—and then smiled in satisfaction as the bird in question went the way of the others. "I had heard that too."

Lili was hopeful Huw and Robbie would recover them. She wanted to know what message they'd been carrying. The sun was hidden behind a cloud now, but it had been a few stray rays that had allowed Ieuan to see so clearly.

Aaron spoke from behind her, his voice gentle, but firm. "Britain, and the CSB, will provide a haven in England for every one of our people, Jacob. David has sworn it, and I am standing here to tell you that you can believe him."

"I do hear you." Jacob swung around to face the old physician. "But I'm thinking now, if the people of Normandy really have risen, and can throw off Paris's yoke and join the CSB, some of us might prefer to stay."

38

August 2023

Day Four

David

David had time traveled a lot. He'd been to war. He had plenty of experience with those moments of utter and total relief and joy at seeing someone you loved alive and being alive oneself.

He didn't love Chad Treadman, per se, but he was very fond of Sophie. Seeing her push open the door of the car, before the driver had even pulled to a complete stop outside the airplane hangar, within seven and a half minutes of David's phone call, was an indescribable relief.

Chad's people had arrived in Oregon and instantly acquired an estate, just as in Wales. It was lovely that Chad too was entirely predictable.

"Hullo." Sophie stood awkwardly before him for a moment before stepping forward to hug him. "Glad to see you're in one piece."

"Glad to be in one piece." He picked up the large bag at his feet and handed it to her. "The seeds Chad wanted."

Then he laughed to see Andre getting out of the car too, since he'd been the one to drive her. Their initial greeting was a bit more awkward, but David ended up giving him a hug too. "I was really worried you were dead."

"Not yet," Andre said, his voice a low grumble and somewhat amused. "I woke up in the little hospital here and called Sophie right away."

"I thought Chad might come himself," David said.

"He doesn't get angry often," Andre said, "but I have never seen him more furious than when he heard what was happening to you."

Sophie looked rueful. "He felt he was in no condition either to greet you or to speak to anyone from the CIA. When we left, he was rushing around like a headless chicken, making sure everything was perfect while literally talking on three different cell phones at the same time." She gave the hangar a side-eyed look before directing David into the car and getting in herself

David laughed, feeling better again, even if he wasn't quite sure what to make of Chad's anger. It was kind of sweet, and thus a little embarrassing, to have someone he didn't know that well care so much about him. "Even I know conference calls exist now. With video even, though I've never been a part of one."

"He didn't want any of the people to whom he was talking to hang up or know he was talking to one of the others at the same time." She made a dismissive motion. "This is normal for him."

As Andre drove away from the airport, David said, "I want to hear everything about what's gone on with you since you got back—and over the last two days. Did you know right away I'd come?"

"We knew someone had come, and the GPS tracker on the plane put it here. Before it was disabled, of course. We feared in those first hours that they'd moved you." Sophie turned in her seat so she could look at him. "This is the middle of nowhere, you realize, even for the United States."

"I grew up here, remember?" Then David amended. "Well, not *here* here. Oregon."

"And then all those flashes, one after another." Sophie sobered considerably. "David." The word came out heavy and soft at the same time.

"Yeah." He covered up his further embarrassment at her pity by taking a drink of water from a bottle from the car refrigerator. "And it isn't over yet. I still have to get back."

That was all the time they had for conversation before they arrived at the estate Chad had acquired, on the edge of a harvested wheat field within sight of the airport. It even had stone pillars and a gate, a combination David had never seen in front of a house in Oregon before, no matter how extensive the grounds. Andre parked in the circular driveway in front of the columned porch and got out to open Sophie's door, guessing correctly that David would have waved him off if he'd come to help him.

"We knew more after George reached out to us yesterday," Sophie said as she stepped out of the car. "He explained everything."

David stopped in his tracks in the act of closing the car door, so stunned he was having a hard time breathing. It was almost as if he was in the void again. "I doubt that. George works for the CIA."

"Not anymore. He says they all but cut him loose." She gave her head a shake. "They took him off the project anyway, which amounts, in his mind, to the same thing."

"So, poor George didn't get what he wanted." David's voice dripped with sarcasm, and then his eyes went to Andre. "How can you even look at him?"

"It's okay." Andre put out a hand to David. "We have him on a short leash."

"Not short enough!" David found his voice growing louder. "He drugged you!"

Sophie bit her lip. "He knows."

"He can't know, or you wouldn't have let George within a hundred yards of this place or me." David didn't budge from his position beside the car. "He tried to abduct Arthur, just like Chad told me the CIA was going to try to do."

"We *know*," she said. "As I said, he confessed everything."

David felt like throwing up. "You sound like you ... *believe* him."

Sophie didn't admit to that necessarily, just gave another shake of her head. "For the moment, Chad thinks he can be useful."

"George betrayed me too, sire." Andre's expression grew more intent. "But I agree with Chad that there's value in keeping him where we can see him. None of us want him telling his story to a foreign power, and that's just about where he is right now. He's lost his faith, and a man in that position is capable of pretty much anything. If we don't take him in, someone else will."

Then Chad came out the front door, followed by George, whose hands were pushed deep in his pockets. He had a sheepish look on his face, and his hair was dark brown instead of his usual sandy blond, indicating he'd dyed it as a disguise. David's feet were frozen to the driveway. At his glare, George's shoulders hunched more.

Then George shook himself, walked straight up to David, who just managed not to take a step back at his approach, and got down on one knee with a bent head before him. "I am sorry for everything I've done, sire. I'm so sorry. Please forgive me."

David stared at the top of George's downturned head. He couldn't think of a single thing to say.

Eventually, after an embarrassingly long thirty seconds of silence, George rose to his feet and backed away. "I see this isn't going to work. I'll go." He started down the driveway towards the gate.

It was exasperating, doing the right thing all the time. David was being played, and he knew it. But still ... "No, George."

George stopped, though he remained facing the gate.

David sighed. "Come back."

George slowly turned around, his look questioning, and then began walking back towards David. "I can go. You have no reason to trust me."

"I don't." David said. "We are going to have a reckoning, you and I, but not right now." He looked at Chad, whom he hadn't yet greeted properly. He looked the same, still hardly older than David though he must be approaching forty by now. "This is about *time*, as it always seems to be, and we don't have a moment to waste."

39

August 1295

Day Four

Christopher

It had been the right thing to send Robbie and Huw back to the boats, and Christopher could only pray that they'd been able to warn Lili and Ieuan about what they were sailing into. Honestly, Christopher was relieved the boats hadn't attempted to sail by already. The fact that they hadn't done so yet gave him hope that Huw and Robbie would be in time. With so many ill people, walking around the city wasn't much of an option, but they needed time to consider it.

It might be that the people of Rouen weren't going to turn on their Jewish neighbors. Maybe all they genuinely wanted was freedom from France. Christopher really hoped so. But the chance of the protesters *not* turning violent—or the authorities not turning violent in response to their protests—was pretty much zero. Rouen had a population of thirty thousand people. At the moment, a significant portion of them were on the streets. While Christopher and Isabelle had been consulting with the Templars, they'd been able to hear the noise all the way inside the stone keep.

Now that he was outside on the battlements, the volume was Friday night football game level. The sun would be setting soon, but it was still light enough to see much of the city, which was lit up with torches anyway. Soldiers from the castle had taken up a position on the Rouen end of the bridge across the Seine, not to stop people from leaving the city but because the green was there, and the stone towers at their backs provided a safe place to which to retreat if the crowd got out of hand.

Below Christopher, the gate to the commandery opened on greased hinges. Creaking would have been more ominous, but even so, forty Templar knights and sergeants (plus William), armed and mounted, were a sight to behold and not one Christopher had seen before. It must have been incredibly intimidating from the other side, especially in the close quarters of the street.

As Amaury had told his brothers, the Templar Order was originally founded to protect pilgrims on the road to Jerusalem. It was only later that the Templars developed a reputation for ferocity and skill in battle in the Crusades. Christopher was very glad the Templars were on his side, even if he no longer wanted to be a Templar himself.

The people outside gave way, though not without some jeering. It was hard to hear anything distinct above the general uproar, but then someone from a window on the other side of the street threw an apple at Amaury. It bounced off his helmet, and Amaury caught it on the bounce, stowing it in his pack as if it were a gift instead of a curse.

From the earlier speeches in the street, the people knew by now that the Templars had been the ones to roust Paris's Jews and send them out of the city, and it only affirmed their conviction that the Templars were no longer independent of the royal court, a distrust that had been a long time coming. It was one of the reasons the people of France had believed the accusations of witchcraft in 1307 when Philippe had abolished the Order.

Watching the path of that apple was like witnessing history in real time.

Then, at a crossroads, the Templar force split in two, with half marching to the wharf to protect the boats once they made it underneath the bridge—if they made it under the bridge—and the other half marching to ensure that they did.

Then Isabelle drew Christopher's attention to the other side of the river. "More Templars, Christopher!"

He swung around, glad not to watch any more abuse being directed at a man he respected, even if he'd met him all of an hour ago. He squinted, just able to see motion on the road on the other side of the Seine, and then drew out his binoculars to see better. The thunder of many hooves wasn't audible above the rushing of the river and the shouts from the streets, but all of a sudden Christopher's heart was pounding enough to make a good substitute.

This was another forty men on horseback, riding towards the far bank of the Seine and the entrance to the bridge across it. They were dressed in the full regalia of the Templar Order, with banners and surcoats emblazoned with the characteristic red cross. If these Templars had been persuaded by a missive from Nogaret too, in another minute Templar might be fighting Templar on the bridge.

Even as this new force approached the southern gatehouse, the portcullis, of which they'd been so afraid, dropped into the river with a mighty splash, one Christopher also imagined he could hear from here, though it also was too far away.

As it dropped, Christopher's heart sank with it. He looked from the Templars on the southern bank, to those headed to the wharf, to the soldiers guarding the mighty towers on the Rouen side of the bridge.

And then, between one second and the next and despite the despair that threatened to overwhelm him, he saw what he and Isabelle had to do.

"Come on! I said I could still help my brothers, and I think I know how!" He took Isabelle's hand and, at a run, led her down the stairs of the tower to the courtyard. Then, despite the protests of the gatekeeper, who preferred now to keep them *inside* the commandery, they went out the wicket gate.

"What are we doing?"

"The portcullis is down. Those boats are coming, and if we can't get it up before they arrive, having the Templars on our side won't help. I don't know what magic words might persuade those other Templars coming from the south or the king's men to allow our boats to pass under the bridge, but someone has to try." He glanced at her. "We have to try."

"I'm a woman, and you're King David's cousin." Isabelle clutched his hand. "It could be your death for them to know who you are!"

"Or it could make them help us! Besides, you are a beautiful woman and Matthew Norris's daughter. Nobody is going to hurt you, and right now, I don't have a better plan."

The commandery took up an acre of the city's waterfront and was nearly as wide as it was long. To reach the wharf, the Templars had exited their commandery and then taken a right onto the city street that ended at the river. By moving to take the wharf, Amaury was ensuring that none of the king's men would be able to get to their own boats, nor have the means to attack anyone on the water or as they disembarked. Between control of the wharf and the commandery's own water gate, which was a matter of a hundred yards downstream, the Templars were giving themselves the best chance of protecting the passengers, who might not have to come into the city itself at all.

Both the street that ran parallel to the river and the one that led to it were full of people, with more coming by the second. Short of dressing in Templar regalia themselves, there was no way Christopher and Isabelle were pushing through that crowd, not to mention getting past the soldiers at the end of the bridge. He had to leave that attempt to Amaury—who wouldn't have seen the arrival of the new force of Templars and didn't know he might have Templar brothers to confront too.

With Isabelle in tow, Christopher entered an alley so narrow Christopher's shoulders almost touched the walls on either side. Nonetheless, he took it at a run until it intersected with another alley hardly wider than the first.

Taking a right so they were heading towards the river, they came out into a narrow yard east of the wharf. Here, pigs rutted and an ancient outhouse perched precariously on the bank above the river, allowing anyone who successfully survived using it to evacuate straight into the Seine. Whether because of the pigs or the outhouse, the whole place stank to high heaven, but at least they were on the bank itself now and could see the river running high below them.

Though the city's defenses were considerable in places, it wasn't walled along the waterfront itself except in a few locations, like at the commandery or the bridge, which Christopher could see to the east of where he stood, with its long span across the Seine. Otherwise, houses and buildings lined the water. Although the Seine was a wide river for much of its length, it narrowed as it flowed through Rouen, with the city itself on the outside curve of the bend.

The wharf, to which the Templars were heading, was now to Christopher's right. He pointed Isabelle to a path that led in the opposite direction down the bank. He didn't really know if it was navigable, and he was pretty sure it was better suited to a goat than a person, but he'd seen from the tower that it led where he wanted to go.

"I saw a child come up it with a bucket of water. It will take us to the bridge."

"Good." Isabelle had a hand to her nose. "If we stay in this yard a moment longer, I might expire from the smell!"

That she was laughing instead of crying at the danger and fear told him in that moment that he could, and would if she asked, go to the ends of the earth and back with her.

Isabelle went first this time, and he followed close in case she needed assistance to navigate the narrow dirt path. They were both running flat out, as they had been since they left the commandery, and at times Christopher felt the path giving way under his feet, since it took them down the bank and right along the water, which lapped at the edge. The Seine was still running high from the storms, though from the discolored band to his left, the path had been submerged at one point, and the water had actually gone down a good five feet from where it had been.

The whole time they'd been running, Christopher had been scanning the bridge for signs of the Templars, hoping he and Isabelle weren't too late. But it seemed they'd been delayed since they were only now being allowed to cross.

When he and Isabelle had started out, Christopher had known full well that their biggest challenge would be getting up on the bridge from the path below. All he'd been sure about was that if they stayed in the commandery, they wouldn't be able to affect the outcome of the evening at all. At the very least, he'd hoped he could get close enough as the Templars rode by on the bridge that he would be able to call up to them, and they would stop and listen. He probably should have said something about this cockamamie plan out loud to Isabelle sooner, before they were both staring up at the bridge above their heads.

The first footing was in the river twenty feet to his right, and beyond that were more footings, each supporting one section of the bridge. Normally the river was much narrower, with the main channel passing underneath the central arch with its portcullis, now down, of course. Much of the time, that central span was the only one with enough flow to accommodate boats and barges loaded with goods, as these boats would be.

As he'd feared, the little path that ran under the bridge provided no way for them to get up onto the bridge without a climber's hook and a sturdy rope. The edge of the bridge was simply too high up to reach by jumping.

But, as it turned out, jumping would not be required today.

With all that high water had come debris. All day as they'd sailed the Seine, he'd seen branches, logs, even downed trees floating with them. One of these had lodged against the bridge, with the trunk at the edge of the water and several branches reaching to the top of the bridge itself.

Without a moment to lose before the lead Templars reached their position, Christopher grasped one of the branches at head height and swung himself onto the trunk. He then walked up it in the posture of a cat until he reached the sidewall of the bridge.

At which point, he looked back down at Isabelle. "Can you manage it?"

"Yes!"

She was shorter than he was, so she hoisted herself onto the trunk a little farther down from where he'd started. He watched her for a few seconds and then decided he'd be in a better position to help her from the bridge itself, so he dropped himself over the three foot high wall. Then, with his feet wedged against the stones of the walkway, he bent at the waist to be ready to put out a hand to Isabelle.

Dresses were not the best tree-climbing garments, but she wasn't wearing the beautiful gown from the French royal court that she'd had on when they'd arrived at the city gate. This was one of Lili's dresses, which had a dozen splits in the fabric and allowed her not only to ride astride but to use her legs. She'd borrowed it before they'd set out from the Paris Temple, and she'd worn it during the journey down the Seine. She'd changed back into her gown only when she'd needed to look the part of a noblewoman. Like his tunic, the dress was becoming ever more filthy and wet, but to his eyes, Isabelle looked as lovely as ever, even shimmying up a fallen tree.

A minute later he was helping her onto the bridge.

Hand-in-hand, they stepped into the center of the span to confront the oncoming Templars, two abreast and faceless in their steel helmets.

But then, at the sight of the two of them blocking their way, the leader on the left removed his helmet.

"Michael!" Isabelle recognized him and started forward before Christopher's mouth caught up with his eyes. Once they reached Michael and Henri, who inexplicably turned out to be leading the company too, they practically tumbled over one another in their haste to explain why they'd climbed onto the bridge.

Not even two seconds after the word *portcullis* came out of Christopher's mouth, Constance, who was riding behind Michael, flung out a hand to point upstream. "The boats are here!"

By way of reply, Michael stood in the stirrups and shouted down the column of riders. "Get the portcullis up! Move!"

As both Templars and David's men dismounted to do his bidding, Michael turned back to Christopher. "How is it you are here ahead of them?"

"We managed to stop at Amaury's estates near Elbeuf and were told of unrest in Rouen, so we rode in advance of the boats to investigate." Christopher flung out a hand of his own to point behind him. "Soldiers of the king stand guard on the other side of that great gate behind us. The portcullis must have come down on their orders. We can't let them stop our boats."

"We won't," Henri said. "We haven't come this far to fail now."

As Henri addressed his men about the dangers they faced, Christopher grabbed a torch from a startled Templar sergeant and ran with it to the western railing of the bridge. Waving it above his head, he could only hope that Thomas, one of the commanders down there, would see him and understand that he was telling them the boats were coming down the Seine right now.

There was no way all the activity could have gone unnoticed by the king's soldiers posted on the top of the bridge's towers. Finally one of them gave a great shout and began gesticulating, first at Christopher and his Templar companions, and then east, towards where the boats were visible in the distance. Until now, the guards' attention had been exclusively towards the streets of Rouen.

Then the great wooden gate began to open.

40

August 2023

Day Four

David

Once out of the shower, David stood before the mirror, noting he needed a trim, but he settled for trimming his beard very short instead. This last year, it had filled out satisfactorily, and trimming it was a far easier way to manage it than trying to be cleanshaven every day. As when he'd been in his suite in the hangar, his clothing had been whisked away to be laundered, and he allowed Sophie to encourage him into yet another blue suit, this one slightly lighter in color, with another white shirt open at the collar.

  Before the shower, he'd laid out the latest course of events in as much detail as he could remember, along with what he'd asked Letitia to do. While he talked, not only had one of Chad's employees been typing madly away on a computer, recording his every word, but another had run a video camera. Chad suggested sending a copy of both recordings to MI-5, David's most likely ally, so that if the CIA didn't cooperate, every intelligence agency would still get the information.

Furthermore, he proposed that the best way to proceed now, if David really was willing to work with the CIA on his own terms, was a video conference call. None of them trusted the CIA a single inch, and David was not going to put himself in its clutches again if he could help it. If they were going to come to terms, he needed guarantees first.

This flurry of activity took place immediately upon David's arrival at Chad's new house. Part of the rush was at David's own insistence, and partly due to Chad's fear, which he expressed, that David at any moment could be snatched from him, either by a black ops team or *time*.

Once these initial issues were taken care of, David called Cassie's grandfather and made an unsuccessful attempt to reach Bronwen's parents. Chad also got him the numbers for the families of his other companions, and he spoke with all of them one by one. After that, he'd dawdled a bit in his ablutions, wanting to give Chad time to sort everything out. Chad was the technology expert, after all. When David finally came out of the bedroom, Sophie was waiting for him, and she straightened from where she'd been leaning against the wall.

He smiled to see the familiar behavior. His companions had a thing for lounging in doorways. He missed Michael and spared a passing thought for what he was doing, hoping he was finding his way successfully across France.

Like every thought he'd had of home over the last two days, he suppressed it immediately. He'd left Earth Two only yesterday morning. It was going to take at least until tomorrow for his family and the refugees to float down the Seine. The river was massively long, and though it wasn't all that far to its mouth as the crow flies, it wasn't dammed or diked, so the channel had been allowed to wend its way through the countryside, taking its own sweet time and David's family with it. But while they'd escaped Paris right under the nose of the French king, that wasn't to say other dangers wouldn't present themselves along the way.

He couldn't think about that now—or shouldn't anyway—in large part because he couldn't do anything to help them other than what he was already doing. Myrddin had dropped him into Oregon for a reason, and that reason was the same one that had encouraged David to allow George to capture him. He needed to see this through and then get back to Earth Two as quickly as he could. While he'd told Chad that tomorrow morning would be soon enough, tonight would have been ideal. The question before them now wasn't *if* he would go back, but *with whom* and *by what means*.

As he walked into the dining room, which was doubling as a conference room for Chad's global enterprise, everybody already present stood respectfully. That was what happened whenever he walked into a room in Earth Two, so he responded with what he did there, which was to lift a hand in acknowledgment and tell them to resume whatever they'd been doing. Also in the room were George, Andre, and several secretarial type people David didn't know. For the moment, their job seemed to be getting everyone snacks and drinks.

The conference call had already started, and Chad had blown up the video images on a screen the size of his wall. The participants' heads were lined up in rows and columns, as in an old television rerun like *The Brady Bunch* or *Hollywood Squares*. This was real life, though, and David had never seen anything like it.

"Sire, if you would." With a short bow and a flourish, Sophie gestured to a chair in front of a computer screen, indicating David should sit at the table opposite Chad.

At some point David would have to tell everyone that the 'sirs' and 'sires' were getting out of hand, but that moment wasn't now, not with the tenuous position in which he found himself. While in Oregon, he was subject to the government of the United States. If these government people branded him a terrorist, they could do as Charles had initially threatened and lock him up at a secure black site for the rest of his life. The gate at the entrance to this estate wouldn't stop them. Chad would maybe have time to load him into another private plane that could take off from the wheat field behind the house, but it was three hundred miles to the ocean or the Canadian border. They could be shot down long before then, and there would be nothing that anyone here could do about it.

Of course, that would just mean David would take everyone in the plane to Earth Two. Not a terrible outcome, but not the one he was ready for in this moment.

Thus, now wasn't the time for wavering. He'd come to Avalon precisely for this purpose.

Chad Treadman sat at the opposite end of the long, somewhat oval table, facing his own computer. Once David was seated, Sophie hovered between them, without a computer screen of her own, though she had a device on her ear that could have been for audio. That, at least, was something David had encountered before. Chad was looking far more serious than was typical for him, which David realized was for the benefit of the other people in the video call. David mimicked him, putting on his game face, and then adjusted his own earbuds and joined the conference.

MI-5 had sent Director-General Phillips; Jack Stine, Livia's direct superior; and Kavya Collins, their liaison to Special Branch, which provided MI-5's military force. It had been her people who'd been the boots on the ground, wearing black and in black SUV's, who typically chased David and his family all over Britain. In facilitating the chase, she had undoubtedly been following orders, just like everyone else, but he himself was not a fan.

Eighteen months ago, David had stood in a grocery store aisle with Phillips. This was a far higher level meeting, and David nodded at them all, virtually that is, acknowledging they'd sent their heaviest hitters. It was an indication of their respect for him and an acknowledgment of his importance. There was a reason Myrddin hadn't dumped him into the UK. MI-5 was, by their standards, tamed. The CIA remained another matter.

They too had sent top people, including the actual director of the CIA, a woman, whom everyone called *Director*. High-ranking generals in the Army and National Guard were included as well, since they were providing support to the CIA, which wasn't supposed to be working inside US borders in the first place. The hangar was actually a top-secret military installation, upon which the CIA was piggybacking, just as David had guessed.

Charles was also present, representing the hangar. Really, he should have been in chains, not making small talk with the director of MI-5. That wasn't David's call to make, apparently. He scanned the faces for Letitia, but he didn't see her. In David's estimation, that was a huge oversight.

It was Charles who began. To his credit, he was straightforward in his enumeration of the order of events, though it was perhaps not as complete as it could have been. In particular, while George was mentioned and commended for his work, *how* George had maneuvered David into the airplane was not. George himself hung back against the wall ten feet from David and out of sight of the cameras, giving no sign he intended to participate or correct the record. Despite David's anger at George's very existence, he accepted that his omission was serving a purpose, even if neither George nor Chad had truly shared with David what it was.

Throughout, Chad kept shooting glances at David, who endeavored to keep his expression as wooden as possible. The recitation was without embellishment, which in a way made it all the more brutal to listen to. And, of course, it culminated in Charles shooting

David, killing one of his own men who was standing behind him instead, and then the death of the man who'd drowned in Earth Two.

"Why are you still here?" Jack Stine was very blunt as he glared out of his little square, echoing David's thought. Then, as Charles didn't reply, he added, "*Director?*"

"You needed to hear this from him." She was matter-of-fact. "He is no longer responsible for this project, however." She gestured to her screen. It was weird the way everyone behaved as if they were in the same room, but it wasn't possible to indicate to whom one wanted to speak without saying that person's name. "Have you landed yet, Paul?"

"Another fifteen minutes, Director." A bald man in a suit leaned closer to his screen.

David was feeling more and more like this meeting was getting away from him. He didn't know Paul and feared terribly that his assumption of authority was going to result in more of the same behaviors David had come here to prevent. "Where's Letitia?"

Nobody among all the screens responded, except for Chad, who looked up. "You're muted, sire."

David was staring at the screen, trying to see how to *un*mute, when Sophie came over and pointed to a little microphone at the bottom of the screen. "There, sire."

While he'd been fumbling with the technology, the conversation had continued without him. He picked it up again as Charles said, "I'm simply here to answer any questions."

"Then how about mine." David's voice was loud in his own ears. Though D-G Phillips had been courteous, the general level of respect David was receiving from the American contingents was just barely an improvement over their former attitude that he was an unsophisticated kid dressed in a suit and pretending to be the King of England. "Did you do as I asked?"

Charles's expression became as wooden as David's.

Taking the lack of overt reply as a *no,* David said, "Why not?"

The Director tsked under her breath. "We are aware of your concerns, sire."

He couldn't help thinking that the *sire* was belated and reluctant. He continued to be frustrated by his inability to actually look at someone when he talked to them. "Are you? Two men are dead, and all sorts of dire threats were directed at my person."

D-G Philipps cleared his throat. "I am authorized to negotiate for King David's transfer from the custody of the United States to the United Kingdom on behalf of Her Majesty's government. He is the ruler of a sovereign nation, ours, albeit in another universe, and your treatment of him violates international law. A complaint has been filed formally with your ambassador."

David eased back in his seat. They were ignoring him again, but this time, he let it go, interested in the CIA Director's answer.

"We have just become aware of the filing." She cleared her throat. "The joint chiefs are meeting as we speak."

David gave a little grunt. *The Joint Chiefs.* If nothing else, he was being passed up the food chain.

Jack leaned forward. Lots of people were doing that, including David, and he made a note to himself next time he answered to stay still. "Sire, may I ask about Livia?"

"She is well, putting what she learned here to good use." He didn't really think it was his place to tell Livia's former boss about her life, but that was certainly safe to say.

"Everyone else—" Jack Stine spoke again, but then cut himself off at what might have been a gesture from Director-General Phillips. Body language was hard to read when all David could see were people's heads.

David answered anyway. "Is well too. Philippe, the King of France, attempted a takeover of Aquitaine, but Callum and Cassie commanded forces that threw his army back." His eyes flicked from one image to the next, trying to read individual responses, without much luck. "As we speak, the entire Jewish population of Paris is being evacuated to Britain in hopes of avoiding the slaughter that happened in Avalon's history."

Everyone's head came up at that. There had been a lot of tension in the room, not all of which David knew the reason for. But this news was greeted with interest all around, and that tension—both in this house and among the conference participants—eased, evidenced by the fact that more people were leaning forward, gesturing with their hands, and speaking animatedly.

"How?" This was from a representative of the FBI, not the director and perhaps speaking out of turn, but he too was leaned forward and earnest.

So David told them, in great detail, about the last eighteen months. He spoke as if he had all the time in the world, which was deliberate on his part. He didn't know these people, and he found video calling a pale substitute for meeting in person, but many of the principles of leadership remained: the more he talked, the more everyone would get used to listening to him.

Then Tom Baker's face popped up on a new screen. "Madam Director, you have to do whatever King David says."

He was speaking one hundred percent out of turn, and the blank stares he received were in keeping with the surprise that one so low on the authority scale would dare address so august a company. Charles leaned back in his seat and spoke to someone off camera, though he was still miked, so everyone could hear him. "What's going on?"

Tom ignored him. "None of you were with us these last two days. Director Makowski"—he meant Charles—"told only part of the story. He was shooting at David, not talking to him. David himself told us in advance that what we planned to put him through wasn't ever going to work, and that we were risking more than his life. From the start, his concern was for everybody but himself." Here Tom made a gesture towards his screen. "He was the one who told us George had left Andre drugged on the floor of the plane. He was the one who cared about the men who went with him the second time, when they ended up in Belize. He begged us to stop and think. He begged us to do it his way, and we didn't listen ..." At this point, Tom seemed to become aware of the level of stares and censure directed towards him and petered out.

David stayed still, his hands clasped in front of him.

Chad leaned forward in his chair. "The man is right, ladies and gentlemen." And then he looked up, into David's face. When their eyes met, Chad's widened. "You—"

He pulled off his headset, laughing, and rose to his feet. As he came closer to David's end of the table, he said. "Mute, if you will, sire."

David hastily did as he asked.

Putting both hands on the back of the adjacent chair, Chad leaned into them. "You *planned* this, didn't you? Every second of it!"

"Not *every* second." His eyes skated to George and back to Chad.

Chad gazed at David for a long moment without speaking.

So David spoke again. "I won't apologize. They wanted to kidnap my son."

"Oh, I know." Chad straightened, now bringing up both hands, palms out. "You won't get an argument from me."

Shaking his head, he returned to his seat and replaced his headset. "Okay, sire." He cut through the conversation on the screen. "It's time to tell us what you want us to do."

Whether because some of the side conversations had ended, or genuinely because of the authority in Chad's tone, everyone fell silent. Even from thousands of miles away, David could tell everyone was looking at him.

"King David," the CIA director bobbed her head, "we would very much like to hear what you have to say."

David smiled. "As it turns out, I do have a plan. It won't please everyone, but—" his voice hardened, "—it's the only way we can move forward together."

41

August 1295

Day Four

Lili

When they finally approached the bridge close enough to see the Templars in the middle of it and the portcullis blocking their path, Lili had to stop herself from bursting into tears.

But then Minna, who was bent over the ship's rail yet again, moaned, "It's over."

Lili tried to maintain a sympathetic and gentle demeanor at all times, and she liked to think it was fundamentally her nature, but this was too much, and she lost her temper. "Of course it isn't over!"

Minna looked up, still well enough to be astonished.

Lili was immediately contrite and put out a hand in apology, but Minna's mother, Esther, waved her off. "You are still breathing, daughter, as am I. With God, all things are possible." For the first time in days, Esther's eyes were bright. "Even if I die, we have still triumphed."

And then, to the enormous relief of everyone in the boats, men on the bridge began to winch up the portcullis. Ieuan had the binoculars to his eyes and, after another long look, gave them to Lili. "It's our people on that bridge: Rhys. Cador. Isabelle too."

"Do you see Christopher or William?"

"No." Ieuan had been standing in the prow since before he shot the pigeons, and with a snap of his fingers, he got some of the younger men up and posted on the rail with him.

While he had little experience with boats overall, mostly avoidance on his part because of his predilection for sea sickness, someone had to make sure the boat made it through the archway. They had few able-bodied passengers, especially after sending five of their most capable young people away. Everyone else was exhausted, sick, or had never been on a boat before in their lives.

From the rear, the captain had to shout to be heard all the way at the front. "I'm going to try to center the boat, but if it bangs against the sides, I'll need strong hands to push us back to safety."

Silence fell among the passengers, as they realized that this entire endeavor came down to this moment. Nobody needed to be told that the stones of the bridge could shatter the boat if hit hard enough, and the current was not going to help them. There was no panic, however, just grim determination and the raised voices of the minyan—a circle of ten—who'd been praying nonstop, people dropping out as others joined, since they'd left Paris.

The other boats lined up behind them, all their captains endeavoring to take the same line as Lili's boat. James Stewart stood in the prow of the ship just behind hers, Mark Jones beside him, his hands braced against the rail of the boat.

They were close enough now for Lili to see Isabelle herself leaning over the edge of the bridge, waving her arms in a fashion Lili interpreted to say, *Come on!*

Then, when they were within thirty yards of the bridge, the men on it convulsed. Some shouted and regained their mounts. The portcullis was all the way up, which was Lili's most immediate concern, but the gate on the Rouen side of the bridge had opened, admitting soldiers and one cavalryman in particular, who had unsheathed his sword and pointed it at the sky. Isabelle straightened, for a moment cocking her head as if listening. Then, just as Lili herself passed underneath her, she swung both legs over the stone wall of the bridge—and jumped.

Isabelle had almost left it too late, but she dropped into the stern of the boat, with a matter of three feet to spare.

By the time she regained her feet, wincing slightly on a twisted ankle, Lili was there to grab her. "What a risk you took!" She clutched the girl to her. "Why did you do that?"

"I wanted to make sure you knew the Templars on the wharf were friendly." She pointed just downstream from the bridge, where men were lined up on the dock, waving frantically for them to come in. "And if there was going to be fighting on the bridge, I was better out of it."

Taking advantage of an eddy forming behind one of the bridge's footings, the captain, who'd overheard, steered the boat out of the main current and into a slip at the far end of the dock, leaving space for those coming behind to fill in the rest.

Lili turned to look up at the bridge, now behind them to the east.

"Christopher is up there." Isabelle had her arms wrapped around her waist, hugging herself anxiously.

Lili squeezed her shoulder. "They aren't fighting yet."

Dock men grabbed the mooring lines, and, once each boat came to rest, began reaching for anxious passengers to help them disembark.

Ieuan was the first to bound out to speak to the commander of the Templars. Twenty knights and sergeants held a line between the dock and the entrance to the street that led to it, where the Templars had erected a wooden barricade, composed of a hodgepodge of crates, carts, and sawhorses, all seemingly derived from whatever had been to hand on the wharf itself. Ordinary citizens of Rouen, rather than the king's soldiers, pressed against it, arms in the air, each asking for attention from those on the other side. The street sloped upwards behind them, and Lili could see more coming by the moment.

"Is Queen Lili here?" A Templar knight pushed his way through the passengers. Many were smiling with relief at being back on solid ground.

"Here." Lili raised a hand and passed Alexander to Dafydd's Aunt Elisa. Ted had a tight grip on Arthur's hand, helping to cross the eight-inch gap between the boat and the dock.

The man who'd called to her put out a hand for Lili to grasp, and she stepped onto the dock with grateful relief. Only then did she recognize Thomas Hartley. With a laugh, she squeezed his hand and would have hugged him if he hadn't been a Templar.

For his part, Thomas stepped back a pace and bowed. He was a few years younger than she, with soft brown eyes and a matching light brown beard. "Greetings from Amaury de Montfort. We are aware you have ill people among you, and we are ready to assist." He gazed around at the people on the wharf and then at those who hadn't yet disembarked because they were unable to rise. "It is our thought that anyone who is too ill to walk should remain with the boats, and we'll transport them a few at a time downriver to the dock at the commandery." He pointed to the fortress a hundred yards away.

"Thank you." More relief flooded her, so much so she felt light-headed. "We have many sick who need immediate attention." She indicated where Aaron was bent over Minna, who was on her knees on the dock. "Aaron ben Simon is our chief physician. Speak to him, please, and he can sort out those who walk from those who need to float."

Thomas turned to another Templar, this one much older. "Do as Queen Lili says."

Beyond the crush of passengers, Lili could see Ieuan talking to a Templar and another man, this one tall with a long beard marking him as Jewish. He was also wringing his hands in an earnest manner not unlike their boat captain had done earlier.

Lili scanned the crowd of disembarked refugees, finally spying her liaison. "Jacob!" She waved an arm to get his attention. "You are needed!" She pointed towards her brother.

Jacob took off in Ieuan's direction at a run, and Lili followed somewhat more sedately with Thomas.

By the time they arrived, Ieuan, Jacob, and the Jewish man from Rouen had already come to an agreement, because Jacob was saying to Ieuan. "That is, if it's all right with you?"

"We are merely the transport and the haven if you want it."

Jacob bent his head with genuine respect before turning to speak to the citizen of Rouen. "We would be grateful, my friend. Thank you."

Ieuan bent towards Lili. "The Jewish community here has offered to take everyone in."

"What about the archbishop's edict of expulsion?" Lili asked.

"We just heard from a messenger sent by Amaury that the archbishop has been run out of town."

Lili's jaw dropped. She had thought little could surprise her anymore, and she's just been proved wrong. "How is that possible?"

"*Even kings rule at the consent of the governed, whether or not the governed or their governors know it,*" Ieuan said, quoting Dafydd—and Meg. "The people of Rouen are not consenting." He gestured towards the crowded streets. "They want a say in their government, and they are making their opinions known."

Lili eyed the crowd behind the barricades, which were now being moved aside so the people could mingle with the refugees from Paris.

Then a shout came from closer to the boats. "They're letting them in!"

She swung around, and she didn't need Ieuan's binoculars to see that the gates were fully open, and the Templars on the bridge were slowly filing into the city. Then a great cheer went up from somewhere on the other side of the gate.

"What you cannot see from here is that Brother Amaury leads another force on the other side of that gate," Thomas said. "Soldiers from the castle were sent by the archbishop to subdue the citizens of the city and to evict Jews from their homes. But they are too few in number to do either against the objections of the people themselves. Nor does their mandate include fighting Templars."

"It isn't these soldiers I'm worried about," Ieuan said. "Normandy is too great a prize for Philippe to let go easily."

"He would march on Normandy at his peril," Thomas said, sounding an awful lot like a Norman revolutionary himself.

"You're that sure?" Ieuan asked.

"The people are ready to fight."

As Thomas made this reply, Jacob looked at him hard. "I am grateful for their defense of my people, but with or without their Jewish neighbors, the people of Rouen are going to fail without real leadership. The Templars *have* to provide it."

"We cannot. You know we cannot."

So Jacob turned to Lili. "You could do it, my lady."

"If we provide it, it means England is at war with France," Lili said.

Jacob threw up his hands. "You're already at war! Look what happened in Aquitaine!"

"We threw back an invasion force," Ieuan said. "This is different. Aquitaine was already independent of France. Normandy is not. Our boat captain was right that what we are discussing is treason if it comes out of the mouths of Normans."

"*Even kings rule at the consent of the governed,*" Jacob quoted back at them. He had never looked more earnest.

Lili met her brother's eyes. "I could do it if it meant saving lives." She made a motion with her head. "But it's Dafydd we really need."

"No, we don't, if you pardon me, my lady." James Stewart appeared from behind her. She didn't know how long he'd been standing there, but she and Ieuan moved apart to widen the circle to include him. "King David knew what he was doing, and I don't think we should jeopardize how far we've come."

"So what do you propose?" Ieuan said.

"I have lands in Scotland and Ireland and no overt connection to the English court other than my country's position in the CSB." James had declined to put his name forward for prime minister of

Scotland or Ireland because he had a different vision for his future. At the time, she'd thought it a shame. Suddenly, he looked prescient. "I think you have to agree that no one is more qualified to bring Normandy into our confederation than I am."

42

August 2023

Day Four

George

The video meeting had ended three hours earlier, which gave each agency barely enough time to get its ducks in a row. Deliberately so. Nobody could have flown from the east coast to the west coast or from England to Oregon. At best, some of these people had traveled from California or Denver. It helped that the little town had a capable airport.

Chad's people had chosen a great spot to meet in person. The park was enormous for a town of this size and entirely flat, with one- or two-story houses surrounding it. There were also dozens of entrances and exits for those on foot, and three different parking lots. The CIA, MI-5, and Chad's people had each parked in a different lot and were converging on the meeting spot from different directions. Snipers were always a problem, since good ones could shoot a mile.

But even they would be stymied by the darkness of the night, poor cover, and nonexistent sightlines.

George was still laughing at what David had proposed. It was so reasonable and *easy*. In short, he'd told some of the most powerful people in the world that he would voluntarily take back one person from the CIA, Chad Treadman's organization, and MI-5 to Earth Two with him in Chad's airplane, which was already equipped for the job. They could bring whatever material or gear each agency thought necessary to institute some kind of *safe haven* for their people in Avalon. He couldn't assure anyone's safety, but he promised to assist within reason in whatever way he could in Earth Two to carve out such an entity, as well as facilitate experiments and data collection. He would bring them home when they were ready if the opportunity presented itself. As time went on, and if things went well, they could include more people from more countries. It would be, in effect, the time travel version of the international space station.

"Only one?" The Director of the CIA had asked, looking put out.

"One," David had said, "and it has to be a woman."

That invoked more consternation than almost anything else he could have said. They'd argued, but David had stood firm.

"*And we are leaving first thing tomorrow. I've been away long enough, so give it your best shot.*"

Sophie was the logical choice for Chad to include, but she shook her head. "Not me. Not again."

"I need a woman pilot too." Chad had rubbed his chin, thinking hard. "That means I get two people."

"Just wait until everyone else realizes it." David laughed. "Sorry about stealing your plane again."

Chad shrugged. "Because you took it to Earth Two, I have orders for that plane for the next five years of production, at a premium price."

David had laughed again at that, as he would.

Chad was more sober. "If you hadn't said only women, I might have come myself."

"Could be that's why I said it."

George didn't believe him, and neither did Chad. Even if the CIA Director was railing at David for wanting only women and pretending she didn't know why, George knew.

It wasn't because David didn't think women were as smart or capable as men. Or that they were softer and less likely to conspire to abduct his children, though that, at least, might give a woman pause more than a man. It was because women were less of a threat to everyone in Earth Two. They'd be underestimated by the medieval people and from the start would also be more dependent upon David and his people. The CIA and MI-5 had the option to send warrior women, but likely they wouldn't be the strategic thinkers the agencies really wanted.

With instituting this provision, George's respect for David had gone up another notch, not that he would ever tell him so. Really, the person the CIA should send was George's old trainer, Paige, except she was dead—

George stopped in his tracks on the edge of the parking lot. In the very moment he'd thought of her, as if resurrected by the thought, he spied Paige Blanchard, alive and in living color, amongst the other representatives of the CIA. "My God. How can she be here?"

At times, David was still looking at George with something as close to raw hatred as to make no difference. George couldn't blame him. He'd been doing his job, but he would be the first to admit that job had been unsavory. In the end, he'd completed it because he believed in the outcome.

It really could be that the end didn't justify the means, no matter how many knots a person twisted himself into to explain his actions. George knew also that he was here on sufferance and that David was merely tolerating his presence out of the hope that he could be useful.

George had been hoping the same, but he hadn't thought it might be for this reason.

"Who?" To his credit, David didn't sneer, but stopped too, allowing several of Chad's people to get ahead of him.

"Paige Blanchard." George gestured to the woman standing in the center of the CIA's delegation. "She's a legend in black ops. She's also supposed to be dead."

"That isn't the name she gave me," David said.

Fortunately, they had a good twenty people with them, so the fact that a handful were still in the parking lot hadn't been noted yet by anyone else. George himself was dressed as one of Chad's bodyguards, with a baseball cap pulled down low over his eyes. In the dark, and with his newly dyed hair, nobody would look at him twice—and if they did, they wouldn't see George Hanson.

Sophie wasn't Michael, but she'd positioned herself as a kind of bodyguard for David, and she had stopped too. Like all the people David seemed to gather around himself, she had a strong sense of duty and responsibility. That George did too—albeit to his country rather than to David—was probably why he'd fit in as well as he had. Competence could take a person a long way. Loyalty was a different matter, and George was newly discovering what it was worth. George had delivered David as promised, and look where it had gotten him.

"What name was that?" Sophie asked.

"Letitia Johnson," David said. "Yesterday when she freed me from the interrogation room, she very clearly said her name, and other people have used it since."

"No." George snorted out loud at how they'd all been duped. "That is not her name. *That* is not Letitia Johnson."

David eyed him. "You're sure?"

George was worried enough that he refrained from giving David a withering look for questioning him. "I'm sure." And then he added. "I don't care what name she gave you when you met. The Letitia Johnson that I know is native Alaskan. *That* woman is Paige Blanchard."

"Will Paige recognize you if you get close?" David said.

"Yes. That's probably why I was sent away before she arrived. And why she wasn't included on that call, in case someone from one of the other agencies recognized her too."

"Is there some reason why she would be impersonating another officer?" David said. "And wouldn't Charles know her real name?"

This whole situation had become a farce, not to say a train wreck. "Well, since, as I said, she's supposed to be dead, her assumption of Letitia's identity was sanctioned at the highest levels. What's more, everything that happened, from my presence in Chad's organization on down, was sanctioned at the highest levels. You can be sure that if Paige is here, she's the one really in charge."

"Why go to all this trouble when David doesn't know her anyway?" Sophie said.

It was a good question, and George gave her a serious answer. "He wasn't the one who had to be convinced, though, was he? Half the battle—more than half, really, since nobody was bothering to try to convince David of anything before now—was getting everyone else on board with forcing him to time travel. Or forcing Arthur if I'd gotten him instead. Paige is famous, not to say infamous, within the

CIA." He looked directly into David's face. "You had no reason to distrust Paige Blanchard if you knew she was here, but others would. *I* would."

"I still don't get it. Why deceive you? You were on board with whatever anyone wanted."

"Was I?"

"Weren't you?"

George shook his head. "The plan to abduct your son was always beyond the pale." Under other circumstances, he would have mocked himself for his casual use of the medieval phrase. He'd actually *been* to *The Pale*.

"But you agreed to it!"

"Did I?"

"You were going to ride him back and forth to Avalon!"

"I wasn't. *I* always intended to exchange him for you."

David settled back on his heels. "It would have worked. I would have given myself up to you to keep him safe."

"You did give yourself up to me to keep him safe. You may note that Nogaret controlled Philippe by the same means. I'm figuring now, however, that Paige has been coordinating this entire mission from the start. She really only ever wanted Arthur or one of the other children because she knew you would be a problem. When I brought you back instead of him, I sealed my fate."

"She's that bad?"

"She's so bad the CIA faked her death rather than allow her to be implicated in any more scandals that have rocked the Agency in recent years."

David's face told George he didn't necessarily know anything of what he was talking about, but he only gave a low tsk of disgust and looked resigned to the knowledge that the CIA had once again played him false. It was a shame, really. A more righteous man had never existed. If they'd tried to get David on their side for real, everyone could have benefitted.

Whatever was going on here now, however, wasn't that.

"She's going to be the woman the CIA sends!" Sophie's mouth fell open in horror.

David let out a low whistle. "I suppose I played right into her hands by insisting that the person who went with me was a woman. Everyone in the CIA contingent must be laughing their heads off right about now."

Since it was exactly what George had been thinking, he merely said, "You didn't know. I didn't know."

By now, most everyone was quite a bit ahead of them. So now he looked hard at David, who was going to have to make the decision about what to do next. Paige's presence put an entirely new light on this whole endeavor. George was starting to think, in fact, that it was irredeemable. "You can't trust anyone from the CIA, sire. They've bargained entirely in bad faith, and they aren't capable of anything better."

"Does that condemnation include you?" David asked dryly, but then made a motion with one hand to cut off George's protest. That George had made to protest—like he deserved the benefit of the doubt—gave him a moment's pause. He had never apologized for anything before he knelt in front of David. It was an odd feeling, and not necessarily a good one. At the same time, it felt a little like being wiped clean after confession as a child. Admitting when he'd made a mistake had never been his strongest suit.

"Okay." Fortunately, David had been around the block a time or two and knew when things had already gone sideways. He tipped his head towards a maintenance shed between them and the meeting place in the center of the park. "Stay out of sight until everyone has gathered. I need you close enough to hear what's going on, so you can step in if I'm being misled. We'll deal with this right now." He set off towards the center of the park, Sophie in tow.

On the whole, Chad's employees had treated George well enough—a little warily, but not condemning him. Of course, only Sophie, Andre, and Chad knew the full story of how he'd gotten David here. George, however, was beginning to wonder if Chad was right that David had set him up instead of the other way around. If so, George was impressed. He hadn't known David had it in him.

That notion, in a flash of insight, gave George an idea—one of his better ones if he did say so himself. And one David certainly hadn't thought of. By now George was alone behind the shed except for a last member of Chad's security team, who was standing a few paces into the parking lot, facing the street and looking for threats.

Two strides put George right behind him, at which point he wrapped his arms around his neck, cutting off the circulation to his brain and rendering him unconscious within seconds.

George dragged him behind the shed, leaving him on his back (and still breathing), but relieved of his thigh holster and pistol, neither of which Chad had seen fit to give George before they came.

Moving back around the shed as if he was merely one of the numerous guards on patrol, he saw that, two hundred feet away near the playground, the various participants in this meeting had come together in a square, whether by design or preference George didn't know. The CIA people faced Chad's people, with MI-5 on an adjacent side and David all alone on another. Most importantly, nobody was standing behind him.

David's plan for an international haven had been a good one. Too bad everything the CIA had told them was a lie.

George circled around behind the line of CIA officials, nodding at their guards, who nodded back, having no idea who he was. Even if they might have recognized him in daylight, he was disguised and out of context here.

Then he changed course in an instant and started marching straight towards one of the corners of the square. Nobody stopped him initially, and by the time he heard a "Hey!" from someone behind him, he drowned out the call with a shout of his own: "Hey, David!"

The officers with their backs to him, both CIA and MI-5, including Paige, turned to look at him, as he knew they would. Nobody can resist the instinct to turn at a shout, even for only a second.

A second was all George needed.

By turning, they also separated, creating a gap wide enough for George to see through.

David himself was looking straight at George and wearing a puzzled expression that said, *what are you doing now?"*

"You need to go back to your family, sire. Leave this to me." Then he pulled his newly acquired weapon from the holster and shot David in the chest.

By the time anyone else had cleared their weapons from wherever they'd hidden them, David was gone and George had tossed the gun into the grass, putting up his hands a heartbeat later. It had been a risk that someone would shoot first and ask questions later, but a calculated one for all that. And he was wearing body armor.

Paige took one look at the place David had been and then advanced on George. Even then, she was two paces away before she recognized him. "What have you done?"

"Hi Paige. Long time no see." George grinned, a feeling of genuine amusement and pride at what he'd done welling up within him. He also chose not to answer her question, which was rhetorical anyway. "And before you arrest me and toss me in a deep pit of despair, might I remind you that I know where your bodies are buried."

43

August 1295

Day Four

David

David came out of the void upright and firmly planted on the stones of a courtyard lit by a single torch.

At long last.

His gratefulness and relief at not finding himself in an ocean, a field, under fire—or dead—would have brought him immediately to his knees if not for the urgency of discovering where he was and why he was here. Above him, the sky was dark and cloud covered, but it wasn't raining. He was definitely in a castle of some kind, and when he looked down, he gave a low cheer to see he'd landed smack in the middle of a Templar cross.

"Qui êtes—"

David swung around to see a very startled Templar sergeant come to a dead halt ten paces away.

Likely, he'd been trying to say *Qui êtes vous?* which was *Who are you?* in French. That question went straight to the central issue and potential quagmire for David. The bit of French the Templar had spoken sounded Norman, which didn't help David determine if he was in France, England, or even Sicily—and might be wishful thinking on David's part anyway. He knew only that he wasn't in London or Paris.

Before he could answer, a voice came from behind him from the other direction, this time with overtones of youth. "Sire!"

That was more like it. Swinging around again, David was opening his mouth to say, "Hi, Huw," when he was almost knocked to the ground again by the force of Huw's embrace.

"We were so—"Huw broke off, his voice choked by emotion. "We saw—"

David managed to extricate himself. "How did you even know I was gone?"

Huw managed a complete sentence. "We saw something your uncle called *a military cargo plane* crash three times into the earth."

David gave that news the respect it deserved. "Lili too?"

Huw nodded.

"Is she here?"

Huw's eyes lit. "She's outside with everyone else. You're just in time!" Then he paused and amended. "Well, we're actually going to be late if we don't hurry."

He started across the courtyard towards the wicket gate and the still stunned Templar gatekeeper. He wouldn't have understood a word they'd said, since Huw and David had been speaking Welsh.

Now Huw stopped in front of him and said in French, "This is David, King of England." For once he didn't say David's name the Welsh way, *Dafydd,* so the gatekeeper would understand. Then Huw gave David the onceover. "I imagine that attire was suitable in Avalon, sire, but here it won't do at all."

David looked down at himself. He'd forgotten in the excitement of returning what he was wearing. This was the second time he'd arrived in Earth Two in a blue suit. Maybe he should stop choosing them because they were bad luck. Then again, from a certain point of view, the suits were good luck too, and they did match his eyes.

Huw, meanwhile, snapped his fingers imperiously at the Templar. "He needs your robe."

"What? I cannot!"

"If you have a spare garment in the guardroom that would be fine too, but we're going now, and he can't go out wearing what he has on."

"But—"

By now, David himself had approached. "It's okay, Huw. It won't be the first time I'm oddly dressed."

"You don't understand." Huw let out a sigh. "For once, it would be better for everyone if you blend in."

Which was how David found himself a moment later stripping down to his underwear in a storage room full of gear, swapping tunics with Huw, who shrugged into the brown robe of a servant, without even the characteristic red Templar cross to distinguish him.

Huw huffed out a breath as the sergeant, now helpful, belted his sword at his waist. "I think you'll be happy to know that we have continued to try not to tie any of us to the Templars more than needful."

"Thank you." David couldn't help feeling relief. "So where is everyone?"

"Those who are ill are in the infirmary here at the commandery. The rest will be sleeping tonight throughout the city in friendly households, but for now they should be at the speech, along with most of the city."

"What speech?"

"James Stewart's speech. Well—" Huw immediately amended his words, "—it's going to be a whole bunch of speeches, but James is going first."

"Why is James delivering a speech?"

"It's actually one Christopher wrote, with the help of his parents. And I think Livia. Weirdly, according to Mark, it wasn't on any of his tablets. He called it *a massive oversight*."

David was feeling more muddled than he usually did after he world-shifted. "Christopher wrote a speech? What are you talking about?"

Huw spread his hands wide. "I've heard it already, and I think you'll like it. He didn't write it originally, though. Something about memorizing it for—and these are his words—*an eighth grade Sons of Liberty test he got second place in.*"

Huw's colloquial American spoken with his lilting Welsh accent was always endearing, but David made a motion with his hand for him to get to the point.

"I don't know anything more about it than that! Christopher said at the time he thought it was *the most useless thing in a whole year of useless things he'd ever been forced to learn.*"

David let it go. He would find out soon enough what Huw was talking about. "So you made it downriver okay? Everyone is okay?"

"Yes. More than okay. You'll see in a minute."

A minute wasn't even a medieval unit of time Huw would know anything about. He was being annoyingly sparse with information.

David was too, in point of fact, but it was better to tell his story once, not just to Huw, and not in front of a stranger.

Finally respectably dressed, they were bowed out the wicket gate on foot by the Templar sergeant, who had warmed to them over the last fifteen minutes, and they headed east down the street. By now, David had figured out he was in Rouen, though the red banners emblazoned with a white sheep carried by the people in the streets would have given it away if he hadn't already known.

They weren't late, as it turned out. In fact, they were just in time, arriving at the giant green in front of the bridge across the

Seine just as James Stewart stepped up on a dais. Other men stood behind him in a row, each dressed formally in their finest robes and sporting excessively flamboyant hats (in David's opinion).

And then James began to speak: *When in the course of human events, it becomes necessary for one people to dissolve the political bands which have connected them with one another ...*

David gaped at the Scotsman. Christopher had written out for him the first part of the Declaration of Independence. For a moment, David was offended that the document was being used to declare the independence of Normandy from France, but then he suppressed his irritation. The sooner it came into this world, the better. If Christopher had really memorized the whole thing, he deserved a medal, never mind first place in that eighth grade contest.

After James had finished, to polite applause, one of the Rouenese rose to speak. Huw leaned in to David, "We heard him before. He's really good."

The man brandished a piece of paper above his head and shook it, claiming it was a captured message from the Archbishop of Rouen to King Philippe, asking for more troops to control the city. Clearly, modern oratorial styles had a long history.

"We brought him that," Huw said proudly, "though it was Ieuan who shot the pigeon."

Clearly, David had missed a great deal in two days.

The speaker continued: "For generations we have withstood abuses at the hands of the French king. These abuses force us now, as our Scottish friend so clearly elucidated, to choose a different form of government. My fellow citizens of Normandy," here he gestured to the men behind him, who'd been joined by three women, "have signed this document, which we will send to the king in place of the archbishop's message."

With another flourish, he unrolled it and began to read.

> *... that Normandy is, and of right ought to be, free and independent; that its people are absolved from all allegiance to the French crown, and that all political connection between them and France is and ought to be totally dissolved; and that as a free and independent country, Normandy has the full power to levy war, conclude peace, contract alliances, establish commerce, and to do all other acts and things which independent states may of right do. And for the support of this declaration, with a firm reliance on the protection of divine providence, we mutually pledge to each other our lives, our fortunes and our sacred honor.*

Even David, who'd grown up with those words, felt his spirits lifting. The last sentence had thrilled an entire planet of freedom-seekers for over two centuries. David rose up on his toes to look around at the crowd, suddenly understanding the difference between James's reading of the first half of the *Declaration of Independence* and this man's rendering of the second half. It wasn't the *words* that were important. It was that a group of people had gathered together in unity and laid their lives on the line for the freedom of their people. It was what had prompted John Hancock to sign his name really big, apocryphally so King George could read it without his spectacles. As Patrick Henry had said, *If this be treason, make the most of it.*

The applause at the conclusion of the speech was deafening, and David was glad to put his fist into the air with everyone else.

The Normans who came next spoke more soberly about the difficult times ahead and the need for every able-bodied man to enlist in the effort. James had already retreated from the dais, perhaps also recognizing that his role had ended. David and Huw made their way through the crowd to where the members of the English court had watched the proceedings without participating. They'd staked out a section of the green somewhat separated from everyone else—present in the crowd but not *of* it.

Everyone was looking at the stage, so nobody was aware of his approach until he was right in front of Lili. At the sight of him, she gasped and then threw her arms around his neck. "You're here!"

"Hello, *cariad*." David hugged her tightly. "I turn my back for five minutes and look at all the trouble you get into."

Everyone laughed, as he meant them to, and then they all started talking at once. He let their words wash over him, not needing to listen so much as feel their love.

"You saw what just happened?" Lili said. "I hardly dare believe it."

"I saw." With her still in his arms, David turned to look at the people of the free and independent state of Normandy. "They're doing this on their own."

"So I told them when they asked where you were." Lili smiled. "But they aren't entirely on their own either, as I made clear when we were hashing out the speeches. If they choose to make their own destiny, we will make room for them in the CSB."

A joy David hadn't felt in a long time—nor expected ever to feel again—rose in him.

Maybe he had more work to do. The fact that Myrddin had sent him back here instead of somewhere else in Earth Two—or killed him—indicated he still had more work to do.

But not today.

Today, the idea of pledging one's *life, fortune, and sacred honor* to the cause of liberty had grown beyond its point of origin.

Today, the medieval world didn't need him anymore.

Thank you for reading *Outcasts in Time* and for continuing this journey into the Middle Ages with me.

www.sarahwoodbury.com

Acknowledgments

First and foremost, I'd like to thank my lovely readers for encouraging me to continue the *After Cilmeri* series. I have always been passionate about these books, and it's wonderful to be able to share my stories with readers who love them too. Thank you also to all my editors, proof-readers, and beta readers. I am grateful for all the ways each and every one of you make the book better.

Thank you to my husband, without whose love and support I would never have tried to make a living as a writer, and thank to my family who has been nothing but encouraging of my writing, despite the fact that I spend half my life in medieval Wales. I couldn't do this without you.

About the Author

With over a million books sold to date, Sarah Woodbury is the author of more than forty novels, all set in medieval Wales. Although an anthropologist by training, and then a full-time homeschooling mom for twenty years, she began writing fiction when the stories in her head overflowed and demanded that she let them out. While her ancestry is Welsh, she only visited Wales for the first time at university. She has been in love with the country, language, and people ever since. She even convinced her husband to give all four of their children Welsh names.

She makes her home in Oregon.

www.sarahwoodbury.com

Printed in Great Britain
by Amazon